THE KING'S MOTHER

Born to a great Lancastrian inheritance, Margaret Beaufort was married at an early age to Edmund Tudor, half-brother of Henry VI. Margaret's son, Henry, was born two months after his father's death, so she reared him in Wales under the care of Jasper, Earl of Pembroke, brother to Edmund. Love blossomed between Margaret and Jasper, but the union was forbidden by the Law of the Church. When Margaret's son eventually became Henry VII, the first Tudor King, she gave of her wisdom and energy to support him, but faced their personal conflict over her reunion with Jasper.

Books by Betty King
Published by The House of Ulverscroft:

WE ARE TOMORROW'S PAST
THE FRENCH COUNTESS
THE ROSE BOTH RED AND WHITE
MARGARET OF ANJOU
THE LADY MARGARET
THE CAPTIVE JAMES
THE LORD JASPER

BETTY KING

THE KING'S MOTHER

Complete and Unabridged

ULVERSCROFT
Leicester

First published in Great Britain in 1969 by
Robert Hale Limited
London

First Large Print Edition
published 2002
by arrangement with
Robert Hale Limited
London

British Library CIP Data

King, Betty, *1919* –
    The King's mother.—Large print ed.—
Ulverscroft large print series: romance
1. Love stories
2. Large type books
I. Title
823.9'14 [F]

ISBN 0–7089–4612–7

Published by
F. A. Thorpe (Publishing)
Anstey, Leicestershire

Set by Words & Graphics Ltd.
Anstey, Leicestershire
Printed and bound in Great Britain by
T. J. International Ltd., Padstow, Cornwall

This book is printed on acid-free paper

Acknowledgements

I wish to thank the following people for their kind assistance in the preparation of this novel:

Arthur Hall Esq.; the Staff of Guildhall Library; Miss O. E. Bunting, Miss T. J. Ash and the Staff of the Enfield Central Library; the Staff of the British Museum Reading Room; the Librarians of St. John's and Christ Colleges, Cambridge; the Staff of the Council Offices of Torrington, Devon; and my family for their continuing encouragement.

Out of the many books consulted the two main sources were Cooper's *Memoir of the Lady Margaret*, published in 1875, and E. M. G. Routh's *Lady Margaret; a memoir*, published in 1924.

Other sources

The Earlier Tudors, J. D. Mackie
The Wars of the Roses, J. R. Lander
Bosworth Field, A. L. Rowse
Life of Margaret, Halsted
Lives of the Queens of England, A. Strickland
Testamenta Vetusta, Nicholas Harris

York and Lancaster, Sir J. Ramsay
Dictionary of London, Harben
King James IV of Scotland, R. L. Mackie
Henry VIII, John Bowles
Letters and Papers Illustrative of the Reigns of Richard III and Henry VII, J. Gairdner, 1861–63
Materials for a History of the Reign of Henry VII, W. Campbell, 1873–77

1

The goblet shattered on the wall behind her with a sharp explosion.

Margaret gasped and her hand went to her mouth. She saw with something approaching awe her brother-in-law's eyes were full of tears.

'Don't speak!' Jasper said quickly. 'All that has been between you and me, I offer as a libation. All that might have been is in God's keeping. Go to your task of helping Henry as the King's mother and rest assured I shall always be at hand if he need me. Be certain also I shall fill my new responsibilities with honour. But look not for heirs, my dearest love, they stay unborn — in you.'

Hours later, Margaret, Countess of Richmond and wife of Lord Thomas Stanley, Earl of Derby, paced the floor of her bedchamber. She had dismissed her ladies and personal maidservant Betsey Massey as soon as they had helped her prepare for bed, pleading fatigue.

She was tired; tired as if her blood were watered and her bones and muscles collapsing within her. She knew the women were disappointed for they would be expecting to sit with her and talk over the wedding held earlier in the day of Jasper, Duke of Bedford and Catherine, widow of Henry, Duke of Buckingham.

Margaret was sorry to deprive her ladies of their simple pleasure but she felt unable to sit and listen to their chatter. Later perhaps she would be able to talk of the day's events without emotion but this night was too soon.

Coming to rest near the window she tugged aside the heavy velvet curtains, noting with her orderly mind they smelt of dust and were in need of shaking in the garden, and looked into the black night. Earlier when Jasper had thrown the drinking glass against the wall she had turned blindly from him and gazed out across the courtyard of the Palace of Westminster to the western horizon, green with the dying light of the November day. The rest of the feast had passed in a miasma of nameless pain as she played the gracious hostess without betraying by even a drooping eyelid her suffering.

The wedding had been the culmination of the anxieties and triumphs surrounding her son Henry since his victory over Richard of Gloucester on the field of Bosworth. Nine weeks had elapsed since the crown of England had rolled in the mire of battle churned up by the horses of men fighting to establish the supremacy of the Lancastrian cause.

Two short months, during which time Henry had worked ceaselessly to restore some order to the confusion left by his predecessor.

★ ★ ★

Margaret drew the curtains over the window and keeping her mind on her son's future as King Henry VII of England huddled her robe about her and went to bed. She closed her eyes, forcing herself to think of the change of fortune that had brought her to the honoured position she now held, but she knew after half an hour of restless changing of position she would be unable to sleep.

However much she tried to push away from her the cause of her own misery it was hopeless. Obtruding into every conscious thought was the knowledge she had relinquished this day her last remaining link with the man who had come to mean so much to her.

'Oh, God!' she whispered into the darkness. 'Help me now.'

Growing a little calmer she realised with a sense of shock she had forgotten to say her prayers. With a wry smile for those who thought her piety unquestionable she forced her heavy limbs to obey and slid from the bed to the floor.

She knelt at the small altar in the corner of her room but the usual devotions in their set pattern deserted her and she found herself saying over and over again:

'In Thee, O Lord, do I put my trust: let me never be put to confusion. Thou art my rock and my fortress.'

Margaret remained on her knees until her body ached with the cold. Rising stiffly she threw dry sticks on to the dying embers of the fire, rubbing her numbed hands as small tongues of flame licked the wood and burst into life.

When she could feel some warmth she took a coverlet from the bed and wrapping it around her sat down in a chair beside the hearth. Comforted in an oblique way by the prayers she had uttered she found she was able to think back over the thirty years of her adult life with less pain than she had imagined.

In her childhood the sun had almost always been shining on her mother's manor house at Bletsoe. Or so it seemed to her now as she re-lived the day Edmund had come to ask for her hand. She could hear again the rustle of lime trees and the buzzing of the bees as they sought the nectar from the sweet-smelling blossoms.

Edmund, Earl of Richmond, half-brother of Henry VI and eldest son of Owen Tudor and Catherine de Valois had been her guardian since she had been nine years old. He had been chosen by the King to take the places of her dead father and the murdered Suffolk, who had been appointed her first protector.

Her lips curved with tenderness as she remembered her joy when in the following autumn she had become Edmund's wife. He had bestowed upon her incomparable happiness and for a few short months she had been transported into a world where only she and Edmund existed.

Almost as soon as her marriage had been celebrated she and her new husband had journeyed into Wales where they might live and keep their heirs safe from the growing threat of civil war.

In Pembroke Castle, home of Edmund's brother Jasper, their love had grown and deepened. The wild and remote countryside surrounding the stronghold had held no terrors for her, for within the walls and in the strong circle of Edmund's arms she was invincible and untouchable.

So she had thought from the secure haven

of her husband's adoring affection. But it was not to be.

In the early summer of 1455 she knew she was with child. The knowledge added to her happiness for she held within herself a part of Edmund's love.

During this time Jasper took upon himself the patrolling of the Welsh Marches and the recruitment of supporters for the Lancastrian King who was his half-brother. When he was called to London at the command of Henry's fiery Queen Margaret of Anjou, Edmund reluctantly took his place in the Welsh countryside but returned to Pembroke as quickly as he was able.

It was during one of these brief absences Edmund had contracted the dreaded plague.

Margaret shivered as she recalled the frightened squire who brought her the news and she saw again the look on the boy's face as she had ordered her pony to be saddled so that she might ride to Carmarthen to comfort her dying husband.

She had nursed Edmund through a terrible night when she had watched the man who awakened her to the joy of living lose his hold in the fight with death.

When he died, the monks had led her away and numbed with shock and despair she had returned to Pembroke.

Here, for two months, in which she existed in a dazed state of semi-awareness, she waited for the birth of her child. Those about her watched her with deepening anxiety until late in January her half-sister, Margery, came from Bletsoe brought by Jasper, who had left his obligations to the King and Queen as soon as he heard of his sister-in-law's plight and hurried to her side.

He had come into her chamber, and the sight of Edmund's brother, his face registering his concern, had, in some way, unlocked the wordless misery fettering her since she had been widowed. Blessed tears, hitherto impossible to shed, flowed down her pale cheeks as she thanked Jasper for coming to her aid and welcomed him to his own castle.

Almost immediately her pains began and a son had been born on the following morning. Snow had fallen in the night and a new peace wrapped the earth and the heartbroken Margaret.

Jasper had come to her and pledged his life in the protection of his nephew and Edmund's widow.

He gave up his active support of the Lancastrian cause and stayed at Pembroke from where he was able to keep alive the loyalty for his half-brother while he cared for Margaret and her son.

Looking back Margaret could not be certain when she had first known Jasper loved her. Perhaps she had always known it from that moment when he had ridden, at tremendous pace, across England and Wales to comfort her and had knelt at her feet on that January night.

Margaret sank a little deeper into her chair as the warmth from the fire increased and she thought of her early years at Pembroke.

If she had not been conscious of Jasper's deepening affection for her when he had first taken up residence with her she knew her life had slowly begun to reawaken under his gentle care for her. Unobtrusively he had helped and encouraged her, bringing her scholars and books to occupy her nimble and logical mind. He doted on his nephew, making every effort to fill the place of his dead father.

Margaret remembered his thought in bringing his own father, Owen Tudor, to Pembroke to see, for the first time, his daughter-in-law and grandchild. She and Owen had become fast friends and it was he who had first taken her for rides beside the broad waters of Milford Haven. She had loved the exulting freedom of the strong air as it whipped fresh colour into her face and Jasper had continued the outings when his father returned to his manor.

It was on one of these rides she had been thrown from her pony and had damaged her ankle. Jasper, in an agony of anxiety, had picked her up from the damp shore and carried her across his saddle, back to the castle.

Alone in her chamber she had slid from his arms and looked up into his face. Fierce delight mingled with swift concern as his arms were about her, crushing her to him. Gasping, she had pushed him gently away. For this, the perfect solution to the vexed issue of her continuing widowhood and her personal happiness, was denied to them as she was his sister-in-law.

For a time she had been threatened with a return to the despair she had known before but with Jasper this was impossible.

Making no secret of his love for her, he was too vital and strong minded to allow misery to swamp her, and when he discovered — as he did, with unashamed humility — his love was reciprocated his delight was unbounded. But from this moment the poignancy of their mutual attraction doubled.

Margaret realised she would have to face up to the increased difficulty of marrying again. She put off again and again discussing the problem with Jasper. Her refusal to do so being bound up with an anguished hope some solution would present itself whereby Jasper would be hers without the relinquishing of her integrity and the responsibility she owed her son in the keeping of her vast estates.

She shifted uneasily in her chair as she thought of the inheritance to which she had been born and the millstone round her neck it had appeared at this time.

But for Henry she would gladly have thrown away the manors and farms, houses and estates her father and mother had given her if she could have lived quietly with Jasper.

Margaret thought of Jasper as he had been in those far off days. She remembered with nostalgia the well-shaped head, the curve of his mouth and the eyes which had looked so often upon her with love. He had been strong, well built, not over tall but fired with a zest for life; warm and compassionate. He had early established himself as a leader of men, courageous without being reckless.

Why when she had wanted him so much had she not sacrificed everything and shared his bed with the same joy as she shared his home at Pembroke?

Setting aside the subtle bond uniting her son, Jasper and herself which joined them while it held Margaret and Jasper apart, what was then, the reason she had not succumbed to the ever present temptation she suffered to become Jasper's mistress?

Unexpectedly, the answer had lain with the Earl of Pembroke. It was not that Jasper was more virtuous than the contemporary men of his generation but she came to realise he saw in their relationship something deeper than that of lovers.

Margaret understood this for she was self-appointed guardian of Jasper's bastard daughter, Helen. The girl, now married with an establishment of her own, had been the daughter of Myvanwy of Narbeth who had died of a miscarriage when Helen had not been nine months of age. Margaret knew Jasper had carried a nameless sense of guilt for the death of this young woman who had given him selflessly of herself and he was very reluctant to burden his brother's young widow with similar misfortunes.

It was this show of strength which helped Margaret to bring herself to consider re-marriage.

On one lovely warm evening when the Castle of Pembroke was filled with the rosy glow of the setting sun she had steeled herself to bring up the subject. She had seen Jasper struggle to speak dispassionately and had heard, through the pounding of blood in her ears, him suggest the name of Henry Stafford, a lifelong friend.

She had grasped quickly at his choice and the decision made threw herself into a whirl of alteration and refurbishing of her apartments.

Henry Stafford, second son of the Duke of Buckingham, took her as his wife in a quiet ceremony at Pembroke Castle. Her sharpest memory of the day was watching Jasper drinking heavily and leaving the feast to go early to bed. When she had retired for the night she had been surprised to find Betsey Massey still awaiting her as she had done since the far off days in Bletsoe. It was as if she had expected her re-marriage to alter everything. In a rush of emotion she had taken Betsey's hand and held it to her cheek. She heard her waiting woman sniff and turned away quickly so that her own tears would go unnoticed.

In the morning she found Jasper had gone to join his father at his manor at Trecastle before leaving for Westminster to resume his duties as an active supporter of the King and Margaret of Anjou.

During his years at Pembroke the contending forces of the Duke of York had openly shown their hostility to the King and discontent had grown markedly. Jasper found much cause for anxiety at Court.

At Pembroke, Margaret heard with growing alarm of the fighting and unrest everywhere between the troops of the King and York and his young sons. She prayed anxiously for the well-being of those she loved.

Henry Stafford lost his father in a battle between the rival forces at Northampton and Margaret persuaded him to return home to his mother to comfort her at this time. He went with reluctance as he was torn with concern for his bereaved parent and the wife he had but recently promised to protect.

Swiftly on his departure came the news of the routing of the King's armies at Mortimer's Cross and the taking of the throne by York's son, Edward.

While stunned by this turn of events Margaret had been shocked first by the unwelcome news of the beheading of her father-in-law, Owen Tudor and later by the taking of Pembroke Castle by Yorkist sympathisers.

She looked back on this period of imprisonment in the once loved place as the most dreary and frustrating of her life.

Only once during the next eight years had she had word from Jasper who had been forced to take refuge in the Welsh mountains when he was attainted by the new King

Edward and had had later to flee to France to bring aid to the displaced Queen Margaret of Anjou.

Their fortunes had taken a happier turn when King Henry had been restored to the throne in 1470 and she had been able to move freely for the first time for over ten years. However shortlived the release had been it had been sufficient to restore Jasper to her.

He had come home with the triumphant Lancastrian forces and immediately sought out Margaret. She could still remember over the span of years the happiness coursing through her when their eyes met after the seeming endless separation.

But their reunion and the King's restoration were not to last. Edward of York gathered sufficient forces to defeat the Lancastrians utterly and succeeded in disposing of Henry VI and his heir by murder and death on the battlefield.

Jasper had sent Margaret back to Pembroke and had brought her son in safety to her there. No sooner had they reached the castle than it was once more beseiged by Yorkist sympathisers and they were beset there for almost a fortnight until friends of Jasper's effected their release and they escaped down the Haven to Tenby.

These fourteen days were the most bitter-sweet of Margaret's life. Alone with Jasper and her child she faced the perils of capture by the Yorkists and all that meant to the three of them who were now the most prominent Lancastrians left alive. Shared danger enhanced the depth of their mutual feeling and it was by sheer strength of purpose they did not succumb to the over-riding temptation to take advantage of their plight and lose themselves in the delights of passion.

She had not broken the news to Jasper that she intended to remain in England while he and her son sought refuge at the court of the French King until they were sailing down the broad waters of the Haven *en route* for the open sea. Later, when a storm threatened to sink the small boat in which they journeyed, she had wished they might all die for the suffering she had glimpsed on Jasper's face had equalled the pain she felt in her heart.

But they had survived and Jasper and Henry had stolen out of Tenby harbour to seek sanctuary.

Margaret's brows drew together as she remembered the anxious months she had passed until she had been brought news of their arrival, not in France, as they had hoped but in the Dukedom of Brittany. Here,

Francois II, in deference to an agreement with Edward of England, imprisoned his noble captives. They had been held as suspect characters until only two or three years ago when the usurper Richard of Gloucester murdered his nephews and set himself on the throne of his late brother Edward. England discovered her conscience once more and began to plot the overthrow of the unscrupulous Gloucester.

The first attempt, set in motion by Buckingham and supported by Margaret herself, who until this moment had taken no active part in the politics of the kingdom, succeeded in drawing Jasper and her son as far as the shores of Britain but had failed when Buckingham was betrayed and beheaded.

Not discouraged by this setback and supported by the hundreds of Englishmen thronging to Brittany to pledge their support of Henry as the surviving Lancastrian heir, he and Jasper amassed an army with French and Breton help and had landed two short months ago on the same shores they had quitted fourteen years earlier.

This time, strengthened with Welsh soldiers and betrothed to Edward's daughter Elizabeth of York, Henry fought his way across Wales and into England and finally overcame

Richard of Gloucester on the field of Bosworth.

Margaret had come out of the confinement in which she had been kept since Buckingham's unsuccessful rebellion owing her life to him for refusing to implicate her in his rising.

She had waited at Collyweston, her home in the Midlands, for the triumphant return of her son and Jasper. She had clasped her fair-haired, gracefully built son in her arms, hardly recognising in the twenty-seven-year-old man the youth she had tearfully sent to a haven in France. While she had fought with the choking emotion of the moment she had been unable to look at Jasper who had stood quietly at his nephew's side but when Henry released her gently and brought Jasper forward she had been obliged to lift her head and regard him.

She smiled into the leaping flames, recalling the pleasure of seeing him again, surprisingly so little changed from the mental picture she harboured of him. True enough, there was grey at the temples and his face was lined and paler but he held himself as well as ever and his figure had thickened but not run to seed. She had wondered, momentarily, of whom he reminded her and then she had known, with a rush of affection, he was exactly as she had remembered his father on the last time he had come to Pembroke.

Later, when the household had retired, she and Jasper had talked over the happenings of the wasted years. He had told her of his despair when he had learned of her third marriage to Lord Stanley before he had discovered she had undertaken the ceremony only after making a vow of chastity.

He was shrewd enough to realise she had made this step to bring Stanley firmly on to the side of Henry when he made his attempt to conquer England and he spoke little of it. Her long marriage with Stafford he found more interesting and she had assured him he had been a true friend and counsellor over the years and when he had died had left her his estate in gratitude for the happiness she had given him.

It was now the pain in her heart began to trouble her once more. For it was during this meeting she had begged Jasper help her repay her debt to the deceased Buckingham by marrying the widow. She held her hands to her chest, pressing against the raw hurt.

How much easier it would have been to have grasped at a little personal happiness now Henry and Jasper were restored to her but she had been possessed by her guilt in the implication of Buckingham's rebellion and her escape at his expense and she felt only by paying the supreme price of giving Catherine of Buckingham into Jasper's protection could she exonerate herself.

There was, too, the matter of the vow of chastity. Always religious, her faith had deepened as her troubles and anxieties increased, and it had seemed a small price to pay for the well-being of those she loved.

The sight of Jasper had shaken her from this complacency. She had realised she might be forty-four years of age but she was still young enough to find her pulses quickened and a warmth suffused her breast as she looked on him.

Before, a liaison between them would have hurt only themselves. Those about them would have been too busy breaking the fifth commandment to have noticed their particular fall from grace but now, as Mother of the King, much would be expected from the Lady Margaret. No breath of scandal must sully the bond between her and the brother-in-law who had guarded her son as his own over all these years. Marriage for him was the safest course for them all.

So, as once long ago, he had chosen a husband for her, she had found him a bride and on this day — or was it now yesterday — ? Jasper and Catherine of Buckingham had been declared man and wife.

With all the generosity of her bountiful charity she had taken the widowed Duchess, with her two small sons, into her protection and had also provided the marriage feast.

It was this last gesture that had drained her of her energy and filled her with nostalgia for the past and what might have been.

Of a sudden she longed for the young husband who had died so tragically long ago. Had she not been widowed when scarcely sixteen years old she would not have found herself in this predicament today. And yet, was it not perhaps because Jasper was Edmund's brother they were drawn to each other?

She sat up abruptly and pushed the poker into the embers sending a shower of sparks up the wide chimney.

Going to the window she threw back the curtains and saw the far horizon lit with a pale, tremulous dawn. Shaking her head at her folly in sitting through the entire night she wrapped herself in the blanket and fell on to the bed, where she was instantly asleep.

2

In the next few months she was to find very little time to brood over her own feelings.

Henry, having strengthened his position by showing clemency to most of those who had fought against him at Bosworth, announced 18th January, 1486, as the day set for his marriage with Elizabeth of York, eldest daughter of Edward IV and his queen Elizabeth Wydeville.

Margaret was, from the outset, caught up in the intricate preparations for the celebration of this union which sought to heal, once and for all, the running sores of the thirty-year-old fight for supremacy between the Red and White roses of the Houses of Lancaster and York.

Elizabeth's mother, the widowed dowager, proved incapable of coping with the organisation of the wedding even if her future son-in-law had considered asking her to do so.

Since the tragic disappearance of her two sons, Edward and Richard, who had been confined in the Tower by their uncle Gloucester, never to reappear, she had lost the lush beauty that had attracted their father to her. She had become careless of her appearance, allowing her fair hair to become lifeless and untidy and her dress slovenly and not over clean.

Henry treated his future mother-in-law with courtesy and showed her every consideration in her bereavement but he confided to his mother he could never feel completely at his ease with her. This, Margaret knew, stemmed from the rumour he had heard during his stay across the Channel of her connivance in the attempt made by Richard of Gloucester to strengthen his slippery hold on the throne by marrying his niece. Whether it was true or not that the Dowager could have been capable of entertaining the thought of her daughter married to the undoubted murderer of her two sons, sufficient evidence remained to prove she had not been strong enough to prevent Elizabeth becoming the centre of some highly scandalous behaviour at her uncle's instigation.

Margaret put the most generous interpretation on Elizabeth's affection for her uncle of Gloucester but could not rid herself of the niggling suspicion Henry's future wife was almost as lacking in strength of character as her mother.

There was no denying Elizabeth was a

pretty girl. She could hardly have been otherwise as a child of Edward of York and his wife. She possessed the clear complexion and blonde hair of both her parents but had not inherited their earlier vitality. She was docile and anxious to please Henry's mother and since she had come from her virtual imprisonment in Sherrif Hutton, had lost over the weeks, the air of strain that had clung to her.

She looked forward, if not eagerly, at least with interest, to her wedding day. She was content to stand for tedious hours while sempstresses fitted her with the magnificent robe she was to wear. If Margaret suggested an alteration here or there she made no demur and seemed almost childishly pleased as the gown took shape.

Elizabeth Wydeville came once or twice to see how the dress was progressing but spent most of her time in her own apartments huddled over a fire with some embroidery lying untouched on her lap. Margaret made several attempts to break through her lethargy but found the Dowager put up an invisible barrier whenever they met.

It was not surprising Margaret became more and more the centre of Court life. At first she sent those who came seeking her advice and counsel to Elizabeth Wydeville but when she discovered, more often than not, the supplicators were refused audience she received them in her own chambers and listened to their problems.

When she spoke to her son of her concern for the feelings of his mother-in-law to be, Henry told her not to worry unduly for Elizabeth Wydeville and spoke of his growing respect for his mother's judgement.

He had formed the habit of coming to her rooms each evening before she supped.

'Do not wonder,' he said to her, 'that your opinions are sought. I value your good sense as much as any of those about the Court.'

She smiled up at him and he thought, not for the first time what an attractive woman she was. Always fastidious in her dress she had no false modesty and liked to wear becoming gowns. Her oval face was serene and her eyes had lost none of the luminous beauty of her youth. She was graceful in her movements and used her hands to emphasise what she said. He knew she possessed a warm, loving heart for during all the long years he and Jasper had been exiled in Brittany she had written to him constantly pouring out her affection and motherly counsel. It was a source of deep regret he had been deprived of so much of her wisdom and companionship.

He was well aware of Jasper's love for his mother and had been secretly amazed when the newly created Duke of Bedford had asked for the hand of Catherine Wydeville. Henry could only guess at the persuasive tactics his mother had employed to bring about the match.

He did not doubt also that Margaret was equally fond of his uncle but he recognised her propriety in encouraging his marriage and helping him to create for himself the family life he had so far been denied. Henry hoped his marriage with Catherine would be happy and complete, but still could not rid himself of the thought of how satisfying it would have been to have had Jasper and Margaret comfortably established as his parents. What sin could there be in a union such as theirs?

He shook off his conjectures about his mother and concentrated on the reason for his visit this particular evening which was to establish the order of precedence at his own wedding. It was some hours before the vexed question was finally ordered and he was able to assure himself all present would be satisfied with their stations and the duties assigned to them.

Margaret wondered, as he stooped to kiss her brow before leaving her, if he knew he had stepped into the routine Jasper had abandoned on his marriage. She tried not to think of the pleasant, companionable hours they had spent talking quietly together in the firelight while they sipped the wine put ready for them on a table between them. She had experienced a sense of real loss when the visits had ceased and although she had chided herself for her melancholy she had been unable to overcome it completely until Henry had taken it upon himself to come to her chambers at almost the same time of day.

Now, when the door closed behind him, she thought for the first time perhaps it was Jasper himself who had sent his nephew to cheer her. Smiling, she picked up a small silver hand-bell and when her page came to answer it said she would take her supper in her parlour and asked him to go to the apartments of her husband, the Earl of Derby, and her Secretary, Reginald Bray, and enquire if they would care to share the meal with her.

Rather to her surprise the boy returned to say both men would join her in an hour.

As she awaited them she thought much of them. Thomas Stanley, whom she had taken as her third husband and who was so different from Edmund whom she had loved with the unreserved adoration of her youth and the gentle Henry Stafford with whom she had shared the difficult years of the Yorkist supremacy. Stanley, Earl of Derby, was a widower with a grown family of his own and shared a common ancestor in Eleanor, daughter of Henry, Earl of Lancaster, with Margaret.

He treated Margaret with gruff courtesy. Since their marriage three years before each had earned the other's respect. When Margaret had insisted upon a vow of chastity being incorporated with the marriage settlement he had made no demur and had not once, since that day, prevailed upon her privacy or bothered her with unwelcome attentions. If he sought his pleasure elsewhere he did so in a manner which was both discreet and circumspect. No breath of scandal had come to Margaret's ear.

Derby had admired his new wife's determination to support her son in his bid for the English throne and although he made no definite moves when she plotted with Buckingham he stood by her when she was attainted by Richard III and relieved the severity of her sentence by seeing personally to her imprisonment and the forfeiting of rights which this inevitably meant.

When at last Henry and Jasper had crossed the Channel and landed in Wales, Derby had kept Richard guessing until the battle of

Bosworth was in progress before tipping the scales against him by sending in his large army to support his stepson. For this stroke of military prowess he had earned Margaret's undying gratitude.

Reginald Bray had been Margaret's Steward of the Household for many years and had played an active part in the despatching of supporters and money to Henry while he had been exiled in Brittany and France. Henry had shown his appreciation of these efforts by electing Bray to the Order of the Garter and making him a member of the Privy Council.

Margaret rose to greet the two men with pleasure when they arrived punctually at the set hour. Derby, portly and balding at the temples of his leonine head, Bray tall and stooping.

After they had eaten a small but excellent repast and the dishes and platters had been removed they stayed round the table talking quietly.

'It is very good to eat in peace for a change,' Derby said smiling. 'Your son, Madame, has gorged the stomach and the eye this Christmastide!'

'But a small way of expressing his gratitude to all those who have done so much to help him,' Margaret replied.

'You had best enjoy the quiet while you are

able,' Reginald Bray said laughingly. 'There is the wedding of his Grace in a few days and I cannot see such an occasion being allowed to pass without the due ceremony it demands.'

'Indeed not!' Derby agreed.

'Yet, although it means we should all spend the intervening days fasting, there is not a man or woman among us who will not rejoice at the union it symbolises between the Houses of Lancaster and York. We have much to thank you for, my lady,' he added turning to Margaret.

She was silent for a moment.

'I pray,' she said quietly at length, 'all may go well for Henry now. After so much tribulation it is difficult to imagine complete peace throughout the realm and I must confess my heart sometimes fails me at the thought of cronies of Richard of Gloucester plotting my son's downfall in secret somewhere.'

'Surely there is very little fear of that!' Derby cried. 'His Grace's leniency should have turned even the most faithful of Richard's men to his cause.'

'One would hope so,' Bray agreed dryly, 'but there are those who would ever seek their own glory.'

Margaret looked at him sharply.

'You are thinking of Lovell and the Staffords?'

'Yes, and perhaps the Earl of Lincoln, Richard's nephew.'

'He who was named as possible successor with young Warwick?' asked Derby.

'But that is impossible! Lincoln swore allegiance to Henry at the Coronation,' Margaret said.

'You are right, my lady,' Bray said reassuringly.

'You will not hesitate to tell my son of your fears at the next meeting of the Council?' Margaret said quickly.

'You need have no concern on the subject, my lady. His Grace has a logical and reasoning mind and is well aware of the inherent dangers of his new reign. He is fortunate in having at his side my Lord of Bedford and you, Sir,' he added turning to Derby.

'His Grace can count on me,' Derby said nodding his great head.

Margaret looked at him gratefully. Then as a new doubt assailed her she turned to Bray.

'Do you think Richard's sister, Margaret of Burgundy, will prove a stumbling block for Henry?' she asked.

Before Bray could reply Derby banged his fist on the table.

'Enough of these doleful apprehensions! Margaret of Burgundy, sister of Kings as she may be, is but a woman and I do not see her aping Margaret of Anjou and gathering an army about her to attack us here! Come, Bray, my lady wife will be completely dejected if we continue in this way. Let us speak of the wedding and the preparations most dear to the womenfolk on these occasions. What are you to wear, my dear?'

Diverted, Margaret laughed.

'A new gown and a secret one, at that!'

★ ★ ★

On the morning of the marriage, on the eighteenth of January, 1486, she went to the room where Elizabeth of York was being dressed by her ladies.

She found the girl composed but with her beauty heightened by the flush of excitement on her cheeks. Her hair had been washed and brushed until it gleamed and it fell in luxuriant strength about her shoulders. The dress they had chosen together suited her to perfection and she seemed happier than Margaret had dared hope.

Elizabeth dismissed her attendants as Margaret came forward and kissed her.

'My blessing on you this day,' Margaret said gently.

'Thank you, my lady. I hope I shall make your son a good and faithful wife and not fail those who have put their trust in me.'

Margaret suppressed a strong desire to look at her future daughter-in-law and busied herself instead with taking a jewelled pendant from the pouch hanging at her waist.

As she fastened it about Elizabeth's neck the girl gasped with pleasure.

'You are very kind, my lady,' she said as she looked down at the magnificent ornament on her bosom. 'I do not know how to thank you.'

'There is no need,' Margaret told her. 'The jewel belonged to my mother and when I realised how well it matched your dress I knew it must be my gift for this day.'

Later, in the cold, hard brightness of the winter day she watched as Henry and Elizabeth plighted their troth at the Abbey door. When they exchanged rings she saw in the ritual the sloughing off the barrier separating their two houses and the promise of peace.

Looking up, her eyes met those of Jasper, who was not attending to the moment rich in future hopes, but regarding her in a way she found difficult to define. Closing her eyes swiftly she found her heart beginning to pound in her breast. She was hardly conscious as the Archbishop of Canterbury pronounced Henry and Elizabeth man and wife and followed them into the packed Abbey almost in a trance.

As they took their places, standing in front of the large congregation and the Dean began to intone the Mass she discovered she was shaking and clenched her fists in an effort to control herself. She had wept openly at Henry's Coronation and it would not do for her to break down again. Opening her book of the Hours she forced herself to concentrate on the familiar words.

By the time Henry and Elizabeth walked down the aisle under a canopy of cloth of gold while trumpets blared in reverberating cadences against the high roof she had regained her composure.

Despite the cold a considerable crowd had gathered outside the Abbey Church and the bridal party were acclaimed with cheers and shouts of goodwill. Margaret smiled with real pleasure for she had been present when ugly incidents had marred occasions such as this wedding and it was not unknown for violence to break out among those who sought to air grievances. The populace's approval showed more clearly than anything she had hitherto witnessed the real need the country felt for a time of peace and prosperity when it might enjoy some of the awakening interest in trade and the new learning taking place in the rest of Europe.

She went into the Hall of St. Stephen's where the wedding banquet was to be held in a cheerful and confident mood. She was glad she had insisted Jasper should sit on the bride's left hand for she could not bear, at this moment, to be reminded by his nearness of her own emotions. Since his wedding she had avoided being alone with him and although they met almost every day in the course of the routine of the Palace, she had seen to it they had no opportunity to speak intimately.

She enjoyed the first course of the lavish feast served to them as they sat on the raised dais at the east end of the Hall but found after this she had lost her appetite. She toyed with the elaborately prepared dishes that followed and signed for her page, standing behind her, to remove her silver plate before Henry discovered her lack of appetite.

She, who prided herself on her excellent health, found to her shame, her head was hurting as if an iron band were clamped across her brow. She carried on a conversation with her husband and Bishop Morton however, despite her feelings and smiled and exchanged greetings with those close enough to call out. The Hall was packed with members of the Court and dignitaries from the City of London and the noise was deafening. Hating herself for her weakness, Margaret longed to slip away and fall into her bed.

The banquet continued deep into the night until at last the bridesmen and women came to bear away the King and Elizabeth of York. Henry bent briefly over his mother and she murmured a few words to her daughter-in-law as she came to bid her good night.

Waiting as long as courtesy demanded she rose quietly and made her excuses. Almost blinded with the pain in her head she gained the corridor leading to her chambers.

She came to the door of her room and, utterly weary, leant against the panelling.

Strong arms came round her and pulled her against a comforting chest.

'Just let go, my love,' Jasper said gently. 'Turn round and weep if you must. It is not every day one's only son marries with so much at stake.'

Tears of relief poured down her cheeks as she held herself rigidly away from him but at length she moved in the circle of his arms and rested her head on his shoulder.

'I should not give way to my feelings like

this,' she murmured. 'Throughout all the long years of separation and difficulties I have striven to be strong and now I melt like any feeble woman at the touch of your hands.'

Jasper moved impatiently.

'My very dear,' he said. 'To seek comfort and understanding from me, who would give his life to protect you, is no mortal sin. Because you are cradled here against my breast for a brief moment of time does not mean I am about to pick you up and throw you upon your bed to ravish you. Although,' he added tautly, 'I can think of nothing would please me more.'

'Don't speak of that!' she cried quickly, while her eyes filled again with tears. 'I have fought the daemon of my passion for you over the years. I am too old, now, to bear the misery of facing it again. When I took the vow of chastity — '

'Vow of Chastity!' Jasper echoed. 'There was no need for that! You are as virginal now as the day Edmund died!'

She said nothing but put her hand trustingly in his and relaxed a little more against him.

Jasper caressed the nape of her neck, easing away the strain and emotion of the day she had done so much to bring about.

'Where is Thomas Stanley?' he asked

suddenly. 'Is he not here to give you the benefit of his husbandly comfort?'

'He has much to see to in his position as High Constable of the realm on an occasion such as this,' Margaret said.

'There is nothing of such importance as seeing to the well being of the King's mother,' Jasper answered her shortly. 'The Stanleys are so jealous of their position they can look no further than their next advancement.'

'Jasper! Jasper!' Margaret said laughingly. 'I do believe I can detect a faint echo of jealousy in that statement!'

'You are perfectly right,' Jasper told her. 'And you know it better than any man or woman alive this day.'

'Yes,' she said simply, 'and I should not tease you.'

She sighed and disengaged herself reluctantly from his embrace.

She looked at him for a long moment. The well-remembered face was dimly lit by the cresset lights guttering in the draughty corridor.

'How is it with you, Jasper?' she said at last.

'You mean, how is my marriage?' he replied.

'Yes. I have no right to ask; but I must.'

'You have every right.'

He took her hand again.

'Catherine is very comely, as are all the Wydevilles. But like the rest of the family one is not certain of what lies behind the fair face and body. If anything.'

'They have suffered much,' Margaret reminded him gently.

'Yes, and not wholly through their own fault. They are fortunate indeed to have you as their champion. Henry tells me he has set aside a generous amount for you to use in the upbringing of Catherine's children.'

'Henry has been most thoughtful. He shows a very sound knowledge of finance which bodes well for the stability of the country. It seems he did not waste his time in Brittany.'

'No, that much is certain. He has too good a brain to have wanted to allow it to run to seed as he could so easily have done during those endless years of banishment.'

'Poor Henry,' Margaret said quietly. 'He has spent more of his life as a prisoner than I care to think on.'

'Let us pray he may now reap the reward of his patience,' Jasper said. 'Will you sleep now?'

'Yes,' she nodded. 'Thank you for your loving kindness to me. It is so very good to know you have not forgotten.'

'I can never do that. Your life and mine are

interwoven with threads that cannot decay.'

He unfolded her hand and putting the palm to his mouth, kissed it. It was a gesture peculiarly their own.

'No, you do not forget,' she said wistfully. 'Good night, my dear.'

Going slowly into her room she discovered her headache had completely vanished.

3

In the spring Henry and Elizabeth set out on a Royal Progress through the Midlands. The new King was determined to show himself among those who had held Richard of Gloucester in highest esteem.

Margaret accompanied them as far as her home in Collyweston. She was pleased to have the respite from court life and looked forward to some time of peace and tranquillity in which to take stock of her life in its new capacity as the King's mother.

When she had wished God speed to her son, who rode off with Derby and Jasper among a large and splendidly attired entourage, she spent several days immersed in the countless household and estate matters awaiting her attention.

These completed she made preparation to celebrate a quiet and secluded Easter. Throughout Lent she had denied herself stringently both of food and the comfort she usually enjoyed. She had given orders for frugal meals and had forbidden her maids to bring her the warmed, scented water her fastidious nature craved for washing. Betsey

Massey clucked round her disapprovingly as she came shivering from an icy toilette, throwing out thinly veiled comments of there being little or no need for further self denial. Margaret ignored her maidservant's asides knowing full well the woman meant them in true kindness. Of all those who had been in her household over the years Betsey knew her best and was cognisant of the love between her mistress and the Duke of Bedford.

Margaret could still remember occasions when she and Betsey had had quiet but heavily charged discussions on the ban forbidding a woman to marry her deceased husband's brother. In the face of the simple reasoning of the countrybred Betsey, Margaret had experienced considerable difficulty in adhering to the doctrines by which she and Jasper were bound. On more than one occasion she peremptorily dismissed her maid for overstepping the subtle division existing between them, only to find minutes later she wished to recall her to tell her how heartily she agreed with what she had said.

It was therefore with no surprise she accepted Betsey's disapproval of her aesthetic life during Lent and quietly continued to deny herself.

Henry sent messengers from Lincoln, where he kept Easter, to say he had received word of the disappearance from Sanctuary of Lord Lovell and the Stafford brothers. He told his mother to have no fear on his account for Derby and Jasper were recruiting men as the progress continued and he saw no reason for altering or abandoning his tour.

Margaret increased the number of daily Masses she heard and prayed Henry might be spared to sit for a long time upon the throne he had so recently won.

For some days she received no further messages and comforted herself with the knowledge bad news travelled considerably faster than good.

The spring days were beautiful in many different ways. Within the space of an hour clear, translucent skies were covered with low scudding black clouds against which the bright new green of the budding trees showed in sharp contrast. Walking through the terraced gardens where the gardeners planted flowers and vegetables and already the bees and the butterflies fluttered in the fitful sunshine Margaret looked with pleasure on the signs of the earth wakening to its age-old cycle. She gave herself several days when she did little but discuss the various merits of one or other position for a carefully nurtured shrub or merely sat, in a well-sheltered corner of the enclosed walk close to the house, and watched the changing sky.

This respite, coupled with the more satisfying diet she ate, filled her with renewed energy and she determined to put in motion the complicated matter necessary to provide almshouses for the needy and sick old people who lived on her estates.

She had always felt within herself the greatest compassion for those not as well blessed with worldly goods as she was. Although there had been many occasions when she would gladly have forfeited her enormous birthright to have her son restored to her or live in anonymity with Jasper, she was sufficiently Beaufort to recognise the great privileges wealth brought her. But her mother, also an heiress in her own right, had taught her from her earliest days to accept her good fortune only as a temporary gift from God and to insure she spent nothing on herself or her immediate household without considering the wants of those who were less fortunate. During the long years of Henry and Jasper's exile in Brittany she had had much cause to be grateful to her mother for her wise counsel and had endeavoured to fill the endless months by personal supervision of her estates. Now that she had seen the fulfilment of her dream of her son's homecoming and had been present at his crowning she realised she must occupy herself once more with the needs of others, if only to counteract the reawakening of her hopeless devotion for the man who had done so much to bring about Henry's good fortune.

Rising early one April morning she went to the small, oak panelled room where she carried out the paper work connected with the running of her home and sent for William Elmer. This young man had recently come into her employ on the recommendation of her half-brother Lord Welles who acted for her as her Chamberlain. Margaret liked William from the start. She found him lively minded and with fresh, uncomplicated views on a wide variety of topics. He was not afraid to differ, with a dissembling charm, if Margaret suggested some measure with which he could not agree completely. In the short time he had acted as her clerk she had found his opinions sound and his reasoning uncluttered by the sentimentality she found occasionally creeping into her own views. He had been educated partly at the Inns of Court and it was this legal training that undoubtedly strengthened the force of his judgement. Margaret quickly learnt to give heed when he suggested alteration or a different approach to the dozens of letters he compiled for her.

Added to his usefulness William was also a social asset to the household; his mop of reddish gold hair and tall, gangling body singled him out from his fellow men and while he possessed a perceptive wit he was too good natured to turn this gift to hurt other people. It seemed impossible to ruffle his easy going manner and he accepted ruefully the endless teasing he received on his singular colouring. At Christmas it had not been difficult for the Steward of the Household to persuade him to take the duties of Lord of Misrule. He had acquitted himself so successfully it was common knowledge several of the women of the Court had tried to attract his interest. Margaret often found herself wondering if any of them had succeeded.

He came into the room now, a smile on his long, oddly attractive face. She waved for him to take his customary stool.

'Good day to you, William,' she said, drawing one of the rolled parchments stacked on the table towards her, 'we had best be writing again to the Bailiff of Ware concerning the almshouses at Hatfield or we shall find nothing has been done at all to start their building. Have you received any messages from him as yet?'

'No, my Lady, but doubtless he is going

about the finding of surveyors and trustworthy masons and tilers.'

'You are trying to tell me I am impatient,' Margaret said wryly. 'I must confess since my son has been restored to me I seem to have lost that virtue that held me in such good stead during his absence. It would appear there is so much to be done there is no time to lose.'

'Shall I delay the writing of the letter for a day or two?'

Margaret nodded.

'What of the deputation who came from the fenlands about the draining of their lands?'

William took up a roll tied with cord.

'This is the latest report from their spokesman. He seems to think the building of dykes could reclaim a great deal of the land covered by the water.'

Margaret took the parchment and studied it in silence.

'Please reply and tell him we shall do all in our power to assist them.'

As William re-tied the seal there was a knocking on the door and one of Margaret's ladies went to answer it.

'My lord the Earl of Ormond is without and seeks audience with you, Madame.'

William stood and looked enquiringly at

46

Margaret. She signed to him and he went quickly from the room, returning almost immediately with Ormond, the Queen's Chamberlain.

He bowed over Margaret's hand as she greeted him. She sent pages for wine while he seated himself.

'You have news for me, Thomas? Good or bad?'

'Some excellent and some a little disturbing.'

'Tell me the ill first and keep the good to lift my spirits.'

Margaret composed herself as well as she was able while the Steward and pages returned with flagons of spiced hippocras and marchpane comfits.

When at last they closed the door behind them and Ormond and she were alone, she turned to him.

'Well, Thomas? My son is not ailing?'

'No, no, my Lady. You can rest quite assured on that account. His Grace is in good health and sends you greetings and letters. What I have to tell you concerns Lord Lovell and some of his followers — '

'There has been a rebellion?' Margaret asked sharply.

'There might have been — shall I say, Madame, had it not been for the preparations of your son and the Duke of Bedford's swift action — '

'Bedford? All is well with him?' Margaret cried, putting a hand to her mouth.

Ormond regarded her gently.

'There has been no battle, my Lady, so no one has been hurt. Perhaps you already know that when we were at Lincoln we received word of Lovell and the Humphrey brothers making preparations to come against the King's forces. Bedford at once made it clear to his Grace this was no time for timid action and he formed up the men he had been gathering during the progress and marched out towards the rebels. It did not take long for those who had promised support to Lovell to realise they were overwhelmingly outnumbered and quite quickly they deserted from their leader and he fled once more into hiding.'

'So he is still at large? And what of the Humphreys?'

'They have taken Sanctuary in Oxford.'

'Holy Church must be an uncomfortable protector for traitors,' Margaret commented dryly. 'I was so afraid this kind of incident would happen. Is my son returning to London to recruit a larger army?'

'No, my Lady,' Ormond said smiling. 'His Grace was so reassured by the action taken by his uncle and the decisive halt put upon his enemies he has taken up residence in York, whence I come with his messages.'

'Henry must be well at ease to stay in that Gloucester stronghold. Was he well received?'

'Undoubtedly. Pageants, bonfires and conduits running with wine greeted the royal party and the King and the Queen rode through the streets to much cheering.'

'Of course, I was forgetting,' Margaret said softly, 'with Elizabeth of York beside, the way would be smoothed.'

'No, no,' Ormond cried. 'His Grace won as much applause, if not more, than the Queen!'

'I am glad,' Margaret replied quietly.

After a moment she looked up at Elizabeth's Chamberlain.

'That is the worst of your news?'

Ormond nodded and drew a small roll from his pouch.

'Here, my Lady, is a letter from your son telling you himself of the good.'

Ormond went over to the window and stood looking out over the stone houses and walls to the rolling countryside beyond.

Margaret broke the royal seal and swiftly read the well-known handwriting. An exclamation of delight escaped her as she took in the full import of the words.

'Oh, my Lord! So the union of our houses

is to be blessed with a child! God be praised!'

'May I be the first to offer my congratulations,' Ormond said kneeling quickly. 'You know you have my sincere wishes for the well-being of the heir of England.'

'The heir of England,' repeated Margaret slowly, 'and I am to be his grandmother! Grandmother!' she said again half incredulously.

'The fairest in England,' Ormond said gallantly. Margaret smiled and took up the letter once more.

'It says here her Grace is in good health. Is that your private opinion, Thomas?'

'I have never seen the Lady Elizabeth look better, and His Grace is clearly delighted with the good news.'

'Then we must pray all will continue so and the realm shall remain at peace.'

On the following morning she resumed her interrupted session with William.

'We have new business to conduct,' she told him.

'If I may say so, my Lady, whatever the matter of the business it gives you great pleasure to judge by your countenance,' William said looking at her with his head on one side.

'It most certainly does,' she answered, 'for it is the ordering of a cradle — '

'A cradle!' William echoed.

For a second their eyes met across the table and they both laughed.

'No, my dear William, let me enlighten you before the household is bursting with the news I am to become a mother. No, don't attempt to deny it was what you thought. I could see it written in the grin you tried so hard to stifle. It is not I but my daughter-in-law who is expecting a child.'

'What wonderful news, my Lady! An heir for England.'

'Good news indeed and therefore the crib must be of the finest design and craftsman-ship.'

'Shall I send the joiner to you?'

'Yes, please; when we have attended to all these other matters which seem now not quite so important. The man we have here is well versed in the art of carving and turning for I would he make for me a cot for the child to use all the time. A homely affair, painted and decorated; not a great State cradle to be covered in rich fabrics and used but now and again.'

She looked out of the window and William watched her, taking in the pale oval of her face lit with a happiness he had not seen before. He found himself wondering, not for the first time, of what else her life consisted beside the management of her estates. Before this morning he would have been prepared to wager the Lady Margaret was completely engrossed in her duties and responsibilities but suddenly he saw she was a very beautiful woman who could be as deeply touched with the emotions of ordinary day to day life as easily as any other woman he knew. Now he came to think about it had he not heard of some liaison between the new Duke of Bedford and his mistress? But of course, she had once been his sister-in-law and had taken care of the King during his childhood after his father died. That was probably all —

'William!'

He sat bolt upright, bringing himself quickly back to the environment of the dark, panelled room.

'My Lady — ' he stammered, for once at a loss.

'Pass me the roll with the accounts for the Cheshunt manor, please,' Margaret said.

As she took them from him she smiled.

'We had best be dealing with the day's work otherwise we shall both lose ourselves in daydreaming.'

'Just what I was thinking,' William assured her, 'now, if you will look at this column of figures here you will see the manor has become almost self supporting as far as vegetables and fish are concerned — '

He stopped suddenly as Margaret clapped her hands.

'What do you think, William, shall I have the flowers on the cradle painted blue or pink?'

4

Elizabeth of York was safely delivered of a son on the 20th September. England went mad at the good omen. The child was to bear the name Arthur in deference to the great man to whom the Tudors looked for their ancestry.

With great tact and a considerable amount of self control Margaret stayed at Collyweston for the event.

Earlier in the year she had been present in Westminster when Henry and Elizabeth had returned from their triumphant progress round their realm and at Henry's wish had compiled a set of Ordinances for every aspect of the new facet of the Royal Household. At his desire she had laid down rules for the conducting of the lying-in period and the feeding and care of the wet nurses who would suckle the babe.

But when Henry had begged her to accompany them to Winchester where the child was to be born, far away from the heat of London and its attendant risk of plague, he found his mother not so pliable. She was never to forget the look of gratitude on Elizabeth's face as she had gently declined the invitation and had insisted on the Dowager Queen being the right and proper person to accompany her daughter at this all important time in her life.

At the Christening, which took place in Winchester Cathedral, the Dowager was godmother and Jasper and Margaret's husband the godfathers.

Although Margaret had elected to stay away she bowed to Henry's request for suggestions of the form the ceremony should take.

It was, therefore, a very colourful and dignified procession following the baby as he was carried down the aisle by his nurse attended by a magnificent train of relatives and courtiers. At the font a mass of men and women held aloft lighted torches while the child clutched in his tiny hand a taper.

Reginald Bray followed behind the Earl of Derby bearing a worked gold cup covered with a handsome lid. His maternal grandmother, for once beautifully gowned and smiling graciously upon all those present, held the babe as he was handed to the Bishop to be taken to the High Altar for Confirmation.

As the procession wound its way back to the castle for the celebration banquet it seemed indeed as if all differences were completely forgotten and the future rich in promise for peace for Henry and his heirs.

Reginald Bray came to Collyweston as soon as the proceedings were completed to report in detail to Margaret. She listened eagerly to what he recounted putting in many questions. Afterwards she went to her chapel and gave thanks to God for His great mercies.

Since Easter her time had been even more fully occupied than before as Henry had increased her already considerable estate by making her a gift of many lordships and manors. At first she had been inclined to refuse his generosity but reconsidered her first thoughts when she realised Henry was probably exercising wisdom for the future and sharing some of his burdens by passing over to her, for her lifetime, the management of such vast tracts of English and Welsh land.

One of the holdings she accepted with unfeigned pleasure was the title of a mansion in Thames Street. This house, backing on the river, fell within the walls of the City of London in the Parish of Allhallows the Less. It was called Coldeharbour and had been the property of the King and his family for some generations.

Giving the Queen and his son plenty of time to grow strong after the Prince's birth

Henry made plans to spend Christmas at Greenwich.

Margaret left Collyweston in October to stay for the first time at Coldeharbour. Since she had taken possession of the house she had given orders for a considerable amount of repairs and new furnishing and she was eager to see what progress the workmen had made. She had sent William several times to London and he had returned full of enthusiasm for her new home.

She was glad to be going south to see her grandchild and to make an opportunity of speaking with Henry about the Coronation of the Queen. She had not mentioned the matter in the many letters passing between them but had questioned Bray closely whenever he had come to her. She well understood her son's reluctance to admit he owed any of his right to the Throne to his wife but she was at a loss to comprehend his hesitation to crown her. Surely Henry could not doubt his wife was completely on his side? Did he perhaps still experience some doubts of her loyalty to his cause? These were the things she could ask him in private where she was too restrained to write them. Many times she longed to see Jasper and talk over with him the whole vexed question. Devoted as Bray was to her and her service only with

Jasper could she speak of her son's shortcomings — real or imagined.

It was now almost a year since she and Jasper had met. He sent her messages whenever heralds came to Collyweston but they told her little or nothing of how he fared or of what his daily life consisted. That he was much with Henry she knew but if he ever went to his estates she was ignorant. She dreaded to hear he had taken Catherine to Pembroke. Somehow the idea of any other woman sharing the remote beauty of the estuary fortress with him was almost more than she could bear.

Catherine's children were now her sole responsibility. Henry had formally made them her wards and granted her the custody of their estates during the minority of the elder. Out of the income derived from these lands she was to provide for their upbringing and education. Her brother, in his capacity as her Chamberlain had been finding suitable men and women to make up the household of the little Edward and his small brother Henry.

Margaret made their acquaintance for the first time when she arrived at Coldeharbour. She felt at home in the stone mansion from the moment she set foot in the arras hung hall. She made a tour of inspection and made it known she was well pleased with the decorations and refurbishing that had been carried out.

When she had eaten and recovered from the journey she had made that day from Hatfield she sent for the Buckingham children and their household.

Their governess, Edith Fowler, led them to make their bows to their patroness and introduced their chaplain and nurses. Both boys, shy and obviously slightly overawed by the gravity of the moment, clung to the young woman's hand but thawed when Margaret spoke to them quietly of the barges lying close beside the house at the nearby wharf. Together they knelt on the padded window seat looking down on to the Thames now dappled with the glow of the setting sun. The boys were fair with the wide blue eyes of their mother and the comeliness of the Plantagenet blood from which they were sprung. Margaret felt an uprush of pity for their fatherless state. How much of their deprived childhood was due to the support Buckingham had given the cause of Henry almost three years ago?

Leaving Edward and Henry looking at the barges Margaret took stock of Edith and the other women. The governess was tall and well proportioned, serene of face and having an air of wholesome good health. As Margaret turned to regard her she was deep in conversation with William Elmer, who though he was paying her every attention, was looking beyond her to a corner of the room. Covertly following the direction of his gaze Margaret checked an exclamation as she saw the young woman who was the object of his interest.

This was Perrot who had been presented to Margaret as the Frenchwoman acting as Edith's deputy. The girl possessed a sinuous beauty subtly underlined by the dress she wore. The gown was fashionable but simply cut and it emphasised the generous bosom and slim waist of its wearer. Perrot was not over tall but she held herself proudly and it was almost possible to touch the air of animal magnetism she seemed to exude. As Margaret watched her the girl became aware of her scrutiny and greeted her appraisal without flinching, returning look for look.

Margaret was glad when Edith called quietly to the two small boys and bade them come and make their 'good nights' to their kinswoman and guardian. Suddenly very tired she waved away her ladies and attendants and bade them call Betsey to help her prepare for bed.

A few days before Christmas she and her

household and that of the Earl of Derby went down river to the Palace of Greenwich. The day was cold and dreary with a biting, salt-smelling wind gusting up the river. Margaret huddled in her fur lined velvet cloak and occupied her mind with the business of keeping warm. She looked forward to the stay at Greenwich with mixed feelings; her delight at seeing her grandchild for the first time counterbalanced by the ordeal of meeting Jasper again after such a long interval. Although she had suffered two much longer and deadlier separations she knew by experience just to have him near her was sufficient to jolt her from the calm in which she tried to pass her days. With this in mind she had drawn up a mental list of matters needing discussion with Henry and her daughter-in-law and with their advisers she would otherwise not have the opportunity of meeting often.

The Buckingham children accompanied her in the covered barge and from time to time she could hear their excited and shrill voices as they saw birds and water rats at the river's edge. Edith Fowler sat at their side pointing out landmarks with Perrot close at hand. Now and again the French girl spoke with the children but spent most of the journey leaning back against the side of the boat and gazing across the bleak water. Margaret was disturbed again by the arresting beauty of her high cheek-bones and the compelling mystery of her heavy lashed eyes. She felt strangely relieved William was in the following barge and she had not been forced to sit and watch the looks, she had come to expect, pass between them. To be in the same room with them was to know, almost at once, the mutual attraction existing between them and although they made every effort to conceal it from Margaret, as mistress of the household, they could not resist the touch of hands and the brush of body against body. Margaret found herself strangely upset by the situation and forced herself to think about it without prejudice. It was not only she liked William and hoped he would find himself a woman worthy of him but some instinct warned her Perrot was of the breed who brought disaster to those with whom they came in contact.

Margaret hoped Henry would see fit to appoint William as Lord of Misrule for the twelve days of Christmas and keep him fully occupied during their stay at Greenwich.

When she was settled in the rambling Palace her son came at once to pay his respects.

Margaret rose with a glad little cry of

welcome as Henry came into her chamber.

'Come close to the light,' she said, 'so I may see how you fare! You look well, my son, but thin. You have no return of the sweating sickness?' she asked sharply.

'No, mother! I am better in health than I have ever been. For the first time in my life I am free to move about at will. Do not grudge me the opportunity to use every moment of the day in the service of the country.'

'Most certainly I would not do that. But take care, Henry, not to use every moment of the twenty-four hours. Even Kings must have their rest.'

'Worry not!' Henry said laughingly. 'I have not come to listen to a sermon on my health but to see how you are and to take you to visit my son.'

Elizabeth awaited her mother-in-law in her parlour and accompanied her to the nursery.

Margaret noticed with pleasure the cradle she had given was in use and the nurses who had the child in their care seemed healthy and comforting. She bent over the crib and smiled with delight on the infant sleeping in peaceful serenity.

'He is a beautiful babe,' she said to Henry and Elizabeth as they went back to the Queen's parlour. 'I think he resembles your father a little,' she added to Henry.

'Would you have had we call him Edmund then?' Henry asked her quickly.

'No, no. There is plenty of time to have a namesake. It was better for your first child to call him for the country rather than for the family. Is your mother here?' she asked, turning to Elizabeth.

'Yes, Madame, she is residing in the chambers of my sister Cecily and your half-brother Lord Welles.'

'I am glad she is come,' Margaret said simply. 'Who else is to be of the party?'

Henry looked at her and she hastily moved nearer the fire as she saw the glint of amusement in his eyes.

'The Lords of Oxford and of Dorset, Suffolk and Lincoln, Derby — '

'But I came with my lord husband!'

'Of course,' Henry said laughing. 'I am forgetting. What do you think of your fine new houses in the City?'

'I cannot thank you enough for Coldeharbour, I hope you and Elizabeth will be able to visit me there before I return to Collyweston. As for Derby House, it is very fine indeed and I am sure affords great pleasure to your stepfather.'

'Then I am delighted,' Henry told her. 'Is there anything else I can do to please you at this Yuletide?'

'Yes, there is; it is only a relatively small thing, but I am hoping you will see fit to ask William Elmer to be Lord of Misrule again this year.'

'Your clerk who was so successful before?'

Margaret nodded.

'That is easily granted. I wish all my supplicants were as swiftly dealt with. Shall I take you back to your apartments?'

'Can you spare the time?' Margaret asked.

'Of course,' Henry told her gently, 'it will be a sad day when I have no time for you.'

'Good night, Elizabeth,' Margaret said kissing the Queen. 'I am happy to see you looking so well. Motherhood suits you, for you look prettier than ever before. Doesn't she Henry?'

Henry stopped with his hand on the door latch.

'Yes, she does,' he said slowly, 'yes, you are perfectly right.'

Suppressing a smile Margaret followed him out of the room.

They were nearly at her door and had been chatting of this and that when he stopped and looked down at her.

'My uncle will be here this evening. He has been with Oxford at Headingham and sent word to say he would arrive tonight.'

'And his wife?' Margaret said in a voice she

had difficulty in controlling.

'Catherine is coming in a day or two. I believe she has been in the country at one of his manors.'

'So I am to be surrounded with old friends and — suitors,' Margaret said wryly.

'The Duke of Suffolk?' Henry said laughing.

'Yes,' Margaret said. 'Although I think I was but five or six when his father, the old Duke, tried to arrange a marriage for us. I do not flatter myself it was my personal charm that enticed the Duke but my Beaufort fortune weighed prettily heavily in his choice.'

'And your proximity to the Lancastrian succession.'

'Possibly,' Margaret agreed. 'Good night, my son,' she said lightly, 'I am happy indeed to be with you and your family and I pray to God we may be spared to see your children bring you much joy.'

She took her supper quietly in her small parlour and afterwards bade Betsey bring her a new cap she had had made of gossamer fine lawn.

She held her head first on one side and then on the other, regarding herself solemnly in the silver mirror Betsey held up for her.

'It looks very well,' Betsey told her, 'although there is no need to dress yourself up. He will be so busy looking at you, he won't notice your new headdress.'

Margaret covered her face with her hands.

'How do you know anybody might come?' she asked in a muffled voice.

'Quite simply. It is not every day you send me for your best bonnet when most folk are thinking of going to their rest. Is there anything else you require or shall I be going now?'

'No, there is nothing more but don't go, Betsey.' Hearing the note of near panic in the well-known voice Betsey busied herself about the room, pulling up another chair and mending the fire. She cast about in her mind to think of something to soothe Margaret and would have liked to launch out into one of her minor tirades against the tryranny of Holy Church but stifled the impulse and grasped with some relief the idea of fetching one of the newfangled printed books Margaret had bought in Westminster.

'Would you like me to bring one of Master Caxton's works for the Lord Jasper?' she asked.

'Yes,' Margaret cried. 'That is a very good idea. I had planned to give him one for the feast of St. Nicholas and he shall have it this night.'

'Has he told you he will visit you?' Betsey

could not help asking.

'No,' Margaret said quietly. 'But if he is unable to come this evening there is always tomorrow — or the day after.'

As she spoke her page came into the room to announce the Duke of Bedford had arrived and sought an audience.

Betsey sniffed over loudly and Margaret clutched the arms of her chair.

'Show him in,' she said.

Unnoticed Betsey went out as Jasper crossed to Margaret and took her hand. He looked at her for a long moment before taking the hand to his mouth and kissing the palm.

'Oh, Jasper,' she said gently disengaging herself.

She motioned him to the chair Betsey had set ready and he sat down, the firelight playing on the furrowed cheek and the eyes which watched her, unwavering.

Neither of them spoke, content to sit, drawing on the rare pleasure of one another's company.

At last, moving forward in the chair, Jasper spoke.

'There is so much to ask and so much to tell you. But first, is all well with you?'

'Yes,' she nodded. 'And with you?'

'Tolerably so. I am plagued with aches and

pains after a day in the saddle — '

'And that annoys you?' she said smiling.

'It does,' he replied. 'I hate to be reminded I am growing older and our time together is shortening by the hour.'

'Don't speak of it,' she said hastily.

'So you are a grandmother,' he said wonderingly. 'It does not seem possible. To me you are still the girl and young woman I took riding beside the Haven in Pembroke.'

'How is Pembroke?' she asked, looking into the fire.

'I do not know.'

Unable to stop herself she smiled.

'I shall not go there again except when there are urgent matters needing my personal attention. But you knew that, didn't you?'

'Yes, I suppose I did.'

'But you wanted to hear me say it.'

'Yes,' she answered huskily.

They fell silent again.

'I have much to ask you of Henry and the Lovell rebellion,' Margaret said.

'That will keep until the next time I visit you.'

He stood up and came to her, kneeling at her feet. Taking her hands he buried his face on her lap.

'Dearest Jasper,' she whispered and bending, kissed the top of his head.

'I must be gone,' he said a moment later. 'It would not do for the fair name of the King's mother to be sullied with suspicion. Good night.'

Margaret leant back in her chair and shut her eyes. When she opened them she found Betsey leaning over her.

'Here, my Lady, dry your eyes and drink this hot posset. What you need is a good night's sleep.'

5

On Christmas Eve as the household were returning from Mass snow began falling in ever increasing flurries. The wide river was obliterated in a mist of white and Margaret watched the lanterns carried by the servants shine eerily through the whirling flakes. When the great doors were opened to admit the worshippers to the Hall and they streamed in laughingly brushing off the drops of moisture on their garments, the welcoming warmth seemed to put them in a party mood.

One young man snatched up a lute and to the air he played some others started an impromptu dance. Immediately the room was filled with men and women who formed circles and lines and dipped and swayed in the rhythm of the music. Henry, delighted with the good start to the festivities, sent for wine to mull and beckoned for everyone to join in.

Margaret found Jasper at her side and took his hand when he proffered it. It was years since she had danced and at first she felt awkward and slightly embarrassed but gradually, as her confidence returned, she discovered she had not forgotten the intricate and sometimes complicated movements and was entering with pleasure into the steps.

She had not spoken alone with Jasper since the evening of his arrival. His wife had arrived from Gloucester the next day and Margaret made no attempt to deprive her of his company. Now she saw Catherine dancing between John, Earl of Oxford, and her own half-brother, Lord Welles, and almost as if he divined her thoughts Jasper pulled her swiftly from the gay throng and steered her towards the anteroom beyond.

Coming into the dimly lit room Margaret caught sight of William Elmer leaving by the other door.

'William!' she called. 'Would you be so good as to go to my chambers and ask Betsey to give you the book I had laid ready for my Lord of Bedford.'

'Certainly, my Lady.'

The tapestried room was already filling with those who had had sufficient of the dancing and Jasper and Margaret sat in two velvet chairs. A servant brought them silver mugs of the hot spiced wine and Margaret held hers warming her hands on its polished surface.

'You are warm enough?' Jasper asked her.

She nodded.

'We could, I suppose, move nearer the fire but — .'

'No,' Margaret said. 'It is very well here.'

She looked up as she heard William cough discreetly at her side.

'Oh, thank you, William.'

She took the small, vellum covered book and gave it to Jasper.

'This is for you,' she said, 'I asked William Caxton to make it especially.'

'What a beautiful thing!' Jasper exclaimed. 'Even if I did not treasure it solely because it is a gift from you, the workmanship would give me constant pleasure.'

He fingered the rich leather, running his strong hands over the cover. As he turned the thick pages slowly he stopped now and again to examine the text. At length he looked up at her, his eyes alight with pleasure.

'Thank you, dearest Margaret. Do you know it is the first printed book I have ever owned?'

'I am glad.'

'Have you been to Caxton's workplace?'

'Yes; when I was at Coldeharbour I went several times to the Almonry at Westminster where he works under the sign of the Red Pale. Have you been there?'

'No,' Jasper replied, 'but I mean to one day,

because I am sure what Caxton is doing will do much to alter the world as we know it. It will no longer be necessary for monks and clerks to spend laborious hours copying at their desks, while many more people will be able to learn to read and think for themselves; although that could be dangerous!' he added.

'I suppose it could,' Margaret said thoughtfully.

'But this doesn't look as if it contains material of an inflammable nature.'

Margaret shook her head, smiling.

'It is a translation from the French, by Caxton himself, of the romance of the knight of Paris and the fair Vyenne.'

'And you meant it as a tribute to the memory of my mother?' Jasper asked softly.

'Yes,' Margaret answered, 'although I never saw my mother-in-law, Catherine de Valois has a special place in my heart as Edmund's and your mother.'

'I have a gift for you, also,' Jasper said after a moment, 'I had it sent to your chambers while we were at Mass.'

'I shall look forward to seeing it,' Margaret said, her mouth curved with pleasure.

Restraining the urge to bend and kiss the parted lips Jasper contented himself with telling her he thought her a supremely honest woman.

'If you mean I did not put up a show of false diffidence at the thought of receiving a present from you, I confess you are probably right,' Margaret agreed, 'I cannot see the point of pretending I do not want your gift when I am made happy by the idea of it.'

'You like having things given to you?'

'Only from those I love. Henry has given me some velvet and cloth of gold to make a robe to wear at Court. Perhaps I shall have it fashioned to wear at the Queen's Coronation — that is, if there is any mention of the day as yet? Do you know of any plans?'

'I do not think a special time has been made but I do know Henry has the ceremony very much in mind.'

'You do not imagine he is putting it off?' Margaret asked anxiously.

'No,' Jasper reassured her, 'I know you understand Henry very well and recognise the necessity he feels for great caution, but I do not believe he mistrusts his wife in any way at all. I think he genuinely intended to have Elizabeth crowned when her pregnancy and the Lovell rebellion intervened and he is now only waiting to have the Christmas festivities ended before returning to Westminster and making the preliminary arrangements.'

75

'I am relieved to hear you speak so,' Margaret said. 'Speaking of Lovell; is there news of him?'

'As far as we know he remains at Oxford in Sanctuary and has given no cause for concern. Henry has shown much wisdom in the clemency he has extended to those who rebel against his authority.'

'I could wish he would release the young Edward of Warwick from imprisonment in the Tower,' Margaret said sadly.

'There must be good reason for keeping him there,' Jasper told her comfortingly, 'Henry has had sufficient imprisonment during his own life to know the effect it can have upon one not to subject anyone to it without cause. You must not forget Edward is the sole remaining heir of the Yorkists — apart from Henry's Queen.'

'Exactly,' Margaret said dryly, 'you have voiced my concern about Elizabeth. But surely, Richard III did not make Edward of Warwick his heir?'

'No. There was some confusion about the whole matter and Suffolk's son John, Earl of Lincoln was named for the succession — '

'And he is with us in the Palace now,' Margaret said quietly and looked over her shoulder uneasily.

'They have sworn their loyalty to Henry

and he has no cause to doubt their sincerity,' Jasper told her. He stood up.

'Are you for bed?'

'Yes.'

He led her out of the anteroom and they walked slowly down the length of the flagged corridor until they came to the foot of the stairway leading to her apartments. Her hand on the newel post she turned and bade him 'Good night.'

'Good night, my very dear,' Jasper said, 'and thank you again for Caxton's book.'

At the turn of the stair she paused and looked down into the corridor. Jasper was watching her. She smiled and with an effort forced herself to continue upwards.

Passing one of the deep alcoves close to her room she was startled by a quick movement and the gleam of a white bosom and shoulder. Turning hurriedly towards her door she had seen enough to know it was Perrot and William Elmer locked in one another's arms.

I am fast becoming an emotionally unstable woman, she chided herself as she went into her room and the faithful Betsey and several of her other ladies came to her.

'Just Betsey,' she said, 'you others go to your rest. You will have need of your sleep to prepare for the masques and disguising I hear we are to enjoy.'

When Betsey had helped her unfasten her dress and she had put on the soft woollen bedrobe, she sat at her table while the woman brushed her hair.

The gentle, hypnotising movement restored her calm. Before she went to her room adjoining Margaret's, Betsey handed her a leather box.

'You don't need me to tell you where that came from,' she said with the touch of asperity Margaret recognised as well hidden curiosity for the contents.

'No,' Margaret said, 'I think not. I'll look at it when I have said my prayers — and show it to you in the morning.'

'Thank you, my Lady.'

Margaret remained on her knees longer than usual, curbing her impatience to see what Jasper had sent her. At length she picked up the box and climbed into her high and elaborately curtained bed, snuffing all the tapers except one burning beside her on a nearby table.

The clasp clicked open easily as she pressed it and she found, nestling in a velvet interior, a magnificent cup of gold. Hardly able to see for tears she traced with her fingers an enamelled marguerite surrounded with four great pearls on the cover.

She set the cup on the table and lay watching the flickering flame of the light catch the pearls' lustre. She was reminded of Perrot's bosom gleaming in the dusky corridor and she found herself strangely disturbed with the remembrance. While one side of her nature grieved for the improvidence of William's liking for the girl she nevertheless envied them the freedom to indulge their mutual passion.

Was Holy Church so right in forbidding the marriage of a widow and her brother-in-law? Who had ever had her interests more at heart than Jasper since he had given her his protection on that distant day of Henry's birth? she thought. Was it perhaps not more of a sin to wed with a man for the protection of his house and name? What have I in common with Thomas Derby? Did I not sell myself to him to bring his support to my son's cause? Why do I lie here, alone and comfortless, when I might live within the compass of Jasper's love and affection?

Unable to bear the sight of the cup, glowing in the dimmed room, Margaret turned over and pulled the silken sheets close about her ears. But she was haunted by the remembrance of what might have been and sleep would not come to relieve her. At length

79

she rose and, taking the golden vessel, went into the parlour and set it on a shelf.

Returning to her bedchamber she blew out the tapers and lay on her back gazing into the darkness. She forced herself to think of her son and his difficulties, pushing the memories of her youth to the back of her mind. She had so much for which to be thankful it seemed ungrateful indeed to carp on what might have been.

There is always a nunnery, she thought. Perhaps when Henry is firmly established I shall take the veil and find serenity in the worship of God. But what was it St. Augustine said? 'Da mihi castitatem et continentiam — sed noli modo!' Later, but not for a little while yet!

Amused at her own cupidity she felt the warmth of the bedcovers soothing her and drifted, at last, into sleep.

She found the remainder of her stay at Greenwich more pleasant than she had thought possible. The discovery of a way to alleviate her troubles, should they become impossibly difficult, served as a palliative. With this new-won defence Margaret entered into the spirit of the Christmas festivities. True to his word, Henry made William Lord of Misrule and although sometimes Margaret caught an enquiring look in William's eye as he regarded her, the young man, nevertheless, fulfilled his role with gaiety and zest. If he and Perrot found time to indulge in amorous interludes Margaret was unaware of them.

When Henry and Elizabeth begged her to come with them to Sheen after Twelfth Night she agreed, rather to her own surprise. The pleasure of being with her family and watching her grandson growing week by week outweighed the necessity to return to Collyweston and deal with the accumulation of estate work piled up there. Trying not to think of her motives she sent her Chamberlain and William to Collyweston to bring back to her first hand news of any matter urgently requiring her attention.

The Queen Dowager elected to stay on in Greenwich and Margaret repressed the sense of relief this news gave her. Elizabeth's mother had not changed in the time since her daughter had become Queen of England; she did not possess sufficient intellect to interest herself in anything unconnected with herself and although her grandson seemed to have momentarily awakened her from apathy she preferred to remain in her chambers and not mix with the other members of the household.

The Royal manor house at Sheen was compact and more homely than the palace at

Greenwich. Warmly dressed in velvet and furs Margaret walked with Betsey, her other ladies and occasionally Henry and Elizabeth when her son could snatch an hour from his duties, beside the Thames.

Jasper and Catherine had returned to Gloucester but Margaret kept the two Buckingham boys with her. They were having their first riding lessons from a groom in the stables and she accompanied them several times to watch them mount their ponies and ride off among the bare trees of the park-like country surrounding the house.

Coming in from one of these expeditions she found the manor seething with excitement. Questioning those nearest at hand she could make no sense of what she heard and she went to her room and sent for Ormond.

It was some time before he came.

'What's afoot, Thomas?' she asked bluntly.

'Men have come from Ireland with strange tales, my Lady — ' Ormond began slowly. 'Strange tales of a King crowned in the Cathedral in Dublin.'

'A King — of Ireland?' Margaret asked.

'Of Ireland and England both; or so it would appear.'

'This is serious indeed!' Margaret cried. 'Is it known who is behind the conspiracy? Who is the man the Irish have proclaimed?'

'King Henry's man says it is Edward, the young Earl of Warwick — '

'But that is quite impossible!' Margaret cried, 'he is held in the Tower.'

'Exactly. So whoever is posing as Warwick is an impostor.'

'Has he obtained much support?'

'Nothing seems very clear from the report his Grace has just received but a Council is summoned to meet here the day after tomorrow.'

'Let us pray it may quickly find a solution.'

Although she did not expect to see Henry he came to Margaret's apartment just before midnight. In the soft light of the candles he looked grey and drawn.

He sat, gazing into the fire for some time before he spoke.

'Our path is not easy, my lady mother, is it? Just when I had begun to hope we had shown wisdom in our dealing with the rebels last year we are brought up sharply to realise it is not as simple as all that. When a priest can take a child and make him believe he is of Royal birth and groom him to that state we are contending with tricky minds.'

'What do you mean by that?' Margaret said quickly.

'It appears an Oxford cleric hit upon the idea of teaching this boy — Lambert Simnel

— all the graces of a noble household so that, one day, if opportunity should present itself, he might be used to further the fortunes of the said cleric.'

'Yes, that much I can understand; but where did he come upon the more exalted project of aiming for the throne?'

'Apparently the priest has always had Yorkist leanings and may, for all I know, have served at sometime in their household. Coming from Oxford he is naturally well adviced about the political situation and from what I hear, the boy is not unlike Clarence's son. Discovering this, the temptation was too great and when he thought he had given the youth sufficient schooling in his role as Warwick, he took him to Ireland. As you well know, Ireland has always had much sympathy for the White Rose and Lambert Simnel was readily accepted as Edward of Warwick.'

'What is the immediate danger?' Margaret asked.

'My informant said an army was being gathered and emissaries sent to Flanders — '

'To Flanders!'

'Yes. You do not need me to tell you the danger that invokes. If Margaret of Burgundy gives her support to this impostor we can expect she will attract those nobles here who are still Yorkists at heart, and once again we shall be faced with war.'

'Oh, no!'

'I am afraid we must be prepared for that. Did Ormond tell you I have called together a Council?'

'He did. What do you propose?'

'The first thing that seems obvious is to show the people the real Warwick. That should convince them they are being tricked. But how?'

'Why not at Mass at St. Paul's?'

'A very good idea,' Henry cried. 'On a Sunday morning when I make it known I shall be attending. What else do you suggest?'

'Your usual clemency,' Margaret said after a pause, 'I am sure you rule more firmly and wisely if you do so without arousing fear in men's minds.'

'Thank you, mother,' Henry said, stooping to kiss her on the brow. 'I'll keep your good counsel and at the same time make all preparation to meet an enemy — should he come. Try not to worry. I am surrounded with those loyal to my cause.'

'Jasper has returned home,' she replied looking up at her son.

'But he will be here again tomorrow. At the first hint of trouble I sent Christopher

Urswick and a strong escort to bring him back.'

'That is well.'

* * *

Jasper came to her as the dusk was darkening her room.

'You have made good time,' she said as she hurried to greet him.

'Not as good as I would have done twenty years ago, but fair enough.'

'You must be exhausted after two days in the saddle.'

'A good meal and a bottle of wine will soon put that right.'

'You have not eaten?' Margaret cried.

Jasper shook his head.

'My first thought was to come to you. There is time for food later.'

'Will you sup with me if I send for something now?'

'Of course. Henry knows I am here and I can go to him later to talk of the morrow's Council.'

'What do you think of this extraordinary business?' she asked as they waited for servants to bring the food she had sent her page to request.

'I suppose one is always on the alert for

trouble makers, but this impostor scheme is a new idea. The Irish are easily persuaded, we know, yet there must be a likeness for those who may have known Clarence well to be hoodwinked.'

'You do not think he is a serious threat?'

'Not in himself. No. The danger lies in the support he may attract from Flanders and power seekers here.'

Margaret dismissed the servants when they had served the meal and she and Jasper sat quietly talking over the events of the past days. When they had finished eating she brought the gold cup he had given her from the shelf where she displayed it and filled it with wine.

He took the vessel from her and smiled the old, familiar smile that touched her heart.

'To Henry's success — and you, Margaret.'

She turned away from him and stood by the window, drawing aside the curtains. A watery moon sent small pools of light moving on the restless water below.

When Jasper came and stood behind her and drew her head on to his shoulder she made no protest.

'Thank God, you are come. Now I am no longer afraid for the outcome of this affair.'

6

The Council met in the Hall of the Carthusian monastery close to the manor. It was soon obvious Henry had not minced his words in the letters of summons he had despatched for all the nobles came hurrying to see what was amiss.

There was about the gathering a totally different air from that which had blessed the Christmas festivities. Gone now was the pleasant and relaxed atmosphere and in its place was present an excited urgency. No women accompanied the men and each man brought with him numbers of well armed soldiers.

Margaret waited for news throughout the day. Jasper had promised her he would come and tell what had befallen so she occupied herself to the best of her ability. The watery moon of the previous evening had kept its promise and steady rain had fallen all the morning and most of the afternoon.

Before she supped she sent for her wards and read them several of Aesop's fables from one of Caxton's books. The little boys sat opposite her with Edith Fowler in attendance.

Margaret had seen little of Perrot since the night she had discovered her in William's arms but she was expecting William to return from Collyweston on the next day and she did not doubt Perrot would be in evidence when he came.

Margaret liked Edith and the way she handled Edward and Henry. Although she could be firm she was also gentle and patient, and it was obvious the boys both liked and respected her. As the children came to bid her good night Margaret was surprised to hear Edith ask them to enquire if William would be at Sheen soon. Margaret looked quickly at the girl but she appeared unruffled and the expression on her face had not changed at all.

'William?' Margaret echoed.

'Yes,' Edith said, her arms about the boys' shoulders. 'He is quite a frequent visitor to the schoolroom and is helping me teach Edward and Henry to write.'

'I see,' said Margaret hiding her amusement. 'Well, we are hoping he will be returned tomorrow, so the lessons can continue in the near future.'

'Good,' said Edward, 'and he can take me stalking as he promised, too.'

'Now, make your 'Good nights',' Edith said and obediently the children dropped to their knees and waited while Margaret whispered a prayer and lightly kissed the bent heads. When the door closed behind them, she sat back in her chair and thought over the new twist in the affairs of her engaging clerk. So Mistress Perrot was not to have it all her own way! Good luck to Edith Fowler.

I must tell Jasper, she found herself thinking while she ate her solitary supper, he does not yet know of my amorous secretary.

But when Jasper arrived over an hour later she saw in a glance this was not the moment to be talking of frivolous matters.

'Is it too cold for you to walk outside with me for a little?' he asked her, 'I have been cooped up all day and the air would be welcome.'

Margaret sent Betsey for her cloak.

'Have you eaten?'

'Yes, thank you. Henry sent for some cold pie and we had that when we returned to his chambers after the Council meeting had disbanded.'

They left the manor by the little-used stairway at the side of the house and passing under the gateway saluted the watch and turned upstream.

For some minutes they walked in silence, heads down against the wind gusting from the north-west. Margaret longed to ask questions but she knew better than to begin the conversation. Jasper had not asked her to walk with him solely for the sake of fresh air but she suspected he had news of such importance it was best whispered to her where no walls could catch an echo.

Coming to the path at the edge of the river they found it enclosed with high bramble bushes. Although they were bare of leaves the entangled branches afforded some protection and Jasper drew Margaret into a hollow where they could speak without shouting against the wind.

He took her hands between his and she stood facing him, the warmth of his body shielding her.

'I have disturbing news for you,' Jasper said, 'it would appear the Dowager is implicated in the plot to put Lambert Simnel on the throne.'

'How can this be!' Margaret cried, 'her own daughter is already Queen of England and her grandchild stands in direct line of the succession.'

'You may well ask; this was the question nobody seems able to answer. Perhaps she has been giving heed to the words of Margaret of Burgundy, who as her sister-in-law probably carries some authority with the Dowager, and has allowed herself to be influenced by what she has heard. Who can tell?'

'What is Henry going to do about this?'

'He has already acted and sent a herald and a force of men to Greenwich to remove her secretly to the Abbey of Bermondsey — '

'Where your mother died?' Margaret said softly.

'The same.'

'Poor foolish Elizabeth Wydeville! She has suffered so much she has all men's sympathies. What can have possessed her to act in such a manner?'

'Probably only God can answer that.'

'What else transpired?'

'Henry made it clear he intended to keep his word to those he had pardoned during the past year so that no incentive would be given to them to join the rebels. This done it was decided to bring young Warwick to London on this next Sunday and publicly show him to the people and the nobles.'

'So the lords agreed with Henry's suggestion?'

'Yes, and St. Paul's is the chosen place after High Mass.'

Margaret made no comment.

'Are the women to be present?'

'At first it was thought it might be too much of a risk to have the ladies with us but it appeared to me if it were to be a perfectly normal attendance at Mass it was better to go as if nothing abnormal were afoot.'

'I am glad,' Margaret said simply. 'Who is to break the news of the Dowager's behaviour to her daughter?'

'You. Henry thinks you are more capable of doing it than anyone else.'

'He flatters me, but I shall do my best. Were any absent from the Council today?'

'No. All the lords who were able attended. Northumberland, Oxford, Surrey, Suffolk, Lincoln, Derby, of course, and the members of the Household.'

'So it would appear there is no disloyalty among our own ranks?'

'It was certainly not apparent today; but who can tell how a man will behave when there is personal gain involved?'

'Do you grow cynical with the years, my dear?' Margaret asked lightly to cover the anxiety his words aroused.

'No more than usual. You and I have seen enough in the past years to wonder at nothing. But, let me hasten to assure you, there was no hint of grudging support for Henry when he asked for it and all present were unanimous in the decision to show Edward of Warwick to the populace of London.'

'I am relieved it should be so. Would it not be terrible, if, after all, Henry's hopes for his country should be destroyed by the machinations of a scheming priest?'

'There is not much fear of that. The Irish are not renowned for their soldierly skill and, should it come to a fight would not last a day against the army Henry could command.'

'Thank you,' Margaret said quietly. 'To return to the matter of the Queen's mother, when do you think I should speak with Elizabeth?'

'Would you find it too much of a strain to go to her this evening?'

'No. It would be easier now, with you close at hand rather than to leave it when you may have returned home.'

Jasper lifted her hands and held them to his mouth. Margaret felt close to tears but Jasper's next words surprised her into forgetting them.

'I do not think I shall be returning to Gloucester just yet. My place is beside my nephew when any danger threatens him or his throne.'

Margaret fought down the joy welling in her.

'I am growing an old and foolish woman,' she said. 'It is time I learnt to stand on my own feet.'

'That is one lesson you learnt earlier than most of us, my dearest Margaret. Of whatever else you may be able to accuse yourself in that critical mind of yours, weakness and cowardice are definitely not faults of yours. It would not be womanly to suffer no anxieties for those you love and since you were sixteen years old it has been my prerogative to help you whenever it has been humanly possible. This is one of those times,' he added simply, 'and God willing, I shall stay where I can be of most use.'

They walked back to the house hand in hand and when they came to her door Margaret turned abruptly away from him to stop herself from putting her arms about his neck and asking for his kiss.

Throwing off her cloak she fell onto the praying stool set up in front of her little altar and buried her head in her arms.

I am worse than Perrot, she found herself thinking fiercely, I am middle-aged and thrice married and should know better than to crave the delights of bed-sport. Oh, God, forgive me and help me. Cleanse my heart and help me forget I am a woman!

She compelled herself to think about her projected interview with her daughter-in-law and formed prayers asking for guidance in what could only be a painful meeting. How was she to break the news of her mother's treachery to Elizabeth when the girl had already suffered more than her fair share of the world's bitterness?

The realisation of Elizabeth's difficulties did a great deal to help her forget her own comparatively minor personal dilemma and she rose from her devotions and called for Betsey to bring her a new robe she had not yet worn. She knew from experience that when she thought herself well-gowned she gained in confidence.

She found Elizabeth surrounded by her ladies, who at a signal from their mistress, made their curtsies and went out of the chamber.

'You wished to speak with me, Madame.'

'Yes,' Margaret told her quietly. 'Henry wished me to come to you with news of your mother.'

Elizabeth looked at Margaret enquiringly but said nothing.

Unconsciously straightening her spine Margaret continued.

'Her Grace has been removed to the Abbey at Bermondsey.'

'Why so?' Elizabeth asked quickly.

'Henry had reason to believe she was become involved with some unfortunate business — '

'But that is long since finished and forgotten! At the time she gave her consent to my marriage with — with my uncle she was distracted and did not know what to do for the best!'

'This matter has nothing to do with your betrothal to Richard of Gloucester,' Margaret said gently.

'What is it then?'

'A plot has been discovered to set an impostor on the throne in Henry's place and Henry has been shown evidence indicating your mother was ready to give her support to the plan.'

Elizabeth shook her head in disbelief.

'What did my mother hope to gain by such an act?'

'It has been given out in Ireland, where the plot has been hatched, that the young man is Edward of Warwick.'

'Edward! But he is in the Tower, is he not?'

Margaret nodded, pity for the vulnerable young woman making her speechless.

'Edward was not even Richard's heir. I do not understand what my mother hoped to gain; unless — '

'Unless?' Margaret prompted quietly.

'Unless she tried to persuade herself the young man was one of my brothers!'

Elizabeth turned to Margaret wide-eyed.

'Oh, Madame, do you think it might have been that? Would we not all clutch at straws if our sons were torn from us without warning? Would we not hope for any miracle to restore them?'

'Yes, we should,' Margaret answered simply, 'you and I as mothers know that to be the truth.'

'Why should my mother be condemned then for doing only what we should do under similar circumstances?'

'I do not think there is any question of punishment. It was thought wiser, for her own sake, to remove her to a safe place where it would be impossible for would-be trouble makers to use her as a figurehead.'

Elizabeth sank down on to a stool and was silent while she gazed into the fire.

'Perhaps it is best so,' she said at last, 'in the Abbey she will be able to find the tranquillity of heart denied to her for most of her life.'

Elizabeth looked up at Margaret, her blue eyes wide as if she saw her mother-in-law for the first time.

'You are very wise, Madame, and have understood the sagacity of keeping your heart in subjugation to your head. Who knows, if my father had done the same, the course of our lives might have been utterly different.'

Startled, Margaret put out her hand to help the girl to her feet and suggested they should go to the nursery and visit the baby prince.

At once an expression of pleasure overtook the perplexity on Elizabeth's face and Margaret watched her as she bent over her sleeping son. Here at least the Queen found some happiness.

Margaret found it impossible to dismiss what Elizabeth had said to her. Putting aside the slight shock of her daughter-in-law's appraisal of her own attitude to life Margaret felt she had stumbled upon an abyss of unsuspected misery in that of the Queen. What did she, Margaret, know of the bitter humiliations Elizabeth had suffered during her short life? Margaret had known nothing but love from those who had surrounded her. She discovered a sense of guilt within herself that she could wish to wring from life more happiness than God had already bestowed upon her. Elizabeth had more to tell of misery than people of twice her age. Margaret confessed to herself a nebulous exasperation at Henry's laggardly crowning of his Queen. Was it possible Henry was so concerned with keeping his tight rein on his kingdom he was ignorant of how his wife suffered? Margaret determined, as soon as the Lambert Simnel threat had been disposed of by presenting the true Edward of Warwick to the nation, she must speak her mind to her son on the matter of Elizabeth's Coronation.

On the following Sunday the King and the Royal household set out from Sheen in a fleet of covered barges. They left the manor so early it was still dark and were glad of the hot, spiced wine and ale provided for them at the Tower.

Jasper and the Earl of Derby went to the apartments where Edward of Warwick was lodged and brought the youth to meet Henry and Elizabeth. Edward bore the unmistakable stamp of his lineage but looked pale and delicate. Margaret wished she could bring him to her household and bring him up with the Buckingham boys but realised, as Clarence's son he presented a lively threat to her son's throne and the restriction he suffered in the Tower was probably in his best interest.

Henry greeted the boy with kindliness and Elizabeth kissed him fondly on both cheeks before he joined them in the King's barge. He took his place somewhat shyly and listened with attention to the directions Henry gave him for his conduct in the great church of St. Paul's. Margaret, casting her mind back, thought the boy must be about sixteen or seventeen and had been born, if she

100

remembered correctly, in a ship attempting to put in at Calais with Warwick, the great earl who had died at the Battle of Barnet, and his daughter and son-in-law Clarence.

What turbulent backgrounds the Yorkist heirs had! All of them had been born under the shadow of mistrust and the males seemed dogged by misfortune. King Edward's sons spirited away to this very Tower, never to reappear; the usurping Richard's heir dying swiftly of some unknown complaint, while this young Edward of Warwick watched hopelessly as his life seeped away in imprisonment.

Don't grow too soft! A warning voice cried within Margaret's mind. You also have known impeachment and confinement while your son has passed the greater part of his thirty years as a prisoner of someone else's will.

But she could not rid herself of a sense of foreboding and was glad when, passing under London Bridge and by her own house of Coldeharbour, they completed the short journey to St. Paul's and came within the shelter of the high wall surrounding the church.

Once inside the lofty building with its graceful columns and jewel-like windows she allowed herself to drift in a miasma of half-aware devotion, repeating the familiar

101

words as a charm. So great was the throng of people and so oppressive the heat from the enormous braziers burning at intervals on the stone floor Margaret was relieved when Henry gave the signal to leave by the South Porch.

Outside they found a great crowd had gathered. In the pale winter sunshine their breath hung on the chill air and there was much stamping of feet and beating of arms to keep warm. As the royal party emerged an eager hush fell immediately; all craned forward to watch the magnificently gowned nobles as the King, accompanied by Lancaster Herald, presented the fairhaired youth to those about him.

Margaret saw Edward smile diffidently as he bowed to Oxford, Lincoln, her own husband with his sons by his first marriage and the other lords who crowded round to see with their own eyes this important prisoner. Glancing at Henry from time to time the boy spoke with several of the men and their ladies and Margaret was relieved to notice a general atmosphere of camaraderie. At the end of the line Henry came up to Jasper and obviously following on some comment the King made to him Edward smiled without restraint and spoke easily and naturally.

Yeomen of the King's Guard, making a splash of scarlet colour against the drab grey of the crowd, cleared a way for the royal party and they embarked at Queen's Hythe for the Palace of Westminster.

Jasper and Oxford returned with Edward of Warwick to the Tower and Margaret watched them until a bend of the river hid their barge from her own. For the rest of the day she was quiet and subdued but was glad to hear from those about her that the encounter at the porch of St. Paul's had been as successful as Henry had hoped.

Within the next few days she returned to Sheen with the household and began to make plans to go to Collyweston. William Elmer had brought her much to occupy her and she could deal more competently with her affairs from her own house.

Henry was closeted with his advisers hour after hour while they produced measures to deal with the Irish trouble-makers and Margaret saw little of him or Jasper for the week after the drama enacted at St. Paul's, but she set herself to be as much with the Queen as Elizabeth wanted. Together they walked beside the river and played with the baby prince. Elizabeth had a half-formed liking for music and Margaret arranged for a band of her own musicians to play for them during the long winter evenings. Elizabeth discovered she could sing a little and coached by the leading player was persuaded to join with them in their madrigals. Margaret noted with pleasure the girl seemed more relaxed than before and the periods when she would gaze with hopeless bewilderment into nothingness seemed further and further apart.

Before I leave for Collyweston I must speak to Henry about her coronation, Margaret thought as she listened with Elizabeth in the Queen's chambers to a new song composed especially for her.

But it was not to be for as they sat, lulled with the gentle melody Ormond was announced with a request both ladies should accompany him to Henry. Startled, Margaret and Elizabeth exchanged glances and followed the Chamberlain to the King's room.

Henry was surrounded with his chief officers of State. Jasper came to greet Margaret and stood beside her as she sat at Henry's bidding. Margaret knew immediately they were to hear grave news.

Without preamble Henry went straight to the reason for his summons.

'We have received news by a courier who has ridden straight from Dover that the Earl of Lincoln and Lord Lovell have fled to the

Court of Margaret of Burgundy.' Margaret closed her eyes and took a deep breath. 'I am persuaded this is no time to hang back and wait for our enemies to strike and for this reason am issuing immediate orders for the raising of an army. I shall leave at once for the east coast so that we may keep watch day and night for any would be invader. My lady mother, I know you had thought to go to Collyweston within a few days, but I hope you will grant my request and stay here to keep the Queen company.'

'Of course,' Margaret replied.

'Should I not accompany you, my lord?' Elizabeth asked.

Henry looked at her swiftly, considered for a moment and then shook his head.

'No, it were best if you remain quietly at Sheen with our son. Perhaps, if I am mistaken, and no trouble is forthcoming it will be possible for you to join me to celebrate Easter.'

'You are certain they mean to cross to England and make war to put this usurper on the throne?' Margaret asked.

'Yes,' Henry replied grimly. 'The traitors in our midst, far from being dissuaded by our showing of Edward of Warwick, seem to have taken heart that he is safely stowed away in the Tower and have gone to Margaret of

Burgundy to pledge their support of Lambert Simnel.'

'Your informants are to be trusted?'

'Undoubtedly so; the man commissioned to discover the facts is well tried and trusted beyond doubt. There is no question that Lincoln and Lovell are already putting in motion the business of recruiting mercenaries.'

With a heavy heart Margaret rose.

'There are many matters, I am sure, needing your attention. Rest assured, however, the safety of your Queen and heir shall be my first concern.'

7

On a splendid May afternoon, when the trees and river sparkled with the gold of the sun, messengers came from the King bringing letters for Margaret, Elizabeth and Ormond.

They bore the news that despite the vigilant watch the royal army had been keeping on the east coast Henry's spies had discovered the rebels had returned to Ireland and were planning their invasion from Dublin. Henry therefore considered it was safe enough for the women of his household and his son and heir to come to Kenilworth where he might have his first sight of them for three months.

Delighted to be rejoining Henry, Margaret and the Queen hurried the household into the elaborate preparations necessary for the journey to the Midlands.

They arrived at the massive castle towards the evening of the fourth day of their ride and wearily stepped down from the upholstered wagonette in which they had bumped over the hard and dusty roads.

Henry with Jasper and the other members of the Council came to greet them. They looked tanned and well with the countless hours they had spent patrolling the fens and sandy wastes of Norfolk.

'Make haste to rejoin us!' Henry told them as they went to wash away the travel stains and put on fresh linen and robes.

Margaret still carried with her to the chambers allotted her the memory of Jasper's kiss of greeting and the unfathomable depth of his eyes as he had looked at her.

'You look very radiant,' Betsey sniffed as she helped her mistress fasten the sapphire coloured dress she had asked for.

'Do I? If I come to think about it, I feel rather radiant, too! It is three months since we have all been together. Isn't that something to make me happy?'

'Indeed yes; and no one is more delighted than I to see you so. Which cap will you wear, my Lady?'

'The butterfly one edged with lace.'

She knew, as she walked down the broad steps into the parlour where Henry had commanded an informal supper should be served, she looked her best for Jasper came quietly to her and taking her hand in his led her into the great Hall.

She made no comment but suffered him to lead her to an alcove where he held her at arm's length looking down into her face.

'You are well, I can see. How has it been with you since we parted at Sheen?'

'Very quiet, and peaceful. I have enjoyed being with the baby and Elizabeth. Sometimes I have felt guilty at the enforced idleness but as long as the news from Henry and you continued good I was content. It is of much more importance how you and Henry have fared!'

'Apart from one incident when Henry was warned of a force coming towards him — which turned out to be only the Queen's half-brother pledging his support — there were no alarms. We swept the fens from end to end. When there was no evidence of an army being massed in Flanders either, Henry changed his policy and sent spies to the west coast of Britain and it was from here he received intimation of a large force being prepared for war in Ireland.'

'Irish soldiers?'

'It would seem not entirely. Lincoln and Lovell had brought with them the force we expected to find preparing in Flanders to invade East Anglia. From what we are told we believe the men to be trained mercenaries from Germany.'

'More dangerous than the untutored Irish!'

'Possibly. But do not worry, we have been levying a mighty army ourselves and they are well trained also. If we should have confirmation of our belief they will land somewhere on the western seaboard and we shall give them more than they bargain for.'

Margaret turned away from him, her pleasure at being in Kenilworth with her son and brother-in-law diminished as she realised the danger was not yet over.

'Forgive me,' Jasper grasped her arms and turned her to face him again. 'I would not add to your anxiety for the world.'

'It is I who am the stupid one. It is so good to be together again I had forgotten the reason for the separation.'

Jasper stooped quickly and held her to him for a brief moment, his cheek against hers.

Back in the parlour Margaret sat between her son and Jasper. Henry had paid his wife and mother the compliment of providing meat and capons cooked in exotic and unusual sauces while fruit and flowers decked the highly polished table.

Everybody talked at once; of the rebels and the Coronation of the Usurper as Edward VI of England; of Henry's visit to the shrine at Walsingham; of his stay in Cambridge and of the change he saw in the little Arthur.

'My husband writes to tell me he has gone to Cheshire to hasten the raising of the levies there,' Margaret said to Jasper.

'He has been absent about a week and should be returning with the men he has mustered in a few days. He works tirelessly in Henry's cause and I am sure has never regretted the decision he took on Bosworth field.'

'I am glad of that; and his brother Sir William Stanley?'

'He does good service as Chamberlain to the King?'

'Henry is fortunate in those about him.'

'He is a born leader, my dear and is possessed of those mysterious qualities that positively commands men to follow him. He most probably inherits the gift from you!' Jasper said with a smile.

Margaret laughed.

'Am I such a dragon then?'

She did not need to have her question answered and went on quickly to ask if Catherine was to come to Kenilworth.

'I do not think so, for the moment at least. I do not think — ' he stopped.

'You do not think it is the right time to bring a woman here?' Margaret prompted quietly.

'But you are a special woman,' Jasper told her, equally quietly, 'Henry wanted you here as much for your counsel as the comfort of having his wife and mother about him.'

'I am honoured, but sorry Catherine is deprived of your company.'

'She is happy enough,' Jasper answered roughly, 'she contents herself with jellymaking and the brewing of beer. She will not miss my company.' His voice rose. 'I have given her the doubtful blessing of my name. What more would you ask of me?'

'Don't speak like that, it hurts my heart to think you other than gentle and kind. Talk of other things to me.'

'Of what?'

'Have I told you of my young secretary, William Elmer?'

'I think not,' Jasper replied a little distantly.

'You remember him, perhaps. A tall, red-haired young man — '

'He who was Lord of Misrule at Greenwich?'

'The same.'

'I do remember him. Is he not the one who is enamoured of your Frenchwoman, Perrot?'

Margaret laughed delightedly.

'You *know* all about it and I was going to tell you the story of their affair.'

'I don't know very much about that, so you can still make my ears tingle. She reminds me, somehow, of Myvanwy and if she is really like her I am sorry for William Elmer. He must be unable to call his soul and his body his own.'

Margaret was surprised to hear Jasper talk of the long-dead mistress who had mothered his daughter, Helen, and she experienced a pang of something she could only describe as jealousy. She said nothing and Jasper turned to look at her, questioningly.

'Well,' he said, amusement creasing the corners of his eyes, 'are you not going to entertain me with the secret amours of your serving woman?'

She shook her head.

'What is it, my very dear?'

But she could not tell him. Suddenly, the affair of William and his enthralment to the heavy-lidded Perrot had become something other than a topic for discussion over a supper table.

'Perhaps I am tired.'

Immediately contrite Jasper lifted her silver wine cup to her lips.

'Drink this, you will feel better for it.'

Obediently she sipped and searched desperately for a topic less dangerous.

'I am thinking of making some extensions at Collyweston — '

'Your favourite among your many residences? Why not? It is a pity to waste your talent for organisation. Do you plan to live there more than in any other of your houses?'

'Yes,' Margaret answered slowly. 'As you know I hoped to live there when Edmund and I were first married and so, after Pembroke, it is where I prefer to stay.'

Jasper turned to her again, his eyes penetrating and swiftly perceptive.

'It is not tiredness that troubles you, but something else, is it not?'

Margaret moved her head with difficulty and picking an orange from the silver bowl in front of her stared down at it.

'Tell me of your ideas to improve Collyweston. Are you going to build some other rooms?' Jasper's gentle voice touched her more than the blunt question she had avoided, but, making an effort to speak naturally she answered him.

'I had thought perhaps a larger Hall where it would be possible to entertain Henry if he should care to bring the Court to be my guests. Then, the existing chapel is small and rather dark, and I should like to make it an expression of my devotion.'

The warmth that suffused her face and breast subsided gradually and Henry, hearing what she said, joined in the conversation. Margaret relaxed her grip on the arm of her chair and leaned back; suddenly, she was as weary as if she had walked the miles from London.

In the days that followed there was little time for private conversation. The castle was filled with the comings and goings of Henry's lieutenants and their officers. Rumours and counter-rumours occupied the interest from morning until night.

Nothing definite could be sifted from the news flooding in until an old and trusted servant of Henry's, Christopher Urswick, rode over the lush meadows to tell of a force crossing the Irish Sea and heading for the Lancashire coast.

Margaret received the information with a sinking heart and watched the preparations of the King's army as they made ready to intercept the enemy with hopeless distress. She had hoped so desperately that once Henry had established himself upon the throne after Bosworth the way would remain plain for him to govern in peace. Instead of this it had been rebellion after rebellion and now she was forced to watch as her son and Jasper left her to face more unknown danger.

Jasper came to bid her farewell on the eve of their departure.

'Come with me and walk on the battle-ments?' he asked.

Margaret nodded and Betsey went to fetch her a thin cloak, for although it was June the dusk brought a freshening breeze.

She stood with Jasper looking out over the trees crowding almost to the moat.

'Where do you make for?' Margaret asked.

'For Nottingham. Henry expects Lincoln and Lovell to cut through Yorkshire and then turn southwards; at Nottingham it will be possible to cover almost all routes they might take.'

'If only this had not to be!' Margaret cried.

'Have no fear for Henry; I shall be always close to him and you know I would give my life rather than harm should befall him.'

'Don't say that! I could not live without your comfort and support!'

Margaret began to walk quickly on the narrow and enclosed path. Jasper followed her until she came to the head of the stone stair where they were saluted by the sergeant of the watch. The man held open the small door for them and they began the steep descent to the gallery below. Neither of them spoke.

In the gallery it was almost dark and very quiet. Somewhere in the misty fields outside a bird sang in uninhibited cadences of joy, welcoming the night.

When Margaret would have walked on Jasper restrained her and pulled her into a recess where a narrow, glassless window showed up the paling sky.

'Stay with me for just a little longer,' he pleaded.

'You have much to do and you will need all the sleep you can have.'

'I should rather sleep in the saddle tomorrow than waste a few moments with you.'

Margaret held herself stiffly upright and kept her eyes on the translucent sky. Despite the summer evening she felt chilled and only repressed a shiver with difficulty.

Jasper put his hand on the nape of her neck and drew her head on to his shoulder.

'Don't be troubled, my dearest; what is between you and me is no sin. In a world where hate seems to be predominant, the love you and I have for one another is a thing of beauty and goodness. We have hurt no one, you and I, and each of us has benefited from the other's affection. Let me go into this battle knowing the golden thread of tenderness still binds me to you!'

With a sigh Margaret put her arms round him and he drew her close, murmuring gentle words of comfort. For a brief moment of time the rest of the world ceased to exist until at last he tilted her face and kissed her very softly on the mouth.

'If I should not return you may know, always, there was no other woman who had my heart but you,' he said as they parted, 'but fear not,' as he saw her hand go quickly to her lips, 'with God's help we shall put down these rebels and return to you as speedily as possible.'

She waited, with Elizabeth, for an endless week. No news came to them and in an effort to occupy the long days they visited the sick and suffering in the village of Kenilworth. In each running sore she bandaged Margaret saw Henry or Jasper wounded and needing succour. This spurred her to crawl through low doorways into evil smelling hovels while an armed escort waited outside. Elizabeth had been reluctant to accompany her but overcoming her fear and nausea of the loathsome sights they were obliged to look upon, she began to take genuine interest when she discovered the reward of the happiness their baskets of food gave and saw festering abscesses responding to the simple unguents Margaret had made in the castle stillroom.

But when evening came their fears reasserted themselves and nothing was able to distract them from the anxiety clutching their hearts. So much depended on the King's army and so little could turn the tide against them.

When, on the seventeenth day of June,

Lancaster Herald came to the castle and was shown immediately to the Queen's parlour, Margaret held her breath as he fell on his knee to Elizabeth.

'My lord, be welcome. What news?' the girl cried.

'The best. The rebels are utterly defeated and the King's forces have won an over-whelming victory.'

'Thanks be to God!'

Margaret sank against the leather support of her chair while Lancaster Herald sat and accepted wine and comfits brought to him by a page. If Henry or Jasper had been wounded would Lancaster Herald not have said so straight away?

Elizabeth's next question voiced her thoughts.

'His Grace, the King, he is unhurt?'

'By God's mercy none of the loyal nobles or the King himself were more than scratched.'

Tears of thankfulness pricked at the back of Margaret's eyes and it was a little while before she paid complete attention to what Lancaster Herald was saying.

'Was the fighting fierce?' Elizabeth was asking.

'Very; and the number of men involved on both sides was larger than expected. This was because the King's nobles had exerted themselves to bring the entire obligatory force. Derby, Madame,' turning to Margaret, 'and his son, Lord Strange had amassed a great many men as had Oxford, Shrewsbury and Surrey. On the other hand the rebels had not only the Irish but a huge force of German mercenaries under their commander, Martin Schwartz — '

'Martin Schwartz!' cried Ormond who had come in with Lancaster Herald, 'he has the reputation of being a fearless and ruthless fighter!'

'Any who spoke of him thus did not malign him. Those present at the battle, which took place eventually at a village called Stoke just outside Nottingham, thought he would have had a real chance of success but for two things. First, he did not receive the support Lincoln is said to have promised him from the countryside he hoped to arouse, and he was hopelessly outwitted by the generalship of the redoubtable Bedford.'

Lancaster Herald looked across at Margaret, seeming for a moment to speak only to her.

'Your son, my lady, has had much cause during his life to be grateful to his uncle, as you know better than anyone else, but yesterday on the field of Stoke he owed most of his swift success to the indomitable courage and strategy of Jasper Tudor. It was he who drew up the front line of the King's army and sent them crashing into the rebels, pressing home his advantage as he saw the Irish and Germans wavering and finally bearing down upon them until they broke and scattered in all directions.'

Elizabeth came to Margaret's side and Margaret was glad when she went on to interrogate Lancaster Herald for she found it difficult to make an appropriate comment.

'Have the rebels suffered sufficiently to prevent them rising again?'

'Yes, indeed, for Lord Lovell and Lincoln were killed as was Schwartz himself.'

'And the child?'

'The child, your Grace?'

'Yes, he who was trained to impersonate my cousin, the youth Lambert Simnel!'

'Forgive me, I had not understood your meaning. Simnel was taken as also was the priest who had tutored him — '

'But no harm has befallen him?' Margaret said quickly.

'No. The King has chosen to extend clemency to the boy, on account of his tender years and has said he will take him into his own service.'

'A novel punishment!' Ormond said and

then laughed in embarrassment. 'Although I would not have it said I ever thought of being your Chamberlain as a trial.'

Margaret suggested the party should move to the chapel where they might give thanks for the victory won on the previous day and Elizabeth sent for the chaplain. Later, when they had supped Margaret found herself walking once more on the battlements.

The soft June evening exactly suited the tranquillity of spirit enfolding her. It was as if a gentle benediction wrapped her heart and mind. She leant against a stone bastion while a light breeze ruffled the gauze scarf about her head. Wordlessly she gave repeated thanks for the swift and fortuitous outcome of the crisis hanging over them since the new year. God had heard her urgent prayers and kept those she loved from the power of evil. In so doing He had given fresh impetus to the hopes Henry had for making his kingdom strong and secure.

When Henry returned he announced his intention of holding a service of thanksgiving in Lincoln Cathedral before setting out again on another Progress. With great pleasure Margaret acceded to his wish she should accompany him but begged to be allowed to return to Collyweston once the service was over. She longed for the peaceful routine of her own household and had been busying herself since the victory with plans for the alterations she had in mind for Collyweston. William Elmer set off for her home with his saddlebag stuffed with rolls and documents. Margaret thought his disappointment, when he had arrived at Kenilworth to discover Perrot was not of the party at the castle, was slightly recompensed when he realised Margaret was returning to Collyweston in the immediate future.

Jasper had not returned to Kenilworth after the battle of Stoke but was expected to join them in Lincoln. Margaret hastened her preparations to return home before the sight of him caused her to falter in her decision.

Lincoln, with its steep and narrow streets and ancient Roman gateways, fascinated Margaret while she found the Cathedral with its soaring towers strangely moving. She admired the foresight of the long-dead builders who had chosen the hill rising sharply out of the fens as the site of their house of worship. She was not surprised her great-grandfather, John of Gaunt, had chosen the Cathedral for the tomb of his third wife, and Margaret determined to find time to visit the burial place once the service was over.

She crossed from the castle across the turf to the Abbey door on the arm of her husband, Derby. Henry and Elizabeth, surrounded by the Yeoman of the Guard, acknowledged the greetings of the townsfolk who pushed and jostled to obtain a view of their monarch and his household. Although it was not Henry's first visit to Lincoln there were many people curious to see this Welsh unknown who had toppled Richard of Gloucester from his precarious throne.

More people thronged the nave as the royal party made its way to the Lady Chapel to hear Mass. When it was celebrated a Te Deum rang out, echoing in the high roof and Margaret, looking at her son, saw him clench his fists and close his eyes while he took a deep breath. At the same moment she saw Jasper regarding her across the dimly lit chapel and they smiled, each knowing the other's thoughts. Once more, the young man who meant so much to them both had been reprieved from the menace of those who sought to overthrow him. There was a great deal for which to give thanks to God.

Coming again into the sunshine they stood on the steps of the Cathedral while the bells rang out and the populace cheered.

Margaret stood close by her son.

'God has blessed our cause,' he said softly. 'Now it is my turn to make amends for my tardiness in crowning my queen. When I return from this journey round the northern counties I shall return to Westminster and put in motion the business of the Coronation. It is possible the capital may wish to express their gratitude for our victory and it would seem a good time to crown Elizabeth.'

'Well said,' Margaret replied, striving to keep the relief she felt from appearing too obvious. This was a day for celebration indeed that at last Henry had announced the crowning of his wife. All doubts were swept aside as he spoke for the first time to his mother of the extraordinary hiatus he had allowed between his marriage and the supreme courtesy he owed to Elizabeth. Whatever he had felt that had caused him to hesitate had been swept aside with his victory at Stoke and Margaret rejoiced it should be so.

Later in the day those residing in the castle sat under the trees in the garden. A band of musicians played while a troupe of tumblers turned and twisted their way through the guests.

Margaret found herself the centre of a group that included Derby and Sir Reginald Bray. Both of them were to come with her to Collyweston when she left on the following day. While they were talking Henry came up to them, closely attended by a pleasant boy dressed in the King's livery.

'My lady mother, may I ask you to take wine from the latest addition to my household, Lambert Simnel.'

Blushing, the child knelt and held out a silver salver on which were several wine cups. Margaret took one and thanked Simnel gravely.

'So you are to follow your King?' she asked kindly.

'Wherever he commands, for I owe him my life.'

'That is well. May God prosper you.'

'Your son shows great clemency,' Derby said to Margaret. 'Let us pray it is not misplaced!'

'Why, surely not!' Margaret cried. 'Our Saviour himself taught us to forgive.' She watched the boy thread his way through the throng behind Henry. 'He was innocent of any crime and was merely the tool of a scheming brain.'

'True enough,' Derby agreed. 'But I am not completely convinced it might not have been better to have made an example of the lad in case there might be other impostors following him — '

'No one would try the same trick twice!' Bray cried.

'Possibly not — '

'Father!' Derby's son interrupted. 'We are celebrating a tremendous victory, why spoil it by vain imaginings of future unlikely events!'

'Quite right.' Derby nodded his great head. 'I am becoming an old cynic,' he said ruefully.

'What's this?' Jasper asked as he and Oxford dropped on the grass beside them. 'Who is becoming cynical?'

'Nobody could be so on such a beautiful evening,' Margaret said swiftly. 'Listen, one of the men is singing.'

The walled garden, sweet with scent of cloves and lilies, hushed as the song filled the night. When it was finished those about Margaret moved away until only Jasper was left at her feet.

For several minutes they sat perfectly still until she said very quietly: 'I am told Henry owed most of his swift success to your generalship at Stoke.'

Jasper shifted impatiently.

'It was nothing. I am old in the art of making war and it so happened I saw quickly what was to be done. More important, I think, was the setting up of the Courts of Justice after the battle and the instructions Henry gave me in meting out punishments and awards. He shows an uncanny instinct for knowing how far to go with transgressors.'

'My husband thinks he is too lenient.'

'It is certainly a charge which might be levelled against him, but only time will tell if he has discovered a new method of ensuring loyalty.'

'Has he told you he is to make arrangements for Elizabeth's crowning?' Jasper shook his head. 'It is to be in the autumn at the completion of this Progress.'

'You were happy to hear that piece of news, I know!' Jasper said laughingly.

'Indeed yes. As you understand very well, it has given me much cause for concern that Henry seemed unable to bring himself to accord his wife the duty to which she was entitled. I hated to think Henry was so unsure of himself.'

'Now you may put that worry completely behind you. You will, of course, come to Westminster for the Coronation?'

'Yes.'

'Don't stay too long in Collyweston. I do not grow younger and I count time when we are separated as lost.'

Margaret did not answer, not trusting herself to say anything lighthearted enough to be other than banal.

'Will you visit me in Thornbury one day?' Jasper asked.

'Perhaps.' Once again they were quiet, the voices of the others sounding far off and hushed. 'My estates in the West Country have been sadly neglected and I cannot put off much longer going to inspect them. If it is at all possible I might be able to come to your manor then.'

'I should like to welcome you, once more, to my home; it seems so very long ago since we shared the roof of Pembroke.'

'Don't!' Margaret cried before she could stop herself.

'Forgive me; but perhaps it would be better if we spoke of those far off days instead of attempting to push them out of our minds. From the long years of imprisonment I have undergone I am well aware it is not healthy for the mind to suppress one's dreams and ambitions. Do you remember my father gathering the seashells to make necklaces for Helen?'

'And the seagrasses we twined into garlands for the children's playthings? We were young then and the simple things pleased us as much as Helen and Henry. What was the name of the pony I rode when we explored the marshes of the Haven?'

'I thing it was Dapple,' Jasper said, 'but surely you do not expect me to remember the name of a horse when my mind was only filled with the girl who rode it?'

Margaret chuckled.

'I remember falling off and hurting my ankle and the look on your face when I stood up, dripping with seawater!'

Once begun, there seemed no end to the memories flooding across the years. Half-forgotten stories became fresh and alive again; the misfortunes and the sadness forgotten in the recalling of all that had been so happy and complete. So lost were they in the magic of the reminiscences they shared they might have sat all night if a discreet cough had not interrupted them and they looked up to see Betsey Massey standing at a little distance with a fleecy shawl for Margaret.

'I thought you might be cold, my Lady.'

'Cold?'

Jasper stood up quickly. 'I am selfish keeping you here, when you need your rest for tomorrow's journey. Good night, my dearest.' Unperturbed by Betsey hovering close by he kissed Margaret on the cheek. For a brief instant her hand rested in his.

'Good night, Jasper. May God bless you until we meet.'

8

The Coronation of Elizabeth was to take place on Sunday, 25th November.

Two days before this the Queen with Margaret and her own Chamberlain and Household journeyed from Greenwich to the Tower.

The Thames was crowded with Londoners, always ready to enjoy a day of pageantry, filling every available barge and wherry. These had been decorated with streamers and huge colourful banners depicting the various Guilds. The Buckingham children were most delighted with a boat cunningly contrived to look like a red dragon which from time to time belched huge tongues of flame across the river. If the boys had had their way they would have stayed by this resplendent monster for the rest of the day. It was only with great difficulty Edith Fowler was able to convince them that other delights awaited them.

On the day before the Crowning Elizabeth set out alone to make a triumphant entry into the City. Margaret thought she had never looked so lovely as she did when she set out from the Tower.

Elizabeth's fair hair was unbound and she had on her brow a circlet of gold embellished with gems. She wore a magnificent gown and mantle of white embroidered with gold and trimmed with ermine. She looked, suddenly, defenceless and ethereal and Margaret felt a return of the slight unease she had experienced before on her daughter-in-law's behalf. She wished, as she had done many times before, Elizabeth's own mother was close at hand to give her support to her child on such an occasion as this important one she was now undertaking. But Elizabeth returned to the Tower in the late afternoon quite happy with the day and talked excitedly of the packed pavements and the richly decorated houses where the citizens had spared no effort to honour their Queen.

'In the Chepe they were especially gay and hospitable,' she told Henry and Margaret.

Not daring to look at one another Margaret was about to make some noncommittal reply when Elizabeth startled them both.

'They probably remember my father and were curious to see what his daughter looks like!' she said smiling. 'I should dearly liked to have stopped and spoken with some of the people but I didn't think it quite the appropriate time for gossiping. My father must have had a considerable amount of charm if all the stories about him were true.'

'Edward of York was a very handsome and gallant man,' Margaret said, 'and had a way with the common folk that endeared them to him; a gift not always given to those who rule.'

Henry glanced swiftly at his mother but she was questioning Elizabeth about one of the playlets she had watched during her ride through the bedecked city and was not to be drawn on the subject.

The following day, Sunday, the royal household were awake early and preparing for the Coronation. Ladies of the Court, pages and waiting women scurried from the wardrobes with their arms piled high with robes and cloaks. Henry had given authority to the Stewards to be lavish with materials and furs so that his wife's crowning should stand out in the memory of those subjects able to witness it as a spectacle without compare.

The Queen was the last to join the procession drawn up in the yard of the Tower. She looked quite different from the maid who had ridden out on the previous day; a symbol of dignity clad in rich purple velvet trimmed at the neck and hem with ermine. She thanked Derby gravely as, in his office of Steward, he stood at the side of her palfrey and helped her mount. Unhurriedly she sat gracefully in the enormous and beautifully caparisoned saddle and bowed her head for the signal to move off.

Henry rode a few paces behind her, with Jasper at his side on a magnificent black stallion hung with a saddle cloth embroidered with the red roses of Lancaster and the scarlet dragon of Wales. Margaret, surrounded with her own ladies and household came next. She had been given, by her son, a length of crimson cloth for the gown she wore and her artistic sense was pleased with the harmony of colour the procession created.

In the Abbey Church Henry and his mother were received by the Archbishop of Canterbury and shown by their chaplains to the especially erected platform between the pulpit and the altar from which they were to watch the ceremony. This carpeted stage was screened from the vast concourse of people gathered in the nave to witness the crowning but was latticed to allow the King and Margaret to watch also.

Henry had told his mother of his intention to concede to Elizabeth the full honours of the day and Margaret could only praise him for his magnanimity. If Henry had shown reluctance to admit his wife had a right — perhaps even a more tangible right — to the throne of England, he was now more than making amends for his omission.

The service followed the traditional pattern laid down since before the time of the Conqueror for the coronation of the King's consort and when the Mass was celebrated Henry and Margaret joined in.

Watching from her concealed vantage point Margaret prayed for blessings on her daughter-in-law, who conducted herself throughout the lengthy and tiring proceedings with a princely bearing. Margaret wondered if she gave thought to the two tragic small brothers who had vanished into the Tower or remembered her Uncle Richard's coronation when both of them had been present. Margaret hoped, once this important event was concluded, Elizabeth would be able to lead a more peaceful life and set about the raising of more children. One small boy, as Margaret knew with sadness, was a precious hostage to fate and she looked forward to the day when two or three more children filled the royal nurseries.

In the evening Margaret and Henry again took up self effacing positions withdrawn from the rest of the distinguished company and allowed Elizabeth to take the seat of honour at the sumptuous banquet in Westminster Hall. Here they were joined by some of their own personal attendants as they watched the glittering scene below them.

It was some time since Henry had had an opportunity of speaking with his mother and Margaret discovered he had much to tell her of what had taken place during her stay in Collyweston.

'You understand, mother, I am sure, that it is wisest for me to consolidate my position in England before listening to those ambassadors from abroad who would embroil our kingdom in the strifes of Europe.' Margaret nodded. 'With this in mind I have concluded peace treaties with France — who helped me so much at the last moments before I set out from their shores to conquer Richard's forces — and with their ally, Scotland while trying, at the same time to keep faith with Brittany. This would appear to be good statesmanship but I have had word brought to me of a revival of French national feeling, unknown since the days of Joan of Arc. This patriotism has resulted in the quiet annexation of Burgundy — ' Margaret drew in her breath sharply. 'And a move against Brittany. I am well aware there are hotheads among us who would wish me to rush immediately to the aid of Brittany and I foresee a struggle ahead of me to keep out of trouble.'

'Surely if you convince your people of the benefits brought to them by trade and commerce abroad they will be satisfied?'

'One would hope so,' Henry said with a wry smile, 'but there are those who still smart under the losses we suffered in France, and who still regard me as titular King of France, and would be only too pleased to cross the Channel and make war to regain our sovereignty.'

'Let us pray that will not come to pass!' Margaret cried. 'You have a unique opportunity to endow England with greatness and it would surely be folly to waste that chance in war.'

'It would indeed and I shall resist any attempts to push me to take up arms. But enough of these miserable conjectures, on this day I have other plans to discuss with you! I am considering asking Ferdinand of Aragon and Isabella of Castile for the hand of their daughter Katherine for Arthur.'

'A marriage with Spain? This is surely a new departure for a Prince of England! What puts you in mind of this alliance?' Margaret asked curiously.

'Spain is filled with the same spirit of nationalism as France. She has succeeded at last in dispelling the infidels from her territory and I have it on good authority that Isabella and Ferdinand are outwardlooking in their hopes for their country. France, with her growing awareness of her potentialities would naturally be regarded with suspicion by Spain, but England is an unknown quantity and I judge that now might be the moment to make Spain aware of her existence.'

'I did not think,' Margaret said softly, 'when I sent you to France with Jasper all those long years ago I should ever sit and listen to you proposing marriage for your son with a Princess of Spain. Have you stopped to consider Arthur's feelings in the matter?'

Henry looked at her quickly but Margaret kept her face without expression.

'Had you any say in your marriage?' Henry countered.

'Not when Suffolk tried to wed his son with me; but later, when I was given as ward to your father I was allowed to state my preference for his suit.'

A slight constraint fell between them until Henry patted Margaret's hand with his own. 'Forgive me. You must remind me from time to time that men and women have hearts and feelings. I am so taken up with the business of statecraft it is easy for me to forget this important factor.'

'Do you find it difficult to remember as far as Elizabeth is concerned?'

'Elizabeth?' he echoed looking down onto his wife's glittering crown, 'I hope she does not find me too unfeeling. Living as Jasper and I did for so long under restraint tended to make me introspective and I admit to finding the expression of emotion exacting. Do you think she suffers as my wife?' he asked suddenly.

'No, I am sure she does not; but with her sad upbringing she needs more affection than usual. Try not to be so busy you deprive her of her fair share.'

'My lady mother you make me feel a veritable boor!' Henry said deprecatingly, and then laughed with relief as he saw Jasper climbing the stairs to join them. 'Thank heaven you are come to relieve me of a further lecture from my mother!'

Jasper raised his eyebrows and regarded them both quizzically.

'What could be the subject for a lecture on such an occasion as this?'

'Marriage.' Henry told him phlegmatically.

'Marriage!' Jasper said with a twinkle. 'A subject on which your mother speaks with some authority.'

'Jasper!' Margaret expostulated with mock severity. 'You know well there are matters I would know more about!'

'Yes, I do. May I sit with you?'

'Of course,' Henry said and beckoned for a page to bring a chair for his uncle.

'What prompted this discussion on matrimony?' Jasper asked as he took his place beside them.

'I was telling my mother I have plans to ask for the hand of Isabella and Ferdinand's youngest daughter for Arthur.'

Jasper regarded Henry for a long moment before speaking. 'You are thinking well ahead with a union such as that. Do we not hear of Isabella as a fiery leader of her people against the Moors?'

'Yes, that is certainly true; but if you are concerned that perhaps we might bring a lion into the dove's nest of our family life rest assured the reports of the Spanish King speak of an ambitious man but one who is less flamboyant than his wife.'

'That might hide a more subtle approach.'

'Possibly; but we have plenty of time to assess the man correctly. So far I have made no official approach either to the Council or to the Spanish Ambassadors.'

'How old is the little girl?' Margaret asked.

'Katherine? I believe she is about a year older than Arthur.'

'Poor children,' Jasper said softly. 'To be

wed before they have had time to look around them and see the world's beauty reflected in the eyes of the well beloved.' He moved impatiently in his seat and beckoned for a servant to replenish his wine cup.

Ormond came up and spoke with the King and Henry moved away to a group made up of the Chancellor, John Morton, Sir William Stanley and the Earl Marshall.

Jasper moved his chair closer to that of Margaret and leaning his arms on the table spoke without looking at her.

'Today moves all of us to a hundred conflicting emotions, does it not?'

'It does,' Margaret agreed. 'I rejoice Henry has done so much to make amends for the tardiness of his wife's crowning. I am sure Elizabeth has enjoyed her day and has made many friends.'

'She looks happier than I have ever seen before. I wonder what truth there was in the rumour of Richard of Gloucester wanting to wed her?'

'I do not doubt the truth of the story. Apart from the fact he saw a true hold on the throne through her, Elizabeth is a comely young woman — as are all the Wydeville women. Your Catherine is no exception and I thought she looked very well today.'

'Yes, she is fair enough,' Jasper said without

expression. 'To judge by the speed with which Buckingham got her with child I am sure her looks do not bely her bedworthiness.'

Before Margaret could comment he went on a little breathlessly: 'And speaking of bedsport your amorous young secretary and your Frenchwoman are as close as ever.'

'Are they so?' Margaret said quickly. 'I have been so engaged with Elizabeth over these past weeks I have not been as observant with the rest of my household as I should have. What makes you comment on them now?'

'It is not that I have actually watched them steal away to a secret rendezvous but they are lost in a world of exchanged glances and the host of other small things that speak of passion.'

Margaret sipped her wine before she answered.

'You sound almost envious,' she said at length, a note of something akin to wistfulness in her voice.

'I am,' Jasper said evenly, 'but I shall not carp against a destiny which denied me the supreme joy of possessing you while it gave me the privilege of being your — '

'Dearest friend,' Margaret prompted.

'Friend and lover,' Jasper added. 'Lover in the true sense of the word and not as a paramour. If we stop to think of our forebears, you and I have some ancestors who put mutual desire before all other considerations.'

'Yes, I thought very much the same thing when I visited the tomb of the Lady Swyneford in Lincoln Cathedral this year after the Thanksgiving Service. It was because she and my great-grandfather, John of Gaunt, carried on their love affair despite the opposition it aroused, that Richard of Gloucester launched such a vituperative attack against me when he attainted me after Buckingham's rebellion. What was it he said?'

' "In double adultery begotten so it is plain to see therein lies no claim upon the Throne of England" or something to that effect. But Richard of Gloucester did not stop at blackening his own mother's name, so I hope you lost no sleep about your own attainder?'

'No,' Margaret shook her head, smiling a little sadly. 'I just wonder what gave them the strength to pursue their own happiness without counting the cost they paid.'

'If excuse is wanted, I think the times they lived in were fraught with the perils of war — both at home and in France — and the danger of the Black Death wiping them out in a few short hours.'

'You are probably right; but I do not believe human nature changes so very much from generation to generation, do you?'

'No.' Jasper turned towards her. 'Margaret, when will you come to Thornbury?'

'As soon as I feel free to relinquish some of the myriad duties which seem to have been thrust upon me since I rejoined the court.'

'I have been hearing about some of those,' Jasper said. 'I was especially intrigued with your Ordinances for the Making of the King's Bed!'

'A bed must be properly made otherwise it is impossible to sleep upon it!' Margaret told him laughingly.

'From what I heard from Ormond you have given instructions for the Gentlemen of the Bedchamber to leap upon the mattress until it is even and properly disposed. The thought of all those lusty fellows jumping about on Henry's bed gives me some cause for alarm at the number of new mattresses the Royal Wardrobe will be called upon to provide.'

'When I said leaping of course I meant pulling and pushing into shape rather than jumping upon it,' Margaret said hastily, 'and I did give instructions for pages to be standing by with beer to quench the thirst of the bedmakers when it was all completed!'

'I am sure you did,' Jasper told her affectionately. 'Never was there anyone who thought so much about the well-being of others as you do. Well, my very dearest, I must rejoin the Queen's banquet; but you will not forget about Thornbury?'

'No. I give you my word. But do not you forget when I go to Collyweston, as I needs must, before too long, that you are ever welcome to come to me there.'

9

It was not until midsummer Margaret felt able to make the long and arduous journey to the West Country.

The Christmas and Easter festivities after the Queen's coronation had been observed with greater pomp than ever before. Henry was determined to show the foreign ambassadors, who thronged his court in increasing numbers, the full splendour of the English heritage. He dazzled their eyes with the magnificence of the elaborate rituals and the splendid attire of his family and their households.

On the feast of St. George the court were at Windsor and the emissaries watched in amazement as the Knights of the Garter set forth to celebrate their yearly Mass in the Chapel of the castle. The Queen, with Margaret beside her, rode in a chariot upholstered in cloth of gold, escorted by men on six chargers also decked out in the same sumptuous material. Following close behind were the ladies of the bedchamber and other women of the court all dressed alike in crimson velvet and mounted on white palfreys with reins and saddles worked in white leather with gold ornaments.

It was not by coincidence that the two Spanish ambassadors, Puebla and Sepulveda were present to witness this display of England's monarch and his family. As soon as Ferdinand and Isabella had received Henry's overture for the hand of their daughter for the baby Arthur the joint monarchs of the southern kingdom had leapt at the opportunity to bring Henry into the orbit of their domination as a possible ally against the growing danger of France. Ferdinand saw in Henry, who owed so much to the Duchy of Brittany, ruled now by a kinswoman of Ferdinand, an extremely useful auxiliary. Although it was rumoured he was at first inclined to look upon Henry's suit as presumptuous he sent messengers with speed to beg permission to send his ambassadors to open negotiations. Henry saw to it they were present at the splendid Garter celebrations.

Margaret hoped, once Easter was past, she would be able to beg permission from her son to go to Devonshire but at one and the same time Henry was beset with crises in his family and in France.

Elizabeth miscarried with a child early in May and almost at the same moment Henry heard of an attempt by the Queen's uncle,

Edward Wydeville, to assist Brittany against the growing menace of French invasion.

Jasper and Margaret had never seen Henry in such a rage as when he received the news of Wydeville's disobedience. For several minutes after Christopher Urswick brought the disquieting information to him he strode up and down his chamber calling down curses on the head of his wife's uncle.

'How dare he flout my authority? What possessed him to gather together this force and pass secretly into Brittany? I told him quite distinctly in the spring when he craved permission to go to the assistance of Anne of Brittany that it was not the time for us to interfere. Here am I trying to keep a balance of peace between the two peoples and this doddering old idiot has to take it upon himself to disobey openly my explicit commands and stir up heaven alone knows what trouble.'

'So far he has done no more than leave the Isle of Wight and land in St. Malo and it could be he has simply gone to visit the little Lady Anne.'

'No one is going to convince me he has gone to Brittany simply for a social visit. What shall I do, Jasper?'

'Nothing,' Jasper told him quietly. 'If you send any force after him now to bring him back the French could misinterpret your action and our countries could be at war in a moment. If you ask my advice it is that we should remain as if nothing has happened and hope Edward Wydeville will think better of what he has done.'

'That is almost too much to hope!' Henry snorted. 'These Wydevilles are the most arrogant, self opinionated family I have ever known; without so much as a brain between them. Oh, forgive me, Jasper, I had forgotten in the heat of the minute that you are married to Edward's sister.'

'And you to his niece,' Margaret reminded him. 'If you will excuse me I should like to go to Elizabeth now, for if she should hear of Edward's escapade she will doubtless be anxious and her health is not sufficiently good to withstand shocks.'

'Go to her, mother and make it plain I attach no blame to her for her uncle's misdeeds. Now that my first anger has cooled a little I must admit Edward was probably only taking the law into his own hands for my sake. He was one of our most loyal friends while we were in Brittany as prisoners and he did a great deal to help us gather together our army. We can only hope, as Jasper so rightly says, he will think again before embroiling Englishmen in this fight against the French.'

When, at length after Whitsuntide, Elizabeth recovered her strength Margaret began a leisurely progress through her many estates and manors to Torrington. It was here, in north Devon, she had passed much of the time after Henry and Jasper had parted with her in Tenby and sought safety in France. It was here she had waited for the first news of them from across the Channel only to learn that they had been driven by storms to take shelter in Brittany and had been made prisoners there by the Duke. It was here, too, she had learnt of the death of her mother and with blow following blow it had been many months before she had felt life held any further happiness for her. Only her simple faith in the ultimate goodness of God had sustained her.

Now, passing through Woking, Basingstoke and Salisbury for the ancient town of Exeter, she experienced a new sense of awareness. It was as if the months of attendance on her son and his family had cocooned her in a silken prison from which she had not wanted to escape but once the bonds were broken she knew again the air of freedom and rejoiced in it.

In her new mood the hazy vistas over miles of undulating and wooded countryside gave her great pleasure touching her heart and filling her with unsuspected longings. When the cavalcade stopped for the midday rest beside some stream she would have been quite content to have stayed there until dusk savouring the sweet smells of the bank and feasting her eyes on the creamy blooms of meadowsweet. She would sit with her back against a bole of a tree letting her gaze drift lazily from the gently flowing water to the clumps of rosy fireweed and ragged robin. She wished, as day after day followed in a succession of warmth and peace, that the journey would never end and she might go out into eternity in the tranquillity it brought her. She realised for the first time how much of her energy was drained by the demands of court life.

Those in attendance upon her took their lead from her and when she lingered in one of her own manors or a hospice along the route accepted the respite with gratitude. They, as well as Margaret, were glad the Buckingham children had preceded them, though perhaps for different reasons. Margaret's half-brother, Lord Welles and his wife Cecily, who was sister to the Queen, headed her household while William Elmer was acting as her secretary. He had been distrait and withdrawn at the outset of the journey but the soft beauty of the countryside and the idyllic weather softened his disgruntled air and he appeared to find again the sense of companionship Margaret and he had once shared in the early days at Collyweston. While she could not help feeling sorry for him that Perrot had been with the advance party Margaret was glad to see him restored to something approaching his old self. She would often discover him sitting not far distant from her while the servants lifted panniers of food from the backs of the mules and distributed it to the company. He would pick out with uncanny accuracy the tree, bird or flower that most interested her and tell her something about it from his seemingly endless fund of knowledge of wildlife. She was grateful to him for his interest and several times wondered if he gave her his attention because he understood her mood and the dreams it awoke in her. For she could not blind herself to the fact that had Jasper been with her her happiness would have been complete.

She had left Jasper with Henry at Windsor; the negotiations for the marriage of the Spanish princess and the baby prince of England now well under way, although the omnipresent threat of Edward Wydeville's disobedience still hung over the King's peace of mind. When she had set out Wydeville had not committed any act of war against the French but Henry's advisors returning from across the Channel spoke of a growing band of those ready to take up arms with Wydeville for the Duchy of Brittany. Yet she thought now, as they sought hospitality in the Abbey of Exeter, how far away and unreal all the anxieties which had pressed upon her appeared from this great distance, and kneeling in the Cathedral on the next day prayed Henry's difficulties would resolve themselves. At the same time she allowed herself the luxury of hoping Jasper would be free to go to Thornbury where she had promised her Buckingham wards she would take them to visit their mother before they all returned to Westminster in the autumn. Even as the half-formed wish forced its way into her conscious thought she smiled at her own capriciousness and bowed her head lower as the Bishop intoned the benediction.

She awoke on her first morning in her Torrington manor and lay quiet in her bed listening to the birds singing in the trees about the house. At length she stretched luxuriantly from the comfort of the down-filled mattress and putting on a bedrobe went to the window. Below the walled garden glowed in the early morning sun. Huge banks of phlox, tansys and yellow-eyed marguerites filled the beds and the lawn was smooth with the constant attention of the scythe.

How fortunate I am, she thought, that even when I am so long absent careful hands keep order in my possessions.

She dressed quickly, steeling herself against the disapproval she would undoubtedly encounter from the faithful Betsey when that worthy discovered her mistress had been ill advised enough to choose her own apparel for the day. Feeling almost an intruder in her own house she crept down the wide oak staircase and let herself out into the garden. Her feet were quickly wet through from the dew on the grass but she took no heed and walked from one side to the other stopping now and again to admire and sniff the fragrance of the roses and lilies. Coming upon a stone bench she sat down and rested against the bricks of the wall behind, already warm with the sun. Closing her eyes she leant back while the warmth stole through her, filling her with a delicious languour. She was reminded of a poem, half-remembered stanzas of which she tried without success to put in order.

'Where I saw walking under the Tower
Full secretly in garden fair
A maiden and the freshest flower

Who in the corner set and while I
So overcome with pleasure and delight
That suddenly my heart became her thrall.'

As she pictured the young man leaning from his turret and seeing below him in the secret garden the girl whose praises he was singing she smiled as she remembered the poet was James I of Scotland and his love none other than her aunt whom he had wooed and carried off to Scotland to be his Queen.

Scotland, Margaret thought, is more wild and unknown than Pembroke but I, too, would have gone there if Edmund or Jasper had called me. We Beaufort women must be fearless when our hearts dictate.

Two chaffinches sped across the garden, their excited chattering rousing Margaret from her lassitude. She opened her eyes and saw two men were already at work in the flower beds. Reluctantly she went towards the house, sorry to waste a moment of the morning's air.

A month went by during which time she rode out to the confines of the estate and interested herself in the affairs of the manor. She began to make plans to donate the house to the priest of the parish for she had been distressed to find he came to the chapel for

Mass on her first Sunday scarlet in the face and having difficulty with his breathing. The man had been hesitant to tell her the cause of his discomfort and she had had to make discreet inquiries before she remembered the walk from his house to the church was steep and difficult. William Elmer had regarded her with an upward quirk of his eyebrows when she first announced she intended to bequeath the manor house to the incumbent and his successors.

'You are very generous, my Lady,' he told her.

'I cannot bear to think of the poor man toiling up that incline when the summer is at its hottest or there is snow upon the ground.'

'But supposing you should wish to stay here again?'

'That is somehow rather unlikely. I should like to return to Collyweston if my duties would allow me and see to the many alterations afoot there. I am sure, should I ever desire to spend a short time here the priest would not gainsay me!'

'I am sure he would not. Most men find it difficult to deny you anything you want.'

'Do they so?' Margaret said wonderingly. 'I must admit I had not noticed.'

Letters came with Richmond Herald for her from Henry and she noted with relief the truce with France, mooted earlier, had been extended until the beginning of 1490 while Henry had made overtures to Scotland for peaceful cohabitation on the Borders where trouble always lay not far from the surface. Henry also told her Elizabeth was well and that Jasper had gone into the Marches of Wales in his position as Commissioner of Oyer and Terminer.

She thought of him riding through the treeless hills and the rain drenched uplands of his father's country. How he had loved his remote heritage and taught her to see the beauty of the desolate countryside! She thought also he was now not so far away from her across the Bristol Channel and it might well be that when she took her wards to Thornbury he would be there to welcome her.

With the feast of St. Swithin's the fair summer had broken with thunderstorms and prolonged downpours. Forced to spend a good part of the day in the house the atmosphere between the occupants became charged with an intangible tension. Betsey Massey told Margaret Edith Fowler was finding it a strain to occupy the Buckingham children, especially, she added, as Perrot was absent more and more often from the nurseries.

Margaret made no comment but later sent for her groom and ordered her wagonette to be ready to take her out with the children and the two women when the skies cleared. She was aware that as soon as William and Perrot had been reunited they were as drawn to one another as before. She often glimpsed them walking swiftly through the yew walks to the gate house and the woods and river beyond. She wished many times she could understand her own misgivings about the outcome of the affair and once or twice was on the verge of sending William back to Sheen, where Henry was in residence, with some papers and documents for her son's attention.

The outing in the wagonette became a daily treat for the children and Margaret sometimes took with them a basket of food for the sick and elderly in the village. The boys enjoyed the giving out of the dole and vied with each other to climb down and deliver the clutch of eggs or slices of cooked meat.

A few days before the date Margaret had decided upon for their return the sun broke through the storm clouds and after a morning of mists shone once again in a cloudless sky.

Margaret told her groom to saddle the boys' ponies and take them out once more to the river and the wooded hills. She took a book and some embroidery and with her half-brother and his wife sat in a corner of the garden. By the evening she began to regret the decision to begin their homeward journey but knew if she delayed the bad weather might set in again and it was possible they could be shut in Torrington for the winter.

On the following day she went alone to sit in the garden. Although she carried a kerchief with some strands of silk and canvas she made no effort to work, content to sit and let the sun warm her body. She would need her strength for the long miles back to Sheen.

She watched, fascinated, as a pair of white butterflies danced close to her above a rose bush. Fluttering their wings they flew together and then apart, until one flew close to the other and followed it whether it spiralled, twisted or wafted upwards on the warm breeze until at last they met and sank out of sight behind a lavender hedge. To her surprise she found tears filling her eyes and she blinked quickly to dispel them.

'Don't hide your tears, my love, in some strange way they become you.'

'Jasper!'

Joy banished the tears as she looked up to see Jasper standing at her side with the sun making an aura behind him.

'I had not looked to see you here!'

'No. When I left London for the Marches and intended to go straight from there to Thornbury I did not mean to come to Devon, but somehow riding over the familiar ground and breathing again the salt laden air we knew so well in Pembroke I was drawn towards you as if you called my name. Now I am here I shall be able to escort you to my home and go with you to London.'

Margaret regarded him with a smile and then shook her head, wonderingly.

'It is said the Welsh people are gifted with a sixth sense unknown to ordinary folk and I am coming to believe you inherited it from your father. Did you know on the journey down to Torrington I almost prayed for you to have been with me?'

'Almost?'

'I never pray for anything I want for myself. Call it superstition or arrogance or what you will, I can only form prayers to ask blessing for those I love and although to have had your company was my dearest wish I could not bring myself to ask God to grant me this extra favour when He has dealt with me so kindly in all my other petitions.'

Jasper touched her cheek with his hand and then glanced behind him to the stone house.

'Will you walk with me to the river?'

'Of course; but are you not weary with the day's ride?'

'I have only ridden from Bideford for I came from Llandaff by sea.'

'Did you? It seems almost another life since I took Master White's ship from Tenby and came here all those years ago.'

'But you are happier now than then, I hope?'

'I have my son restored to me and you are by my side — could I be anything but contented?'

They walked through the trimmed hedges to the cornfield where the garnered grain stood in stooks and rabbits scuttled away at the sound of them. The heat beat down on them and the sun shone blindingly on the bleached stubble. When they came to the woodland bordering the river the cool wrapped them as a balm. They walked slowly now, hand in hand, talking very little.

Margaret had asked for news of the King and his family but Jasper could tell her very little more than she already knew and she dropped the topic, savouring his company.

Coming to a cleared space where piles of stacked branches told of the woodsman's labours they sat down on a fallen tree. It was very still, the tall ferns dappled with the sunlight falling through the leaves over their heads. Far below as the Torridge curved towards them they could glimpse the river. After a while Jasper slipped to the earth and rested his head against Margaret's knee. She ran her fingers lightly through the strong hair now streaked with grey.

'You grow more like Owen each time I see you.'

'Do you think so?'

'Yes, the shape of your head is identical.'

'Strange you should mention my father just then, for I was thinking of him in our days at Hatfield. This forest reminds me of the woodland around our home and I can recall a similar day when Edmund and I could not have been more than about six and seven when he took us with our mother for an outdoor feast. I suppose I have not thought about that day for years but the quiet and the smell of the moss and the mouldering leaves of the centuries beneath our feet suddenly recalled it vividly.'

'I often think perfumes and smell are more evocative of past events than anything else.'

'They are. I think that day we spent in the Hatfield forest was one of the last we were ever to enjoy as a family. It was soon after that Duke Humphrey of Gloucester tore us away from our father and mewed us up in Bermondsey Abbey. What a mixture he was, lewd and cruel on the one hand and possessing a great thirst for knowledge on the other. It is said the collection of books he has left to Oxford University is among the finest in the world.'

'There must have been some goodness in him because he was far seeing enough to realise education of the young is a very important duty of the older generation. Have you ever been to Oxford or Cambridge?'

'To Cambridge, yes. When Margaret of Anjou was interested in founding her college there she used to send me down to confer with the master and the surveyors. It was while I was staying at the inn there that Edmund told me you and he were to be married.'

'I did not know that.' She was quiet a moment. 'It must be very gratifying to see a place being built where young men may be taught to acquire wisdom.'

'Why do you not interest yourself in something similar? With your talents you are the ideal person to set in motion such a college. Far better than Margaret of Anjou who had no scholastic bent whatever!'

'I might think about it one day. Just now there seem other things to occupy my mind and heart.'

Jasper took her hand and held it to his mouth.

'Oh, Margaret! If only things had been other for you and me who knows what we might have accomplished.'

'Who knows?' she echoed softly.

He stood up and pulled her to her feet; stooping he kissed her forehead. For an instant she stood still and then turned as if to go towards the manor.

'Don't go back to the house yet. We are not allowed many hours to ourselves. Walk as far as the river.'

'Very well.'

He set off a little ahead of her, pushing aside the trailing brambles that clutched at his hose. The sound of the river came nearer. Margaret almost slipped as the ground sloped slightly towards it. Jasper held her arm. They came out into the bright sunshine, blinking at the sudden brilliance.

As their vision cleared they caught sight of a movement below them. In the same moment they both saw a naked man and a woman on a flat rock at the water's edge; as they watched the woman stretched her arms above her head and dived into the river. She swam upstream with leisurely strokes, not looking behind her, while the man poised gracefully on the rock and followed her with powerful strokes until he overtook her and she turned into the circle of his arms. The sun burnished the red gold of the man's hair.

'William and Perrot,' Margaret said dully.

'Don't look like that,' Jasper said, as with his arm about her shoulders he led her upward and back into the cover of the trees. 'They are young and unfettered.'

'I do not understand what it is about them that makes me fear for the future — '

'Now who is possessed of necromancy? I thought it was I who could see into the future! I do not believe you are so concerned for their wellbeing as you are involved emotionally in some strange way and their actions colour your own feeling.'

She stopped suddenly and looked up at him.

'How well you know me! Not to anybody else in the world would I admit there is reason in what you say.'

'No other person in the world would have sufficient knowledge of you to begin to understand. But, if I am not very much mistaken, you see in those two some of the passion that has lain dormant between you and me since Edmund died and you mistrust the demonstration of such deep involvement.'

'Yes, it is exactly that although I had not been able to explain it to myself or would not have expressed it as you have done.'

Margaret put her arms about Jasper and put her head on his breast. Through the thin shirt she could hear the strong beat of his heart. Jasper made no move to touch her, for it was the first time since he had returned from Brittany he could remember her making an unconscious gesture towards his protection, and to interrupt her now would be heartless.

'At first,' she was continuing against the warmth of his chest, 'I thought I saw in them the parallel of your affair with Myvanwy and I put my emotions down to jealousy.' Jasper kept his arms to his side with difficulty.

'But now you know that that was not the case and it is easier.'

'Yes,' she murmured, 'it is slightly easier but I am still afraid for them.' She clung to him, her nails biting into the flesh of his back. 'Don't go too far away from me, Jasper. I do not think I could live without your love!' she cried suddenly.

Gently he disengaged himself and taking her hand led her slowly homewards. He spoke to her quietly, comforting her with the age old words of a man to the woman who is his life.

At the manor house the shadows were lengthening and John Welles hurried to meet them as they came in.

'I am glad you are come, for Richmond Herald is here with letters from the King.'

Margaret and Jasper went into the oak lined parlour where the Herald awaited them. Margaret took the rolled parchment from him and went over to the window. As she read she turned quickly to Jasper.

'Henry says Sir Edward Wydeville has launched an attack against the French with the Breton army!'

'Good God!' Jasper shouted. 'The man must be mad; he'll have the whole French army in arms against us. Does Henry say anything about going out to France?'

'No, he doesn't mention it here in so many words but he is obviously very concerned indeed.'

Across the darkling room their eyes met. Both knew that in one letter came the blow to their hopes of going to London in each other's company.

'I shall not go tonight,' Jasper told her later when the household had supped and were preparing to go to bed, 'but I shall be gone by the first light in the morning.'

'And I shall come straight to Sheen rather than go to Thornbury with your stepsons. I shall send them to their mother with their own household and let her enjoy their company for a short while without their guardian.'

'I would wait for you but — '

'Our rate of travel would only hinder you. You had best be gone and see what is to be done. Thank you for coming even if it were for so short a time.'

'Thank you, my dearest, for this most happy day. Do not be too long behind me.'

10

By the time Margaret came to Sheen the King had sent Christopher Urswick to apologise for his subject's behaviour in France and news had been received of the complete rout of the English force and the death of its instigator, Wydeville.

Henry had not wasted his time and had sent emissaries to all three countries surrounding the kingdom of France, strengthening his alliances with them. He had separate agreements with Spain, Burgundy and Brittany. While strategically encircling France he was leaving nothing to chance in his own country and Bedford, Oxford, Northumberland and Surrey were despatched into the countryside to bring together the men promised the King by parliament.

At this juncture it seemed as if Henry's efforts to bring his kingdom to the forefront of the European powers were being noticed even as far afield as the Holy See for word came that the Pope, Innocent VIII, was endowing him with the coveted prize of the hallowed sword and cap of maintenance. These symbols were regarded as honouring their wearer with pre-eminence in the Pope's opinion among the princes of Christendom.

Margaret found herself once more caught up in the demanding activities of the Court. From Sheen she went to Windsor, from Windsor to London and thence to Sheen for Christmas. By Easter the King and Queen were at Hertford.

Outwardly it appeared as if all were the same as before Edward Wydeville's abortive attempt to come to the succour of the helpless Duchess of Brittany but Margaret knew this was not really the case. Henry, while working into the night to keep the peace, sending emissaries in a constant stream to those with whom he was allied, nevertheless extorted from parliament a large sum of money with which to wage war against the French should it be necessary. Spain and the Low countries certainly encouraged him to do this, promising they would give their support in any effort Henry made to free Brittany from the French yoke.

Henry was shrewd enough not to believe all he heard from those who had newly joined with him in amity but Margaret was concerned lest he should commit himself to war against the French only to find the other allies mysteriously melting away.

He was deep in the tangled web of

diplomacy when he received word from Yorkshire of the death of Northumberland in a riot over the payment of dues to the King granted by the Commons. Henry set forth immediately but when he arrived found Surrey and the other lords had restored law and order. Staying for a short while to thank those who had taken care of his interests he came back to Sheen in time to receive the ambassadors he had sent to Medina del Campo to sign the treaty binding him to help Spain and uniting his son and Catherine of Aragon. Henry was delighted to find Isabella and Ferdinand had not quibbled about the large dowry Henry had asked for Catherine but not so pleased when he found they were adamant about retaining their daughter until at least her twelfth birthday.

'How can we turn her into an English Princess if she is allowed to remain in Spain until she is almost a woman?' he growled to his mother.

'Surely you did not expect Isabella to part with a child of two?' Margaret asked in some bewilderment. She had to admit there were times when her son's reasoning baffled her.

'If Catherine could come here now she would be used to our ways when it came time to marry Arthur. Besides she would be becoming used to our climate which from all accounts does not measure up to the heat of Spain.'

Whether or not Henry was satisfied with the political aspect of the Treaty Margaret did not discover and she was wise enough to ask no questions. From what she saw of Henry's negotiations with the Courts of Europe she could only surmise he had a firm grasp on what he intended to do.

It was shortly after this Elizabeth the Queen became pregnant again. Margaret, longing to go to her own home in Collyweston, could not find the heart to leave her daughter-in-law at such a time.

She was particularly pleased she had elected to stay when she heard, with something approaching hopelessness, that Henry had despatched a large number of troops to Brittany in an effort to help the young Duchess clear her territory of the French invaders. Margaret recognised this was the only course open to her son but wished fervently some other means might have been found of reconciling the two parties.

At first all went well and Oxford sent back glowing reports of the Breton towns recaptured for the Duchess but just when victory seemed inevitable the young woman quarrelled with her own advisors, who were always seeking to marry her off to the most advantageous suitors, and lost faith with her allies from across the Channel. The English shut themselves up in one of the towns they had captured while the Bretons were defeated everywhere.

Henry received ambassadors from the French who pressed him to bring home his troops. Henry hesitated. Just as his mother had feared both Spain and Maximilian had made excuses and had not joined in his fight to help Brittany and he found himself alone. He kept the Frenchmen waiting while he debated behind locked doors with his members of Council. At last he sent them to Charles of France promising to give due thought to renewing the truce.

It was at this time the Queen was brought to bed of a daughter. Elizabeth begged Margaret to stay with her when her labour began and Margaret was present when the child came into the world and responded to the midwife's slap on its buttocks with a lusty cry.

Both Henry and Elizabeth asked Margaret to stand as godmother to the child and she willingly did so, holding the baby up to the Bishop of Ely to christen in Westminster Abbey on the following day, the thirtieth of November. Margaret watched as the Bishop poured water from the silver font on to the child's brow and afterwards made a presentation to the infant, who was named Margaret in her honour, of a chest of gold and silver.

Christmas was celebrated at Westminster in great state. Despite the uneasy situation existing with France the French ambassadors were guests of honour.

Margaret's husband, Derby, and most of the other nobles were at hand when the Court made a state visit to Westminster Hall for a service to mark Candlemas. Later in the evening they were entertained with a play and a supper.

Jasper was not present on any of these magnificent occasions, being absent on the King's business in the Marches once more. He spent the Holy festival at Thornbury, sending gifts for St. Nicholas to Henry and Margaret from his home.

Margaret missed him more than she cared to admit. She was drawn immediately to her new granddaughter and longed to tell Jasper of the infant's progress. Although Derby was in Westminster she could not bring herself to talk to him of the shape of the baby's nose or ask him whether he thought she favoured her father or mother's side of the family. She discovered she went more and more often to the royal nursery and was quite happy to sit with a book while she rocked the cradle of the little Margaret with one foot.

Soon after Candlemas the royal physicians reported an outbreak of measles and suggested it might be wise for the King and his family to go down river to Greenwich.

Margaret agreed with this suggestion for she was concerned, not only for the young but also for Henry, who, since his early days had shown a tendency to chesty complaints which had not been helped by his long confinements in Brittany. The air in Greenwich was strong and touched with the salt from the sea.

She did not accompany the royal party when they left from the landing stage outside the Palace but waited for William Elmer who had gone to Collyweston to collect dues and accounts and was visiting Cambridge for her on his way back to London.

On her return from Torrington she had acted on Jasper's advice and had snatched sufficient time from Court to go to the University town to see for herself how it was conducted. She had been nobly entertained by the corporation and by the University authorities and had come away determined to help the colleges in any way she could. She had visited the splendid chapel built by Henry VI and had been almost conscious of his ghost as she knelt to pray for the unfortunate young man whom she honoured in her memory as the instigator of her alliances with Edmund and Jasper. It was he, who as their half-brother, had appointed them to be her guardians when she was a small child and had predestined her marriage to Edmund. She thanked God for the wisdom of the aesthetic King who had given her of the very stuff of human happiness when he had been so pitifully denied it all his harassed life.

William Elmer came to Westminster with a roll of letters from the University.

'Who received you?' Margaret asked.

'One of the proctors, John Fisher. He seemed very pleased to have your interest and has sent much material for you to look into.'

'Good. I shall take it with me to study at Greenwich. Tell me now of Collyweston. Is all progressing favourably with the building there?'

'For the first time I began to have some idea of how the manor will look when it is finished. I think it will be a very worthy home for you, my Lady.'

'Think you so? What of my wards? Has the young Northumberland arrived as yet?'

'He has and appears to have come to terms with the Buckingham boys.'

'He is as pugilistic as his forebears then?'

'It would appear so, but is amenable to discipline. Edith Fowler says he does not make much extra work for her but I think she is overtaxed at times.'

'It will not be long before they have outgrown her schooling and I shall have to look for a tutor for them. You had best be keeping your ears open for the mention of a suitable man. But what of Perrot, is she not giving Edith all the help she needs?'

William turned to her with an expression she found completely enigmatic.

'Perrot is Perrot and she is as she has always been.'

'Well then,' Margaret said crisply, 'shall we deal with the accounts?'

With some misgivings she sent William back to Collyweston on the eve of her departure for Greenwich. She was making some preparations for her stay there when Betsey came to tell her Jasper had arrived in the Palace and sent word to say he would welcome the opportunity of supping with her.

He came into her parlour as the servants finished putting the last touches to the table. For the first time she could remember he looked tired, but she said nothing and led him to a chair by the fire. Margaret signalled for a page to pour wine and Jasper drank it and sat back. While they ate they spoke of the Christmas festivities and the visit of the French ambassador. The food was tasty and plentiful but Margaret, impatient for the meal to end, hardly noticed. When at last the door closed behind the last of the servants she sank back against the velvet cushions and looked at Jasper with solicitude. He returned her look for look until he said: 'I am tired, that is all. Travelling in this weather is not always easy and the courts I have attended have been dreary and long winded. There is nothing wrong with me a few days in your company will not put right.'

'I am glad,' she told him simply. 'For I do not like to see you weary. We are not so young any more and a little rest now and again will not hurt.'

'It is I who am old, not you, Margaret. You forget I am eleven years your senior.'

'Yes, I do forget, because you have always been so active and full of energy. How came you to Westminster rather than going straight to Greenwich?'

'It so happened I met up with young William Elmer as we came through Hatfield and he told me you had not yet joined the court. It did not need any persuasion for me to delay my Greenwich visit to accompany you there when you leave tomorrow. As we were denied our journey together from Devon, I think fate owes us tomorrow!'

'How fortunate your paths crossed. William was no doubt in a great hurry to return to Collyweston?'

'Why so? Is Perrot there?'

'Yes. I despatched my wards thither as soon as Twelfth night was past for I have taken the little Northumberland into my wardship also and I think it better for the boys to live quietly at Collyweston for most of the year rather than at Court.'

'You are probably right. On the subject of William, have you overcome your aversion to his affair with Perrot?'

'Not wholly, but it is easier to bear with when it is not under my nose!'

She rose from her chair and drawing up a stool, came and sat at Jasper's feet. He took her hand, caressing it between his own.

'How have you been since last we met?' he asked her gently.

'I have been too busy to really know. The new baby — '

'Ah, of course! Your new granddaughter. Is she thriving?'

'Yes, she is a stronger child than Arthur and not very like him to look at. I think she favours our side of the family rather than Elizabeth's.'

179

'She is not fair then?'

'No, her hair is brown and her complexion darker than her brother's. She is a lively little thing and already looks about her quite knowingly.'

'Spoken like a truly fond grandmother. I am glad you find happiness in your family for you were deprived of so much of Henry's youth and young manhood. Is he well?'

'Moderately so. He works too hard and lets no one rest — least of all himself — in his effort to convince those from abroad what a stable government he is building up. I do not think Elizabeth sees very much of him but she appears to be content enough and is really fond of her babies.'

'But she likes to have you at hand to help with them?'

'Yes, I think she is basically lacking in self-confidence and if I am on hand to turn to she is helped,' Margaret said simply.

'Meanwhile you stay at court and have no time to lead a life of your own?'

'It could be it is best it should be so.' She was quiet. A log fell with a small shower of sparks and she leant forward and pushed it back on to the fire with the poker. She watched for a moment to see it was safe and then turned to Jasper, putting her arm across his knee and looking up at him.

'Enough about me; tell me of yourself. Your Christmas was quiet?' He nodded. 'And since you have been occupied with the Courts again?'

'Yes. I find they grow tedious nowadays. When I was younger I enjoyed the clash of differing opinions and the meting out of justice but who knows, perhaps since I was at Torrington I have discovered within myself a longing to be at peace. It could have been the sight of William and Perrot that sparked off the malaise; I am not sure. I thought often of them on my ride back to Westminster and since. Their obvious enjoyment brought home to me how very much you and I have missed.' Margaret looked away from him quickly. 'Don't move,' he said very quietly, 'just to have you close makes me feel better.'

On the following morning she dressed with great care for her journey to Greenwich, choosing a new robe of fine white blanket trimmed with miniver covered by a cloak of the same fur. Jasper smiled at her with real pleasure as he helped her step aboard the barge. In the morning light he looked more rested.

In the curtained boat they were joined by their waiting women and officers of their households. The tide was falling and they made good time down the Thames. As they passed Coldeharbour Jasper asked her if she spent much, if any, time at her house. She shook her head and replied she had not slept in the place for weeks.

'You do not see very much of your homes, do you?'

'No,' she told him smiling, 'but I hope the day will not be too distant when I shall be able to spend more of the year at Collyweston.'

But it was to be more than two years before she was able to stay longer in her home than a few days at a time. The intervening months were momentous in the fullest sense of the word. Brittany sorted out her differences with her own advisers and Anne sealed her alliance with the Emperor Maximilian by a marriage of proxy. France realised this was the hour to strike and mounting a large offensive against Brittany took Nantes and the towns held by the English. Anne and Maximilian appealed to Henry who was only able to send the few troops he had at the ready.

The English Commons voted more money for Henry to raise a better army but it was too late. The Lady Anne of Brittany, impoverished and tired of the war which had dogged her short reign gave in to the importuning of the French and even went as far as to have her marriage by proxy to

Maximilian cast aside so that she might wed with King Charles of France. This she did in December, 1490, in the Castle of Langeais where Henry, five years previously, had enlisted the same King's help to win the English throne. Now Brittany subjected herself to France and the two countries became one.

Margaret prayed Henry would now abandon his plans for war with France but she discovered he had no intention of so doing and was in fact pressing his people for more money with which to equip an army. Further to astonish his mother he announced he intended to lead the army himself and take Jasper with him to France.

He was spurred on to make this effort for he felt his pride was touched. If Margaret hoped the people of England would grudge him the money she was mistaken for the funds poured in. The English, hereditary enemies of France, were quite happy to see their King try to recover territories lost since the reign of Henry V and he prepared for war with their blessing.

Henry had another reason to prove himself, for from the Netherlands, the home of the Dowager Duchess Margaret of Burgundy, sister to both Edward IV and Richard III came rumours of a youth who claimed to be Prince Richard, the younger son of Edward, who was supposed to have perished in the Tower with his brother. Rumour was sufficient to rouse the hopes of latent Yorkists and Henry was aware of gathering consolidation in their ranks.

Margaret would have been more worried than she was but for the fact the Queen had given birth to another child and she was constantly in attendance on Elizabeth and the babies. The latest addition to the royal nurseries was a beautiful golden haired boy, Henry. From the start he captivated those who tended him, lying gurgling in his cot and only resorting to fits of temper when he could obtain his own way by no other method.

As the child grew Henry went to Southampton and set in motion the moving of the huge force he had gathered across the Channel. Hundreds of ships had been commissioned and breweries created to meet the thirst of the army. Not since the time of Henry V had Southampton seen such activity in the smithy and forge.

At last, waiting in Greenwich Margaret and Elizabeth were brought the news of the sailing of the fleet. Margaret almost ill with anxiety for her son and Jasper, who she privately considered too old to fight. Mercifully she did not have long to worry for Henry sent Richmond Herald to tell her a peace had been concluded and he was bringing his victorious army home. Bewildered by the quick turn of events Margaret curbed her impatience until she could speak with someone who knew the full story.

When she heard it from Jasper she could hardly believe her ears. Had it been anyone but he who told her the facts she would have doubted their veracity.

'We landed,' Jasper told her, when he came straight to her chamber after he and Henry with their army had received an ovation from the citizens of London, 'sending troops to Boulogne from the beachhead at Calais. Henry, with Oxford and myself under him, led the army to Boulogne and dug in outside to begin a siege. We expected to be there for the winter but to Oxford's and my astonishment we had been but a week in the place when Henry summoned us and told us his ambassadors had been treating with Charles ever since we arrived in France and they had come to terms with them!'

'Do you think he ever intended to fight?' Margaret asked shrewdly.

'You speak my own thoughts. What worries me is that we are not alone in our opinions and there are those who will be set against him on account of the spoils they have been denied.'

'What of payment for the troops?'

'As you know, Henry has been extremely active in raising the large sums needed to fit out such an army as we led to France but you need have no fears he will be short of gold.'

'How so?' Margaret asked sharply.

Jasper was silent and walked slowly away from her to look down on the river.

'You remember Henry was most pressing in his demands to the Lady Anne of Brittany for the reimbursement of the army he sent to her aid previously?'

'I have not been allowed to forget the matter. Has he obtained promise of its payment?'

'He has done better than that. Charles has agreed to pay the whole debt and any other outstanding monies his wife owed Henry — '

'Henry has been bought off?' Margaret asked looking away from Jasper.

Choosing his words carefully Jasper answered her after some thought.

'There are those who are bound to put that interpretation on his actions, but I think he has shown the cleverest statesmanship of his reign. We lost but one man, and that in an accident. Henry has recovered all the gold owing to him and has obtained as well, a signed agreement from Charles, he will not give any help to future rebels against Henry's crown.'

'That I am glad to hear. There has been much talk during your absence of this impostor in Flanders. Tell me one other thing, what do Ferdinand and Maximilian think of their ally's action?'

'To the best of my knowledge they are as yet unaware of it!' Jasper chuckled, 'but doubtless, when they *are* made aware of what has transpired they will look upon your son with different and more respectful eyes!'

'I hope that is the case. Sometimes I think Henry has qualities beyond my understanding.'

11

The court spent the Christmas of 1493 at Windsor and from there Margaret wrote to the Chancellor of Oxford asking for the authorities of the university to release to her Maurice Westbury to be tutor to her wards.

She had interviewed several young men for the post but she knew, as soon as Westbury had been shown into her chamber, that here was the man she sought. Not over tall, but well built, dark with large brown eyes fringed with outrageously long lashes for a man, he was intelligent, calm and possessed of the right ideas about the discipline required by boys approaching puberty. Destined for the Church he was quite willing to postpone his priesthood until he had completed the task of educating young Northumberland and the Buckingham boys.

The University were not slow to recognise the compliment paid them by Margaret's choice and in February Westbury came to Windsor. With the family he stayed there for a few days before Margaret's household set out for Collyweston.

Margaret could hardly believe she was

really going to be permitted to stay in her home when once she arrived there but she kept her fears to herself. One thing gave her hope that she might be mistaken. Henry had announced he was to make another royal progress and had asked her, a trifle hesitantly, if she would be prepared to entertain his Court at Collyweston at the conclusion of the tour. Margaret had happily agreed to this visit but when she left Windsor nothing definite had been arranged about its date.

Jasper accompanied her party as far as St. Albans and took leave of her at the gatehouse of the hospice.

'You are joining Henry at Sheen?' she asked.

'I have some business in Westminster first and intend to go to Sheen at the end of the week.'

'Will you be accompanying him when he makes his progress?'

'Doubtless; and I shall do my best to persuade him to come to Collyweston. Do you think your building will be completed by the autumn?'

'I sincerely hope so! It seems to have been so long since I first visualised the changes.'

'Will Derby join you?' Jasper spoke without a change of expression.

'He left several days ago for Lathom. I

know he intends to stay there for some time and then go on to Knowsley; when he comes south again, doubtless he will spend a few days at Collyweston. He has as many interests as I have and his time is perhaps even more occupied than my own.'

'I trust it may remain so!'

Maurice Westbury came up to tell her his charges were ready and Margaret presented him to Jasper. She knew by the quick appraisal he gave the younger man he approved her choice and when he had moved off to join the boys he told her so.

'That is a very fine young man. He reminds me of someone, but I am at a loss to think who it is.'

'Edmund,' Margaret said quietly. 'He is more thick set than Edmund but he has the same bearing and sincerity of manner. I am sure he will be the right man to tutor the boys.'

'Catherine must surely appreciate all you do for your wards. Not everyone who takes the children of other families into their household goes to such pains to see to their education.'

'There are extenuating circumstances where the Buckingham boys are concerned. I shall never be able to repay the debt I owe to their father.'

'I hope I have helped a little.'

'By your marriage to Catherine? Of course. I count her the most fortunate woman in the land.'

'Wedded to me on my terms?' Jasper asked.

'Wedded to you on any terms,' Margaret told him laughingly.

'You are balm to my heart,' Jasper replied sombrely. 'Your words will stay with me as I return to Westminster.'

'You do not want to go?'

'How could I wish to leave you — for Heaven alone knows how many months with the possibility I might never see you again?'

'Don't speak like that, my dearest Jasper. We must keep faith we shall be spared to one another for many years to come.'

'I hope you are right, but — '

'You are not ailing in any way?' she cried quickly.

'Nothing at all. My health is good.'

'Then have no fears. I, too, am strong and seldom suffer so much as a headache.' She stopped and looked at him perplexed. 'Perhaps I had best not go to Collyweston after all and return with you to Sheen.'

'Of course not! I am ashamed of myself for speaking as I did. I would not spoil your pleasure in going to your home after so long for the world.'

'There would be no pleasure in life without you to share it. What would possessions be without love to illumine them?'

'As soulless as the dust, my love,' he told her quietly. 'See, take my hand and I shall help you to your horse.'

But she lingered, her hand in his, until reluctantly she put a foot in the stirrup and sat in the saddle. She looked down on him, unsmiling.

'It is not like you to fear for the future. Where would you have been through all the years of Henry's and my exile if you had despaired then?'

'I was young then and life was a challenge.'

'You are not old now, although infinitely more fair!'

Margaret smiled and Jasper laughed quickly to despatch the real misery he had seen in her face.

'See,' he said, 'I have brought you a visible sign of the golden chains binding you to me!'

He opened the pouch hanging from the girdle at his waist and took out a beautifully wrought necklace of fine chain.

'Bend your head!'

Jasper slipped the long necklace over her head, winding it until it nestled against the soft fullness of her breast. Margaret touched the chain lingeringly, her eyes on Jasper's.

'Thank you,' she said with difficulty. 'Thank you.'

'Go with God and rest assured I shall bring Henry to Collyweston if I have to carry him there as I did when he was a child.'

Setting off when at last the whole party were mustered, Margaret looked over her shoulder until she could no longer see Jasper standing at the hospice gate. Once free of the houses the road took its way through narrow lanes and undulating countryside. Several times Margaret wished she had listened to those who had wanted her to ride in a chare for the cold spring wind tore at her coif and blew tendrils of hair across her face. She was in no mood to exult in the exercise or enjoy the awakening signs of life in the hedgerow and field and however much she tried to think of other matters her mind returned again and again to the conversation she had had with Jasper. As each mile took her further and further away from him she longed to be turned in the other direction and hastening to meet him. She was oppressed with a sense of the futility of her actions and her own involvement with the material aspect of her life. The visit to Collyweston which had appeared so vitally important suddenly seemed of no moment. She had houses enough without wanting to make any of them larger or more ornate and she was assailed, as she had been on previous occasions, with the burden of her vast inheritance. She was glad she had carried through her intentions of giving her manor at Torrington to the priest and decided to set aside more of her income for the benefit of the needy.

They arrived at the Gilbertine Priory of Chicksands as the brief spring sun was setting and Margaret was grateful to slip wearily down from the saddle and seek the comparative warmth of the hospice. The Buckingham boys with Northumberland, came to help her dismount and Margaret smiled at them as their household joined her. She was aware as they went into the antechamber of Edith Fowler, now acting as the boys' housekeeper and Perrot talking animatedly with someone. Too tired to take part in the conversation it was not until she was almost asleep she realised with a pang of dismay it was Maurice Westbury who had been the object of the Frenchwoman's interest and she had looked, if Margaret could recall, especially attractive and pleasing. Margaret, who prided herself on the calm atmosphere usually prevailing in her domestic life forced herself to remember to take steps to see it was not endangered by Perrot's behaviour. Not for the first time she wished she had not taken the young woman into her employ.

The remainder of their journey to Colly-weston allowed no time for dalliance of the romantic kind for it rained almost without ceasing throughout the two succeeding days. Margaret still refused to ride in a covered cart and wrapped herself in a hodden cloak that was heavy but kept out the worst of the downpour. In some strange way she enjoyed the feel of the rain in her face more than the searching wind of the first day.

Betsey Massey regarded her attitude as foolhardy and stayed close by her side. Margaret brushed off her anxious solicitude but had to admit she was grateful to leave behind the beautiful town of Stamford and turn west for her home.

When they arrived she was too tired to make a tour of inspection and much to everyone's relief said she would accompany her comptroller of the household to see the additions and alterations on the following morning.

It was almost a week before she was completely rested but she kept the women of the house and her retinue occupied from morning to night as she ordered the furnishing and appointment of each room. She had brought with her tapestries and beautiful materials with which to make hangings and bedcovers and she spent much time in the wardrobes of the beds overseeing the sempstresses as they cut and sewed the curtains and drapery. She undertook also the unpacking of her silver and precious plate and chose places to show them to their best advantage. The cup Jasper had given her she took to the small chamber outside her bedroom and put it on a cupboard close to the fireplace. Here, she felt, was the very heart of the great house she had created and it was to this small room overlooking the walled garden she would retire for quiet and solitude. For she discovered almost as soon as she arrived her attention was in demand for countless matters throughout the day; she found herself thinking her life with the King's court had been exacting but in a quite different fashion from the demands now made upon her and she hoped that once they had settled down her household would be restored to the order she loved.

She kept William Elmer at her side wherever she went, taking note of any alterations she wished to make. She was full of praise for what he had accomplished at Collyweston and promised him a visit home to his parents after the King's projected stay. Perrot she took away from the boy's menage and made her second in command under the comptroller of the household as head woman of the sewing room. Perrot was an accomplished and fine needlewoman and Margaret hoped to catch her interest with the skill she would now be able to demonstrate.

At last she looked round the house and told herself all had been done to create an atmosphere of restrained splendour. In the great parlour she had had hung the arras depicting Nebuchadnezzar and in the chambers she set aside for her son and his wife other tapestries of Paris and Helen and chairs covered with velvet and softened with silken cushions. She had most pleasure arranging the books she had brought with her in the new library. It was here and in her own parlour she spent most of her day.

Towards midsummer she received, almost on the same day, a herald from Henry and a messenger from Jasper, telling her the King intended staying at Collyweston on the completion of his progress before his return to Westminster. Henry gave details of the number of retainers he would be bringing while Jasper asked what he could do to help her provide for the added number of people who would be residing in Collyweston.

Happy to have definite news of when she might expect her son and his family Margaret set about the business of laying in stores. She had several meetings with her chamberlain, comptroller and William where they discussed the best means of having ready vast quantities of food and drink. Merchants came from Stamford to receive orders for spices, dried fruits and wine. Messengers were despatched to the manors where stews held the best supply of fish and tenants of the home farms were asked to state how much produce they would be able to bring to the manor kitchens when it was needed.

The small band of musicians she employed spent hours a day practising airs while William sought entertainers to keep the royal party amused.

Yet with all the preparation Margaret was relieved Henry and his train did not come to Collyweston before the end of September. She felt if they had come a moment earlier than the stated time she would have been not ready for them. As it was, on the morning of their expected arrival she was able to tell herself the house and gardens looked their very best. Once the mists had cleared the trees, tinged with early gold, glowed in the soft autumn sunlight and the flower beds were filled with pale, mauve michaelmas daisies and the sharp, yellow spikes of golden rod.

Margaret's husband and his brother Sir William Stanley had already taken up residence in the house and Thomas had been most complimentary on the arrangements she had made for receiving her son.

'I shall be hard put to it to come up to the standard you have set, Madame,' he told his wife as they stood on the flagged terrace looking across the deep valley to the pastures beyond. 'His Grace promises me he will honour my homes with his company when he comes North on another progress and I fear me neither Lathom or Knowsley are as fine as the mansion you have created here.'

'I do not altogether believe you, Thomas, and am more than certain when Henry comes to visit you, you will show your usual hospitality.'

'I shall try!' Derby promised her.

Richmond Herald came in the late morning to tell her Henry and his entourage were leaving Stamford and would be with her within the hour. Margaret lined up her personal household to greet her guests, sending the other servants to the gatehouse to await the royal party.

She had a new robe of soft red velvet for the occasion and had had new suits made for her wards, who stood with her at the house door. They were as eager as she to see the

Court arrive for their mother was to be of the party. Margaret wondered how the years had treated Catherine and genuinely looked forward to speaking with her; she hoped she would be pleased with the healthy look of her two sons now aged fifteen and thirteen and their scholastic progress under the tutoring of Maurice Westbury. Margaret glanced round the waiting household, noting William stood at her elbow with Maurice behind the boys. She saw Perrot standing with the other women, her eyes lowered although Margaret could have sworn an instant earlier she was looking in the direction of the doorway. Margaret just had time to think how unsuitably cut Perrot's dress was for the autumn, exposing most of her bosom as it did, before cheering coming from the gatehouse told the head of the procession was coming down the slope to the house.

Henry leapt almost boyishly from his horse and kissed his mother affectionately on the cheek. Elizabeth, with Arthur and the little Meg close behind her, stepped down from the open wagonette in which they had travelled, followed by a nurse leading the two-year-old Henry. Even in the swift look Margaret gave all the family she saw this child, smiling on those about him, was the best looking. Meg, oval faced and slightly overawed, greeted her grandmother warmly and Arthur bowed over her hand but the golden haired Henry captured the attention, rolling forward on chubby legs and holding up his arms for her to pick him up. Laughingly gathering the child Margaret stepped back and allowed her son to enter her home.

They dined in the Great Parlour, an elaborate feast of many courses and free flowing wines.

It was late before it finished and when the boards were cleared Margaret walked among her guests bidding them go to their bedchambers as soon after her son had retired as they chose. She was certain they were tired after the morning's travel and although she had much to say to Henry it could wait until the following day. Although she hoped she would be able to snatch a few words with Jasper she saw her chances dwindle as the court lingered, reluctant to break up the conviviality of the evening. She had greeted him briefly on his arrival knowing that with his coming came a warmth otherwise missing in her life. Catherine had been at his side, more comely and more sure of herself than Margaret remembered. She had given every appearance of pleasure in gathering her sons to her and before the feast, while it was still light, had walked to the

Welland river with them.

'You take good care of my sons, my Lady,' she said now to Margaret as she joined the group of men and women comprising the Bedfords and Oxford, Lord Welles and Cecily, Catherine's niece.

'I am glad you think so,' Margaret answered simply, 'we enjoy their company and they attend well to their lessons. Maurice Westbury tells me — '

'The good looking young tutor?' Catherine interjected.

'Yes,' Margaret told her, smiling. She did not pursue the subject of the Buckinghams' tuition in Latin and mathematics because it was patently obvious their mother was not over concerned with their prowess in the schoolroom. Taking care not to meet Jasper's eye Margaret moved on to speak with her son who had about him Derby, Sir William Stanley, Ormond and Sir Robert Clifford. They parted to make way for her and Ormond brought her a chair.

'You have made great improvements in your house,' Henry told her. 'The workmen you have employed are skilled and daring in the methods they have used. I look forward to making a thorough tour of inspection on the morrow. Ormond tells me you have a full programme of gaiety to entertain us while we are here. Although I am glad to hear that I shall also be happy to stay on with you for a few days when the festivities are finished. The summer has been busy and one or two days of rest would be heaven-blest.'

'Nothing would give me greater pleasure than to have you here for as long as you wish,' Margaret said; she looked quickly into his face to see if she could detect any signs of strain but Henry was relaxed and she went on, 'there have been no alarms since last we met?'

'No,' Henry told her reassuringly. 'I am not allowing this Perkin Warbeck to lose me any sleep.'

'Perkin Warbeck?' Margaret echoed. 'Who is he?'

'You have not heard of him?' Derby asked incredulously. 'I thought all of England had heard of him who styles himself Richard of York!'

'Oh! The Flemish impostor. Of course. If you know his proper name then surely there can be no menace?'

'It would have appeared so to me but while we are satisfied he is no son of Edward IV there are those who are equally certain he is sprung of Plantagenet stock and are prepared to back his cause.'

'Margaret of Burgundy?' Margaret said.

'Yes. She has stated publicly she believes the boy to be her nephew and fetes him like the prodigal son. He wears clothes outshining any other about her and has his own retinue. From the accounts brought to me he is a well mannered and graceful youth, personable and charming.'

'I thought when you took Lambert Simnel into your service you had finished with impostors.'

'I hoped so, but with the mysterious disappearance of Edward's sons the way lies open for people to resurrect them. Fortunately Perkin does not, as yet, anyway, seem to have aroused much Yorkist sympathy in England although he has gulled even Maximilian into believing he is really the younger son of Edward. From that it must appear the boy possesses looks which are akin to those of Margaret of Burgundy, for Maximilian married to her stepdaughter would be familiar with the cast of features of the house of York. I suppose I must not rule out the possibility Perkin may be a bastard of Edward's or else a lovechild of Margaret of Burgundy herself. This latter would explain very thoroughly her desire to push the youth. We must keep a most vigilant eye for backsliders to the Yorkist cause but that is for the future — now I intend to shelve my worries and enjoy the hospitality of my mother's house!'

Margaret climbed the stairs to her chambers rather wearily, when, about an hour later the last of her guests had gone to their rest. Despite her fatigue she was pleased with the smooth-running of the banquet and the obvious enjoyment of those present. She hoped the following day would be pleasant and dry so that the men might enjoy some hunting and the women the tour of her domain.

As she turned the last flight of stairs she found Jasper leaning on the carved balustrade watching her.

'I did not dare intrude on your parlour in case Betsey Massey sent me packing. I know she frowns on anyone who keeps you from your rest.'

'Poor Betsey, the older I get the more trial I become to her. But come and drink a posset with me and I'll send her to bed.'

Despite the lateness of the hour, Betsey was still sitting in a chair beside the well-tended fire. On a stool was a bedrobe and in the hearth a copper ewer and linen towels.

'I sent those other damsels to their couches,' she told Margaret, ignoring Jasper. 'I don't know what young women are coming to! No stamina, that's what it is! What can I get you, my Lord Jasper, for doubtless you will be staying for a while?'

'Thank you Betsey; a tankard of ale would not go amiss and the Collyweston brew is very good indeed,' Jasper said, smiling.

'So at last we are met in Collyweston. It has seemed an interminable progress. I do not grow more patient as I get older and when my mind is set on one goal everything else becomes a stumbling block.'

'But now you are here and I shall do everything to make you happy. Did you hear Henry ask me if he might prolong his visit when the Court has left?'

'No, but he mentioned it to me before we arrived. May I remain also?'

'You do not have to ask.'

Betsey returned with a jug of foaming beer and two pewter tankards.

'I'll be saying good night, but mind, Lord Jasper, my Lady has many duties to perform during this week and she needs her rest!'

'Thank you for reminding me, Betsey. I promise I shall not overtax her.'

When she was gone Margaret leant against the padded back of her chair. She put up a hand to remove the coronet and gauze veil covering her hair. Without speaking Jasper lifted the circlet and took out the pins binding her hair and before he drew his chair close to hers, bent and kissed her forehead.

'At least I shall not be accused of giving you a headache. Those headgear must be very wearying.'

'They are! Many is the time I have sat at some important state occasion and longed to do as you just did. It is heavy enough at any time but when it has pressed down on the brow for an hour or two it appears to have trebled its weight. I am only glad it is no larger.'

'Like the Crown?' Jasper said quietly.

'Yes. I do not think the wearing of the token of majesty is easy either in fact or symbolically.'

'You are thinking of Henry, of course and yet, you might so easily have claimed the right to wear it yourself. You do not ever regret you did not assert your own title?'

'No. I never imagined for one instant it was my right to do so. I am more than happy to be Henry's mother.'

'The power behind the throne?'

'Does anyone think that? It is surely Elizabeth's privilege to be so called.'

'You know as well as I that your daughter-in-law is a pleasing, ineffectual young woman who has no ambition to rule anyone.'

'But Henry is happy with her?'

'Yes. She is the perfect wife for him. She makes no demands on his time or energy and is lovely to look at which is of vital importance with the populace. She bears healthy children and to boot, has Yorkist blood in her.'

'I hope when you make jest of me being the power behind the throne you do not think of me now as a veritable termagant who is forever issuing orders!'

'No! Nothing is further from what I think. To me you are womankind, all that is best in the sex. Could you really believe, loving you as I have done since the day you were betrothed to Edmund, you could ever assume any guise but that of my heart's ease? You know it is impossible and while we have been separated I have begrudged every moment of time away from you.'

'Did you go to Thornbury to fetch Catherine?'

'No. I sent my chaplain and chamberlain. She has been with us since we left York. What think you of her?'

'Why do you ask?'

'I know you are mulling something over in that mind of yours and I would know what it is!'

'It was merely I thought she looked

— different in some way.'

'As if she had lost the numbed patina that enfolded her?'

'Yes, exactly.'

Margaret looked at him suddenly.

Jasper put out his hand and took hers, lifting it to his mouth.

'No, you do not even have to put into words the thought crossing your mind. It is not I who have aroused her from her apathy. It could be some other man. I do not know. I suppose I hope it is, for she is young to be burdened with a husband who shares his title and estates with her and denies her all else. But let us not talk of Catherine or next we shall be discussing Derby and Henry's projected visit to Lathom! Will you be acting as his hostess when the visit takes place?'

'If he asks me I shall have no choice!'

A few minutes later Jasper said he must leave her to her rest.

'I am thinking of what Betsey said; you have a great deal to do with such a vast concourse of people under your roof and it would be selfish to keep you talking half the night.'

'Very well, if you think you should go, I shall not try to detain you, but you know well I would prefer to keep you here.'

'Don't!' Jasper cried and Margaret saw

with concern his eyes dilated with pain. 'It is not like you to play a heartless jilt.'

'Jasper! I did not mean to sound enticing. I would you might stay with me and — '

'And?' The simple word hung between them. She slumped back in the chair biting her lip to prevent the tears of strain and pent up emotion. Jasper looked at her and then suddenly knelt before her, putting his arms about her waist and his head on her bosom.

'Forgive me, forgive me. We grow too old to jest and speak foolishly with one another. You touched the raw hurt of my need of you. There is nothing in the world I would rather do than stay here with you, not for this night only but all the others God will spare me. Perhaps now I want your love more than ever before. Before, I was strong and could fight the daemon of passion but now, something of my strength has ebbed away and I long only to clasp you in my arms and seek oblivion in the warmth of your nearness. Forgive me.' He rose from his knees, drawing her to her feet beside him.

'Go to bed and try to forget I have behaved so badly.'

But when she saw him again on the following day she knew he had not slept for his eyes were dulled and his face drawn with fatigue. It was with a great effort she dressed with added care and set her mind and hand to the entertaining of the King and his Court. Outwardly calm and smiling she knew an inward turmoil she had imagined she had long since outgrown.

The climax of the visit was to be the feast on the last evening of the official stay. Extra men had been called in to help Henry Ludlow, her cook, prepare the gargantuan meal and William had kept the best of the entertainers to delight the Court and other guests invited from the surrounding countryside.

Margaret sat at her bed table while Betsey dressed her hair before she went to the Hall to be ready to receive her guests.

'You look drawn to a string,' Betsey said as she picked up a coil and pinned it in place. 'I hope his Grace will not think of coming to your house too often if you are going to be tired out each time.'

'My son is welcome in my home at all times. You should know that better than most.'

'I do know it and it is not the Lord Henry I would keep away but the multitude he brings with him. It is impossible to move anywhere without being pushed about by some graceless knave who haughtily says he is about the King's business! — King's business indeed! I would have them know, I was minding their precious King before they were swaddled!'

'So you were,' Margaret said soothingly. 'They think only to do their duty.'

'And that's not all from what I hear,' Betsey went on, darkly, as if she had not been interrupted. 'Some of these entertainers are no better than they should be; there are tales going round this morning of fires in the churchyard and strange songs coming from among the tombstones.'

'Too much drinking of the wine and ale we have provided would account for that.' Margaret picked up her hand glass and turned her head sideways. 'That will do very well, please give me the coronet and I shall put it on myself.'

She did not want to listen to more of Betsey's superstitious stories. Never before had Collyweston entertained on the scale of the present visit and the unlimited food and drink handed out to all who dwelt in or near the manor was sufficient to cause fantasies in the minds of those who over indulged. Margaret felt she had sufficient to occupy her mind without adding the burden of servants partaking in drunken revels.

At the feast she sat on a raised dais with the King, Elizabeth, the great officers of the

Church and Court who were present, her husband and Jasper and his Duchess. With Henry on her right hand she had Archbishop Morton on her left. The conversation was agreeable and polished; no one missing an opportunity to show a turn of wit or quote a passage from some of the books now becoming increasingly popular.

'You have a very fine library, my Lady,' Archbishop Morton told Margaret. 'I must confess to envy of some of the works dedicated to you by Master Caxton. But then, you deserve his bounty for you have been an inspiration and most generous patron.'

'I should like to think that was the case, for I truly believe his work will do much to stamp out ignorance which I am convinced is one of the main causes of heresy and heathen thinking.'

'You foresee the freedom of all to read the Scriptures one day?'

'I trust so.'

'What do you think of the voyages of Christopher Columbus?'

'He who's brother begged for assistance when we were not able to provide it?' Morton nodded. 'If I were a man I should like to have accompanied him on his voyage of discovery to the Indies — as I should like to have gone on Crusade against the infidel Turk, if only in the capacity of menial to those who were prepared to give their lives for Christianity.'

'You are brave, my Lady, and adventurous.'

'What of you, my Lord Archbishop, would you have journeyed with Columbus across the uncharted sea?'

Margaret listened as Morton warily replied to her question. Chancellor of England and holder of the highest office of the Church in England, a cardinal of Rome and Chancellor of the University of Oxford, he had a brain far outstripping most men of his time. Henry leant more and more upon him as an adviser but Margaret never found herself completely at ease in his company. She had long since forgiven his subjection to the Yorkists when Edward had sat upon the throne for many other men had done the same thing at a time when the Lancastrian cause looked hopeless. She thought, rather, it was the involvement of Morton and herself in the Buckingham rebellion which irked her. Richard III had sent Morton as a prisoner to Buckingham's house and it was here the Duke had listened to the tale told him by Morton of the imprisonment of the Princes in the Tower and set out to free them. On this fateful journey he had fallen in with Margaret returning from a pilgrimage and together they had hatched the plot which had ended in Buckingham's beheadal and Margaret's imprisonment and attainder.

And now Buckingham's widow was married to Jasper and all of them sat at her board while Buckingham rotted beneath the earth. Margaret shivered and picking up her wine cup, leant back against her chair and drank deeply. She looked up to see Jasper watching her from the end of the table. He smiled and her fears retreated into the recesses of her brain. Taking another mouthful of wine she gave her attention once more to Morton.

The musicians had played from the gallery throughout the feast but when the ornate marchpane confections had been served jugglers, tumblers and singers appeared in lively succession to much banging on the table and shouts of appreciation. The Hall was hot and the wine had flowed freely; many of the men and several of the ladies were flushed and askew in their seats. To a clash of cymbals a youth, dressed simply in black, came into the place to announce the advent of the Master. He ignored the cries of 'Master? The Master of What?' and held out his arm to welcome a figure who glided into the Hall dressed in a voluminous cloak of rich oriental silks that changed colour as the light from the flambeaux caught it.

An unusual hush fell on the company as the man, masked but bearded, faced the high table and held both arms over his head. Unhurriedly he caught two lengths of rope from the youth who had announced him and showed them to the guests. Drawing a knife from his cloak he cut the rope in several places, threw all into the air and presented two whole pieces to his audiences. A restrained banging on the trestles greeted this show of his skill but the magician held up a hand for quiet while the boy bowed before him and placed a wicker basket on the flagged floor. The man performed a complete circle and brought out of the folds of the cloak a reed pipe. He put this to his lips, nodding to the boy to pull off the lid of the basket. The youth, somewhat reluctantly complied and stepped back. The pipe's eerie music filled the Hall and plucked at the listeners' ears, speaking strange magic and weaving patterns of mystery. A woman shrieked and a man shouted as a hooded snake uncoiled slowly from the basket and followed the end of the pipe as the man moved it upwards. With a shrill discordancy the air finished and the snake flopped into the container. The boy put out his foot and shut the lid; stooping, he carried it away.

The Hall was filled with excited comments

and half-smothered exclamations of fear. All at once the majority of the torches were extinguished and a greenish smoke rose from beside the cloaked man; when it subsided a girl, clad only in a robe of scarlet gauze stood revealed. The guests murmured among themselves for no one had seen her enter. In the dim light the magician and his black-suited assistant melted to the shadows. The thin wail of the pipe once more filled the Hall and, with eyes fixed into the furthest corners of the room, the girl began to gyrate to the music. There was no sound from the onlookers as she twisted and bent from side to side in exact imitation of the snake. Her movements were foreign to those who knew only the steps of the courtly dances or the more lusty prancing of the country romps. At once there was something evil and compelling in the sensual rythm of hips and undulating form that would not allow the eyes of the beholder to waver.

Margaret held her breath, gripped in a strange ring of fear that kept her rigid in her seat. She longed to call out and tell the sorcerer and his familiars to leave the Hall and restore their peace but she found herself unable to speak.

The weird wail of the pipe bubbled suddenly into a melody of such purity

Margaret was near to tears. In a second she could smell the salt laden air of the Milford Haven and hear the cry of the curlews as they made for the open sea. Half-conscious of the girl who knelt now and threw her body in a circular motion, her naked arms swaying and dipping in time to the haunting music, Margaret was back in Pembrokeshire, racing down the strand on her pony with Jasper beside her on the magnificent stallion he had owned in the far off days of her youth. She clenched her teeth on the exclamation rising in her throat at the same moment as the girl rose to her feet, pirouetting on her toes. As Margaret watched, hypnotised, there was a flash of light and the girl vanished. Immediately the Hall was a babel of excited chatter. Men pushed their way from the tables to the place where the magician and his assistants had been, only to be met with the acrid smell of burning gunpowder and no sign of the man and those who had been with him. The noise in the room became deafening and Margaret signalled to the Comptroller of the household to take round more wine and command the musicians to play. Gradually the ferment subsided and the disturbing atmosphere melted.

'My lady mother, you have certainly

excelled yourself in the remarkable entertainment we have witnessed this night. I doubt if any man has ever seen a more extraordinary display of the magician's art than you have given us this evening. Who found these gifted people for you?'

'William Elmer. Although how he came by them, I do not know. I only trust no offence will be given to the more susceptible among my guests.'

'Why so? It was surely only a display of the most cunning ingenuity.'

'Think you so? You detected no hint of sorcery?'

Henry looked at her with a puzzled air.

'Sorcery? No! I found it highly entertaining; as I am sure did everyone else. I should like to say a few words to thank you publicly for your hospitality here — may I say them now.'

Margaret shook her head. 'There is no need. I have had little enough opportunity to look to the welfare of my son and this I have done from the heart.'

'Be it as you will then, Mother. I can only say how honoured I have been by all the preparations you have made for my Court and I shall enjoy to the full the quiet we may enjoy when the others have departed for Sheen.'

It was some hours before the last of the company sought their beds. Some so much the worst for the lavish hospitality they had received they went ignominiously in the joined arms of their own and other men's squires. Margaret had longed for the peaceful privacy of her own chamber as soon as the feast was finished but carrying out her role as hostess stayed to watch the last of her guests depart.

Jasper sought her out when he saw her, briefly, unattended and came up to her quietly as she grasped the back of a chair for support.

'Did the air of Pembroke smell as sweet to you as it did to me?' he asked.

'Jasper!' she spun to face him, her aching back forgotten in the shock of his words.

'So they did,' he said smiling. 'What witchcraft was practised here this night that you and I were transported to Arcadia?'

'I know not; oh, I know not, but I am afraid, my dear one!'

'You and I have nothing to fear when the magic of music but recalls a treasured memory. Those who should take heed are those who saw bottomless pits and smelt the fire of burning brimstone. But enough of mystery; you are weary and should have been in your bed hours since, I shall bid you good night and do my best to hasten the laggards among your revellers. God be with you, dearest Margaret.'

Betsey rose, sleepy eyed from the truckle bed she had dragged into her mistress's chamber, to help Margaret undress. With her usually nimble fingers thickened with sleep she took out the pins in Margaret's hair and brushed it soothingly. Margaret undid the bracelets and the chains about her neck, her eyes closed in weariness.

'Were you pleased with your first reception for his Grace?'

'Do you mean am I pleased it is over?' Margaret looked up into Betsey's face. 'For if that is what you mean, I am happy it appears to have been successful and glad, very glad, that tomorrow we bid them farewell.'

12

In the next year Margaret received a letter from Henry telling her of his desire to knight his younger son and bestow upon him the Dukedom of York. The message was sent from Woodstock where the Court was in residence and asked the King's mother to come to Sheen as soon as she was able and before the worst of the weather. Henry also requested the presence of the Buckingham children as he intended the young Duke should take his place among the nobles in his first public duty.

Margaret began the intensive preparations for her departure to Sheen. She discovered herself quite ready to take up again the Court duties from which she had been resting.

Collyweston had wrapped her in a peace that had rejuvenated her, renewing her energies and giving her again the wish to be with her son and her grandchildren. She was, also, anxious to see how Jasper fared. Since the visit of the Court to Collyweston she had not seen him. Once the host of guests had left for Westminster he had remained with Henry and his Queen and the family had spent a few quiet and intimate days. These had filled her with nostalgia and she had been secretly glad when, after about a week, Henry had announced they must depart to rejoin his Court. When they had gone she had spent several hours of each day on her knees in her newly constructed chapel; praying for she knew not what, other than for inward tranquillity. This she had at last been granted and the calm environment of her home began to work its magic upon her. Now she felt able to take up once more the responsibilities of her public life and looked forward with pleasure to the coming celebration and festivities.

She did not need to enquire into the reasons for the making of the three-year-old Henry into the Duke of York. Ever since she had received the Court there had been growing evidence of the influence Perkin Warbeck was having upon the royal houses of Europe. In some capitals he was given the palaces usually reserved for the reigning monarch of England or his children and was receiving great sums of money from Margaret of Burgundy to enable him to live as the son of Edward of York would expect. With royal aplomb Perkin wrote letters to Ferdinand and Isabella expressing his faith in their belief in his cause and asking for their support. Henry, not unnaturally, did not take kindly to this intrusion into his territory — more especially since he did not seem able to convince the sovereigns of Spain of the honour he was doing in offering his son to their daughter — and he acted with the customary wisdom and foresight his Council were coming to expect. He sent Sir Robert Clifford to make discreet enquiries in the Lowlands about the English Yorkists who were reported stealing away from England to pledge themselves to Perkin and set about making his second son a true Duke of York.

As far as Margaret could make out from the letters Henry wrote to her her son was less concerned with Perkin's effect upon the loyalty of his subjects than the worsening — because of Margaret of Burgundy's adherence to the Pretender's cause — of the trade situation between the two powers. It was becoming increasingly evident Henry firmly believed the stability of his country depended very largely on the commerce between England and the continent of Europe. With the ever growing sums of money thus pouring into the coffers of the realm it was clear any interruption was most unwelcome.

Margaret thought she knew Henry well enough to understand he would have no fear for his future from a young man who was so obviously a false hope for the Yorkists but that he might view with serious alarm the real threat to the economy of his kingdom.

When she came to Sheen she looked around the familiar chambers set aside for her use with pleasure. Care had been taken to make her rooms shining and sweet smelling; the furniture shone with beeswax while bowls of marigolds and beech leaves made splashes of colour against the panelled walls. Henry sent for her a short time after her arrival.

Entering his room she checked an exclamation of dismay for Henry was gaunt and stooped. She received his affectionate kiss and sat down restraining the anxious enquiries she longed to make. She had difficulty in remembering her son was thirty-six years of age and might well resent her concern.

When at last she had enquired for Elizabeth and the children and listened to his eager plans for the forthcoming ceremony she ventured to make what she hoped were casual seeming questions for his own health. He had always been prone to complaints of the chest since his childhood and had been struck down immediately following his victory at Bosworth with the sweating sickness which had resulted in the postponing of his

Coronation. Margaret could never dismiss from her mind the dread of lung sickness that could overpower him in a few short weeks.

'I?' he said with some surprise to her questioning. 'I am very well.'

'You have had no coughs or colds?'

'Perhaps one or two, but nothing to worry about. I am too busy to be overconcerned with my health.'

'Why are you so busy, Henry?'

'To make England the great power she should be.'

In the face of such simple reasoning there seemed nothing more to say and she kept her counsel hoping it would not be too long before Jasper would come to the Palace and she could unburden her mind to him.

Jasper was absent in Westminster making final preparations for the many days of feasting and splendour to mark the occasion of the little Harry's knighting. Henry told his mother Jasper had spent much time journeying between Eltham, where Henry was at present residing with his household, and the Palace of Westminster.

'He has been invaluable in the organising of the Tournament I am holding and in the finer points of the ceremony of the bestowal of the Dukedom.'

'I hope he has not overtaxed himself.'

'Jasper? I have never heard him complain.'

'Have you ever?' Margaret said dryly.

'No; that I have not.'

Now Henry stopped in front of his mother and looked down at her. 'You appear very anxious for the health of your family of a sudden!'

'Your uncle and I do not grow younger and it is not so easy to shrug off anxiety when one has passed the salad days.'

'I do not think of either of you as changing. Come to the light and let me look at you properly.'

Smiling, Margaret gave him her hand and he drew her to the casement where already the short day was fading into dusk.

'In fact,' Henry told her, 'you look younger than before. I can see the peace and quiet in Collyweston suits you and I shall have to be careful not to keep you too long at Court.'

It was to be several days before Margaret heard from William Elmer that the Duke of Bedford had arrived in Sheen. Within the hour Jasper came to her apartments.

'I did not know you had arrived three days ago, otherwise no business would have kept me from your side!' he cried as he came quickly into her parlour. Without appearing to notice her waiting women he kissed her on both cheeks. Margaret signed for the ladies to leave them and Jasper turned as he heard the click of the latch behind them.

'So you were not alone!' he said unrepentantly.

'They should be used to us by now.'

'If they are not, I am only concerned for the effect it has upon you. For my own part no tittering or vile gossip could sully our relationship. Let me look at you.'

Jasper took the branched candlestick from the shelf above the fireplace and studied her face without comment. Putting it in place again he took her in his arms and held her tightly against him. Neither of them spoke until Margaret put up her hand to wipe the tears she felt on her cheek.

'You cry, my love,' she said gently.

'I cry for the wasted years. God grant, if there be a hereafter, He spoke truly when He promised us in His house are many mansions and there shall be no giving in marriage.'

'My dear, when our Lord spoke thus to His disciples He was educating them in the broadest sense of the Christian faith and Mercy is His second name.'

'You are wise, dearest Margaret, and shame me with the depth and breadth of your understanding.'

'How so?' she said lightly from the circle of his arms. 'From what Henry tells me you have been applying all your skill and knowledge to the matter of the little Harry's bestowal.'

'That but comes in the day's work and is small hardship compared with the making of war and the rotting of one's flesh in the prisons of Brittany.'

'Tell me what plans you have been making for the jousts,' she said hastily. 'Come, sit here.'

Reluctantly Jasper released her. He brought another velvet covered chair to the fireside and placed it close to the one Margaret had been sitting in when he entered. When they sat he took her hands, fondling them between his own and holding them against his face. She sat quietly, her strength ebbing out to support him, her heart contracting at the sight of the multitude of white hairs among the strong grey.

'Tell me of Collyweston.'

'There is not much to tell. The usual routine of estate matters; the granting of requests; the settlement of disputes and the disposition of those who seek preferment in various church and other benefits. Not very much when I set it against what Henry is attempting for England.'

'He succeeds, I truly believe.'

'Think you so? But at what price? Do you

not think he looks bent and unwell?'

'Do you?' Jasper countered.

'Yes, but I have not seen him for some time and perhaps notice differences not apparent to you.'

'He has suffered one or two colds but nothing more.'

'No coughs?'

'No, dearest. I know you cannot help being anxious for him but he will not come to much harm through hard work.'

'He is caught in the web of helping his country.'

'But the web was of his own making and he is proving how well able he is to manage his affairs from the heart of it.'

'It comforts me to hear you say so. I confess to feeling guilty with my life of idleness at Collyweston while he is overset with affairs at Westminster.'

'Henry has always had the gift of attracting men to his side and he now has a most capable set of advisers; men of the Church and of the Law, well suited to give him counsel and carry out his wishes.'

'He does not seem much concerned with the threat from the Pretender across the Channel.'

'He makes light of it but in the spring two or three men were brought home from the

Low Countries and tried for being ready to pledge loyalty to Perkin Warbeck — '

'And some paid for it with their life?'

'You know about that?'

'My half-brother told me. It is not like Henry to be vindictive.'

'But these were men in whom he had placed his confidence. In his time he has shown much clemency but there comes a moment when if all else fails a show of strength is necessary.'

'I suppose you are right, but I do not like to hear of such happenings.'

'Tell me of the lovelife of Madame Perrot!' Jasper said laughingly. 'I am sure she makes better listening than the traitorous dealings of Henry's subjects.'

'Yes, you speak truly,' Margaret said after a while. 'Judging by the solemn conduct of William Elmer of late all cannot be well between the two. I put Perrot to work in the sewing room at Collyweston in the hope of giving her less opportunity to entice the young man and my scheming seems to have borne fruit.'

'You have not seen them so much in each other's company?' Margaret nodded. 'But you are not entirely happy in your mind about the situation?'

'No, I am not. But how did you guess?'

'It is not difficult to explain when your voice betrays you with that little breathlessness I associate with doubt.'

'It is hard to put into words why I doubt my wisdom in the matter. I do not like to feel there is an undercurrent of ill will among either my personal retainers or my servants and I usually go to some lengths to resolve any dissension that arises; but with this — I do not know.'

'You mean they appeared so happy in each other's company that you may not have been right to interfere?'

'Exactly that. It is showing a pride beyond one's encompassing to set oneself up to judge all men's actions.'

'I understand perfectly,' Jasper said quietly. He dropped her hand and kneeling at the fire threw on a few, well dried logs; when the flames caught hold he sat back on his heels and regarded her intently. She did not flinch but held his gaze, unsmiling.

'You think, don't you, that in denying them the happiness they found in one another you acted in a spirit of envy?'

'Yes,' she whispered, 'and I did envy them! Envied them their youth and the proud beauty of their bodies so well attuned one to the other; envied them their freedom to swim naked in the river and lie afterwards in each other's arms — ' Her voice broke on a sob. Jasper swiftly gathered her once more into the circle of his embrace, kissing her gently until she was quiet.

'Don't think about it any more. We all do things we wish we had not and we do ourselves no good by perpetual recriminations. Think now of how much you have accomplished and what there is still for you to do; there can be no other woman in the realm who has done more for the common weal!'

Margaret thought about their conversation many times as they journeyed by boat to Westminster. Perrot, with the other waiting women accompanied her, and she found herself again and again drawn to look at the young woman. Margaret realised with a sense of shock that Perrot had changed from the vibrant person she had been and wore now a sullen air. Her dress also was strange and instead of the flamboyant robes she had always favoured she was dressed in black with a voluminous cloak tied high in the neck. Throughout the journey she spoke to no one. Margaret tried to push her anxiety from her and determined, when she had the opportunity, to ask Betsey if she had any knowledge of what might ail the girl.

At the Palace landing stage the Prince of

Wales and the little five-year-old Meg waited to greet their parents and grandparent. The sight of their fresh young faces quickly dispelled Margaret's gloomy preoccupation with Perrot and she watched with pleasure as Arthur, clad in a replica of his father's garments, came forward gravely to give his speech of welcome. Glancing first at his tutor he spoke a few words in commendable Latin and bowed with becoming grace; this accomplished he turned to lead his sister and handed her to Henry. The King patted his heir's head and commended his learning before stooping to kiss his daughter who stood on tiptoe to receive his salute. The Lord Henry, very wisely Margaret thought, had not yet been brought up from Eltham and would doubtless find the ensuing days exciting enough.

Before they dined they attended a service in the Abbey Church and the royal family joined in the singing with the eighty Royal Choristers. Special chants and anthems had been composed to mark the occasion and the orchestra was supplemented by musicians borrowed from Margaret's own players.

On the morning of the Procession to the City to meet the little Harry Margaret was woken by the manifold tapping of countless hammers and the shouts of the workmen employed in building the stands for the tourneys. Out of her casement she could see the corner of one stand and when she had broken her fast her granddaughter came to ask her to accompany her to see the progress being made. Margaret went willingly for the child was to be the Patroness of the Tournament and was to present the prizes to the successful jousters. Anything that helped Meg to be familiar with the quite exacting task in front of her would be an asset.

They arrived in the yard at almost the same moment as Jasper came from the Hall. He greeted them both and hoisted the child on to his shoulder.

'It looks very pretty from here!' Meg said.

'Come with me and I will show you where you will be sitting.'

Jasper led them through the maze of new timber and climbed with them to a box set prominently high and over the lists. It was already hung with magnificent azure blue arras worked all over with silver fleur-de-lis.

Meg clapped her hands with delight when she stood on a small stool and looked down into the arena just in time to see two horsemen make dummy play with hooded lances. After a moment of rapt attention she turned to Margaret with a little frown between the delicate eyebrows.

'Could it be dangerous, my Lady?'

'It was, most certainly, in days gone by, but this tournament is to be more of a display than an actual contest and nobody should get hurt.'

'Ah, there might be one or two sore seats and a cracked head or two!' Jasper said laughingly. The child regarded him quizzically until Margaret also laughed and chided him for being warlike enough to hope for a real display of arms.

'Your great-uncle but teases you,' she said reassuringly to Meg.

'Are you returning to your apartments?' Jasper asked. 'For if you are I will accompany you to seek out my stepson to discover if he is well enough versed in the part he is to play in tomorrow's ceremony.'

They walked through the cloisters and through several stone passages. They were about to turn into the small staircase leading up to the King's mother's chambers when Margaret stopped and pointed down the long flagged walk.

'This is the very spot where I first saw your grandfather,' she said softly to Meg, 'and if I remember aright, Uncle Jasper was with him at the time.'

'Is that really so?' Jasper asked wonderingly.

'Yes. I was going to the Friar who taught

the children of the Court. What a lifetime ago it all seems now! I must have been very little older than you are, Meg.'

'What were you doing here, my Lady Grandmother?'

'As well as learning Latin and reading French and English I was sent here to be with my first guardian, the Duke of Suffolk, to acquire the ways of the Court.'

'Did you enjoy it?'

'No. I missed my mother and the life I had known at Bletsoe.'

'Were you here long?'

'Not very. The Duke of Suffolk was disgraced — '

'Disgraced?'

'He did something very wrong and was sent out of the country.'

'And then you had no guardian?'

'Yes, I had,' over the child's head Margaret and Jasper exchanged smiles, 'because the King made me a ward of your grandfather and Uncle Jasper.'

'That must have been much better!'

'It was!'

Filled with nostalgic memories Margaret came to her rooms and sending Meg back to her nursery with one of her waiting women, waited with Jasper for Edward of Buckingham and Maurice Westbury while a page went to seek them out.

'Do you wish me to accompany you?' Maurice asked when he brought the youth to them.

'No, thank you. Edward is old enough to present the spurs at tomorrow's knighting and I think he can remember what he is asked to do. Isn't that so, Edward?'

'Yes, sir,' the youth said fervently. 'It will be an honour to learn from you.'

Jasper raised an eyebrow at Margaret as he went out and Margaret and Maurice spoke a few words on the boys' progress in their scholastic life. They had moved on to discuss some new works coming from Caxton's press when the door was flung open and a flushed and vivacious Perrot stepped across the threshold.

'I heard you were here and — !' she stopped as she saw Margaret. In an instant the life faded from her face and the lascivious mouth drooped in pique.

'You wanted me?' Margaret said quickly to cover the awkard moment.

'It can wait, my Lady; some trivial matter of the fastening of the robe you are to wear for the ceremony.'

Perrot curtsied hurriedly and with eyes downcast backed from the room.

'What was it you were saying?' Margaret

said evenly to the young tutor.

'We were speaking of the new translation by Caxton of the romance of King Blanchardye and his Queen.'

'Yes, I remember.' As she went on, with an effort to collect her thoughts on the subject she covertly watched Maurice's face but his expression did not alter and the dark eyes were as candid and clear as usual. When he left a few minutes later Margaret leant back against her chair perplexed by this new turn of events. Here, she saw, was the reason for Elmer's gloom and Perrot's air of frustration; tried of the conquest of the engaging young man who was Margaret's secretary the waiting woman had now turned her attention to the more difficult business of overcoming the celibacy of the tutor. Here, Margaret could see, was the challenge most enjoyed by a woman who lived for sensual pleasure and while she thought Perrot would be hard put to accomplish her designs Maurice Westbury was a man, dominantly and handsomely male. If the situation persisted Margaret realised she would have to consider dispensing with Perrot's services for it would not do for open scandal to touch her household. Perplexed, she rang the bell to summon Betsey and her ladies to begin dressing for the day's events.

In a chare she was conveyed to Temple Bar and waited while the youngest of Henry's children was brought up from Eltham and escorted to them by the Mayor, aldermen and members of the crafts in the liveries. From a long way off they heard cheering which grew louder and louder as the procession escorting the little Harry came nearer.

The child, honey haired and rose complexioned, rode in the saddle before the chamberlain of his household, and smiled and waved to the populace crowded on the narrow street. When he caught sight of his parents he bowed and doffed his velvet hat as he had been instructed and kissed his father's and mother's hands as they came close before bending to Margaret. He looked pleasantly wholesome and gave every appearance of enjoying the animated scene. Margaret hoped he would not be over-excited and develop the tantrums his nurse, Ann Luke, had confided to his grandmother was his only fault.

For the next two days the little boy was prepared for knighthood with the other nineteen young men who were to be honoured by the King. Harry was bathed and royally clad and took part in the complicated ceremonial of the Bath; he was attended by Oxford, Northumberland and the Earl of Essex and while the others fasted and made their vigil was allowed to rest in preparation for the ordeal ahead of him. With the others, however, he came to St. Stephen's Chapel and to the foot of the Star Chamber where he was lifted on to a horse and conveyed to the Hall where his father waited to dub him.

Carried aloft by Sir William Stanley and accompanied by Lord Courteney who bore the sword and spurs of the child, they came into the presence of the King who signed for Oxford to take the spurs and sword. At this signal the Duke of Buckingham, his back straight and his face accurately registering the responsibility he felt, came forward and placed the spur on Harry's heel.

Henry smiling benignly, girdled the small, fat waist with the minute weapon, and after touching his son on both shoulders with his sword, lifted him up and set him upon the table beside him from which vantage point the child watched his fellow knights kneel and receive the accolade.

Later, while the King ate a frugal meal with Margaret and the Queen, Harry feasted with the new knights in the parliament chamber and was allowed, by the King's own dispensation, to eat meat as it was Friday and therefore a day of fasting. When Margaret enquired of his nurse towards evening how her grandson had stood up to the very exacting day Ann Luke told her he had chattered happily to her of all that had occurred, muddling some of the sequence of events but obviously very proud of his participation and had gone willingly to bed and to sleep.

On the following day Margaret waited in her bower while the enormous procession that was to walk into the Chamber was prepared. Henry had suggested she and Elizabeth should not tire themselves by standing about unnecessarily while the nobles and ambassadors formed themselves into a sequence where all parties were happily satisfied with the positions allotted them. Remembering other occasions when precedence had resulted in near chaos Margaret had agreed readily to wait until she was called.

Harry had been already proclaimed Duke of York by the King in the presence of all the nobility of his realm and now prayers and thanksgiving were to be offered to God in a celebration of the Mass.

Elizabeth, growing more comely as the years passed, wore a robe of white velvet and a splendid and heavily jewelled crown on her head. She spoke quietly with Margaret while they waited to be called to take up their positions and Margaret thought, not for the first time, she had matured with more serenity than had seemed possible remembering the troubled girlhood and marriage with a man she knew little or nothing about. The older woman had no delusions about her son's qualities as a husband, for fond though Henry undoubtedly was both of his wife and his children he had very little time to spare for them.

At last Ormond came to tell them the procession was formed and they took their places directly behind the judges of the land and in the forefront of the other ladies of the Court. In a swift glance at Henry and Jasper who followed straight after his nephew Margaret was amused to see both she and Jasper were dressed in identical cloth of gold with trimmings in similar devices.

Harry was carried to his place by the Earl of Shrewsbury and looked around wide eyed at the nobles who carried magnificent wands of office, crowns and swords. Margaret, too, felt a certain element of pride in the display of her son's estate. As she knelt to pray for the new Duke of York she asked God to preserve her son and his lineage to the future glory of the realm.

As the household made their way to the feast following the service the stands were already filling for the tournament of the day.

Under the awnings emblazoned with the bright reds, green and white of the Tudor badge the people of London, who had paid well for the privilege, ate the cold meats they had brought with them and waited for the proceedings to begin.

Henry ate alone with Archbishop Morton but the rest of the family dined together while the city dignitaries and other nobles of the realm were entertained separately.

Margaret and Jasper were shown to adjoining places at the board.

'Did you know I was to be dressed in the same cloth of gold as you are?' Margaret asked him with a chuckle.

'Yes. Henry thought it was fitting his nearest relatives should resemble Castor and Pollux and as I knew it would amuse you I kept it secret.'

'The Mass was very touching, did you not think?' Jasper nodded. 'How did my grandson behave during the bestowal of the Dukedom?'

'Very well. At first he seemed slightly overawed but that soon passed. I am almost persuaded if he were not destined to fulfil the duties of the second son he would command recognition as a leader of a troupe of mummers!'

'Quite possibly. Even in the chapel when he glanced round at Ann Luke from time to time it was more in the manner of seeking commendation than asking for prompting or reassurance.'

'All three of Henry's children are intelligent and quick to learn.'

'I could wish Arthur looked stronger than he does!'

'Worrying again, my dearest? I always think of you as confident and unafraid for the future; able to bestow comfort and give of your inexhaustible supply of compassion.'

'I only fear for those I love.'

'I know!' Jasper cried swiftly. Under the cover of the table he took her hand and pressed it. 'Oh, God's Grace, I grow weary of these state affairs. I would gladly forgo the remaining years of my life to spend a week with you in Pembroke and die in the enchanted encirclement of your arms.'

'Pembroke!' Margaret said in a voice only a little above a whisper. 'Happy Pembroke. The long day's magic passing almost unaware as the soft winds filled our hearts and minds with the delicious wellbeing of living. Was it not strange we should both have returned there when we heard the strange music of the magician's pipe at Collyweston?'

'Strange perhaps; but very understandable. The air he played conjured up memories of joy that almost tore at my loins with their poignancy and it was not surprising my thoughts went to that place where love was my life.'

Jasper fell silent and Margaret found herself unable to speak. She was glad when he looked up at her and smiled.

'Speaking of magicians reminds me that one of my squires told me Allhallowe'en was celebrated in high style by certain members of the Court.'

'Apple bobbing and the burning of tapers to find the name of their trueloves?'

'Yes, but from what the boy said I gathered there was more to it than that! He hinted there had been darker doings in an unused chapel on the Southwark bank and the boatmen were kept busy ferrying masked and cloaked men and women to and fro.'

'Is Hallowe'en a witches' Sabbath?' Margaret asked.

'I believe it is; I think they meet for some very special rites and ceremonies on this day and it has not been unknown for them to offer sacrifice in the shape of goats and hens.'

'The curious among us would be eager to watch such evil practices and I am not surprised the boatmen were kept busy.'

'As long as those from the Court were merely spectators I do not suppose much harm will be done.'

'Surely you do not think any could be more involved?' Margaret cried.

'It is not unknown for those who have special petitions to seek the aid of the powers of darkness when they are unable to see the fulfilment of their plans through divine intervention,' Jasper said lightly. 'It has crossed my mind more than once to seek the Devil's alchemy to aid me in my search for a solution to the problem of a lifetime of loving my brother's widow!' He smiled and spoke jestingly but Margaret felt there was more than a hint of truth in his words. She was reassured when he went on quietly. 'Do not fret, sweetest love, I am as good a churchman as you would have me be and I shall not go to the sorcerer's den and exchange my soul for charms to waft us both to an Elysium beside the the waters of Milford Haven. Although God knows — ' He broke off as his chamberlain coughed discreetly behind him. 'What is it?' he asked testily.

'My lord, it is time you were supervising the entry into the lists.'

Jasper rose heavily from his chair.

'Forgive me; I must go to inspect the weapons to see no private quarrel finds its satisfaction at the end of an unprotected lance.'

Margaret watched him make his way to the

screens masking the main doorway of the hall. His going dimmed the brightness of the feast and left her with a yearning pain in her breast.

It is best we do not meet so very often, she thought as she attended to the conversation about her, for I am sore at heart when we are parted. All my life is bound up in the care and trust he has bestowed upon me. In him lies my youth and my love for Edmund; my struggle to rear Henry and the short happiness of those long ago days in Pembroke.

She took her place with her family in the box prepared for them and found more pleasure in watching the children enjoying the brilliant spectacle of the jousting than the sport itself.

Meg and the small Harry watched round eyed as the combatants rode out on splendid chargers caparisoned in the richest materials and hung about with goldwork and spangles. The pale sunlight gleamed on cloth of gold and silken damask and picked out the red rose where it twined in a riot of colour with the white of York. The Challengers, led by the Earl of Suffolk, were as richly clad as their horses and so too were the Answeres when they streamed from the yards into the lists. The crowd clapped and cheered at the magnificent spectacle before them; it was obvious they felt they had not paid over their hard gained earnings in vain and they settled down to enjoy themselves.

The Prince of Wales tried unsuccessfully to preserve his youthful dignity but when the horses charged and lances met with a metallic clang he sat forward eagerly and shouted encouragement to the competitors.

After supper, dancing followed. Margaret elected to sit beside her granddaughter and watch. The child had come shyly to her side when it became time for the presentation of the prizes and put out her hand to Margaret.

'Courage, my little one!' Margaret smiled down on her. 'Never were prizes given by a sweeter princess — not even in all the fables of King Arthur — and you will delight the heart of the lucky combatants.'

Meg closed her eyes and took a deep breath. 'I should not like to — how did you say it — disgrace my lord father.'

'You will not do that, sweeting!' Margaret told her fondly. 'See here comes Lord Ormond with the day's reward.'

Ormond brought up a velvet cushion on which sparkled a ring set with a glowing ruby. He held out his hand to Meg and led her to the front of the dais. A hush fell on the company as the Lady Anne Neville accompanied by the Lady Anne Percy led forward with silken ribbons John Peche. The young man knelt to the little princess who took the ring from the Chamberlain and pushed it, with smiling concentration, on to the champion's finger.

When it was finished Meg rejoined her grandmother.

'You did very well,' Margaret told her as the musicians began to play again for the dance. 'See, here is one of my own girdles to remind you of this happy day.'

She took a chain fashioned with fine links and ornamented at intervals with daisies in enamel and put it into the damp palm of the child.

'Oh, it is beautiful! May I wear it now?'

'Of course. Come here and I will help you.'

The feastings and tournaments went on until the middle of November. The anniversary of Edmund's death being marked with solemn remembrances and a cessation of the festivities. To complete the celebrations Henry ordered the royal barges, with those of the prelates, to be ready at the Palace landing stage to accompany the new Duke of York part of his way to Eltham.

Margaret too sat amid the down filled cushions with Henry close beside her.

'These days should have done much to render useless the claims of the Pretender,' Margaret said quietly.

'That is certainly my hope,' Henry told her. 'I find it disquieting to think there are still those in the country who would rather see a false Yorkist upon the throne.'

'Was the rumour I heard about Sir Robert Clifford being in favour of Perkin Warbeck's cause correct?'

'Yes,' Henry said after the slightest possible pause. 'His name was called among the other traitors at St. Paul's.'

'I find it almost impossible to believe he could turn against you. He came to Collyweston and partook of the hospitality there; how could he come to change his mind?'

'I know not. The greater cause to call him traitor!' Henry spoke more sharply that Margaret could recall and she dropped the subject drawing his attention to a bonfire that blazed on the river bank and lit up a circle of men, women and children who waved and called out greetings.

'Will you come again to Collyweston next summer?'

'If you ask me! I have promised your husband I will go to Lathom in the course of the year's Progress and I am minded, if it pleases you, to come to your home after the official visits.'

'I should be made very happy indeed if you would do that. When you come, leave behind you your state papers and your advisors and petitioners and give yourself time to restore your energies.'

'Thank you,' Henry said. 'Not only for the offer of peace beneath your roof but for all the loving support you give so generously.'

13

Margaret went to her manor at Woking for a short time before Christmas and then returned to Westminster for the Christmas celebrations. She lodged in her own house at Coldeharbour immediately after Twelfth Night and visited from here her almshouses at Hatfield and Cheshunt. The weather was cold and the rutted roads made passable by the ice that froze the puddles to resemble iron. When she found the inmates of her charity houses huddled together for warmth she ordered extra wood to be brought from the neighbouring manors and sent Perrot to the wardrobes for discarded gowns and warm hose.

'What ails that woman?' Margaret asked Betsey bluntly as her waiting woman helped her prepare for a supper party she was giving in her Thameside mansion.

'Well,' Betsey said slowly, 'I do not know the truth of it but there are those who say — '

'Say what?' Margaret asked patiently.

'That she is in league with the troupe of magicians who came to Collyweston and steals out at night to keep company with them.'

'How does she pass the watch?' Anxiety touched Margaret's voice with severity.

'There are means, Madame, of tempting men known only to women like Perrot.'

Margaret said nothing; a nameless suspicion half formed in the back of her mind. Quite suddenly she was reminded of the conversation she had had with Jasper at Hallowe'en.

'Where did she fall in with the troupe?'

'At Collyweston. If you remember I mentioned to you strange noises had been heard coming from the churchyard and there were villagers who swore they had seen half-clad men and women cavorting among the graves.'

'I see. Please do not speak of this with any of my other ladies.'

'You know me better than that!' Betsey said with dignity.

'Indeed I do.' Margaret agreed, instantly contrite. 'I am much concerned that none of my household should be mixed up with such base born mountebanks and I must think of the best way of protecting Perrot and anyone else who might be tempted to fall under their spell. Do you think they were here in London at the time of the knighting of the Duke of York?' she asked.

'I am sure they were; it was common gossip

a witches' sabbath was held across the river in Southwark and one of Lord Oxford's pages hid in a ferry and followed those who went to take part. He swore the chief priest was the same man who practised the magician's art at the feast at Collyweston and the girl and the young man were also present.'

Heavy of spirit Margaret went down to her parlour to greet her guests. With her half-brother and his wife she had invited her own husband, Sir William Stanley, Jasper and Catherine, Archbishop Morton and some other clerics with the young John Fisher with whom she was in correspondence about a chair of divinity she wished to found in Cambridge.

She had heard from William Elmer, Fisher was in London on University business and had sent to the chapter house at Westminster where he was lodging to beg him to attend her supper.

He was among the first to arrive and he came quietly into the parlour in the wake of the steward who announced him and bent over her hand. Margaret was struck with Fisher's calm demeanour and the great depth of the eyes which shone from a thin face softened by a wide and generous mouth above a firm jaw.

The young man was tall and the gown he

wore hung about him in folds, revealing large feet and bony, blue veined hands. When other guests were escorted into the room he stepped discreetly into the background but spoke easily with any who engaged him in conversation.

Derby and his brother and his wife came just before Jasper and Catherine and Margaret's chamberlain led them, with a wand of office, to the small hall where a long trestle had been set with gleaming napery and silver candlesticks. Resisting the temptation to have Jasper at her side Margaret had placed him in the centre of the table and put Morton and Sir William on either hand. As the meal progressed she saw with pleasure her guests gave every appearance of enjoying themselves and the food and wine she had chosen personally seemed to be meeting with the appreciation of those who ate it.

John Fisher, sitting across the table from Jasper, spent much of his time speaking with the older man and Margaret guessed they were talking of Cambridge and the distant days when the young Earl of Pembroke, as Jasper had been, was sent down by Queen Margaret to report on the progress of the College she was helping to found.

'Has Fisher been interesting you in his

plans for enlarging the University of Cambridge?' Morton asked, divining her thoughts.

'So far I am only contemplating the endowing of a chair but, as you know, I believe learning to be the true way to teach men to help themselves and am therefore ready to be called upon to play my part.'

'Your son has done much to finish the work of Henry VI and his proposals for a chapel to extend the Abbey Church of Westminster are magnificent indeed. I pray I may be spared to see, at least, the beginning of his noble conception.'

'My lord Cardinal, your looks are enough to tell me you should be spared to us for many years to come! Let us hope we shall all live long enough to see the commencement of the building.'

Margaret had decided to have no entertainers to round off the feast but her musicians played softly and one of them occasionally walked about the trestle singing extracts from popular ballads. He had just finished one such verse, standing behind the chair of Lady Stanley, when Margaret's Comptroller of the Household came up to his mistress and bent over her.

'What is it, Bedell?' she asked sharply as she noted the expression on his face, 'Is something amiss?'

Her mind flew to the possibility of illness in the King's family and she had to ask the man to repeat what he was saying before she fully comprehended what he was trying to tell her.

'My Lady, the Earl of Oxford and Sir Richard Edgecumbe are come with urgent messengers from the King. He wishes the Duke of Bedford, the Earl of Derby and Sir William Stanley with Cardinal Morton to return at once to the Palace.'

'What's that; what's that?' Morton said quickly.

'My son has sent word requesting you and Lords Bedford and Derby with Sir William to come at once to him. Oh, I am afraid! What can have happened with such speed to require urgent action?'

'There was nothing untoward when I left him this afternoon. Do not fear Madame, his Grace has probably heard of a possible landing by Perkin Warbeck and wishes to send out commissions of array.'

Jasper and Derby with Sir William had risen in their seats as the Comptroller spoke to each of them and they now came up to Margaret to tender their apologies for leaving her hospitality so peremptorily.

As Jasper kissed her hand he told her he would ensure she should not be kept waiting overlong to know the reason for their recall.

'Why did Henry not tell me the reason?' she asked.

'In the heat of the moment he probably thought he had,' Jasper said comfortingly.

Margaret took her remaining guests into the parlour and they sat in rather uncomfortable patches of silence and forced conversation until Catherine said the hour was late and she would like to be escorted to her chambers in the Palace. With almost tangible relief the other guests made their excuses and Margaret sent one of her waiting women to summon the servants to transport their mistresses homeward.

'Thank you for the honour you have done me in asking me to partake of your hospitality,' John Fisher said as he prepared to depart. 'I am truly sorry you have been discomfited in this way and pray you may soon be relieved of the anxiety it has caused you.'

Despite the cold of the February night Margaret stood at the watersteps and watched as the barge left her landing stage and made its way upriver. When she could no longer see the lantern at the vessel's stern she went to the chapel of her house and prayed earnestly that her son and his country might be spared further bloodshed in the threat of war.

She saw with some surprise the clock in her parlour gave the hour as half past twelve and going to her bedchamber told Betsey she would undress and prepare for bed but would return to the parlour downstairs until she was certain no messenger was coming from Westminster. She could not believe Jasper would fail to keep his word.

'Shall I come with you, my Lady?'

Margaret hesitated.

'No, you go to bed, Betsey, you have already been kept waiting long enough. If I should need you I shall call you.'

But Betsey insisted upon coming down with her and only returned to her chamber when she saw the Comptroller was not yet abed and had ordered the parlour fire to be replenished and the pages of the day replaced by others who had been roused from their slumbers.

When the door closed behind her maidservant Margaret found she could not settle in the chair in front of the fire but walked restlessly from the window to the hearth. She drew back the curtains and looked out on the Thames, now almost at flood, and the dark outlines of the small houses on the opposite bank. The city slept and only on London Bridge could she catch a glimmer of light from the warning flares hung up to remind boatmen of the hazards of the stone piers and the swirling currents. As she waited she thought of all those who slept within the safety of the city walls and wondered if they were to be left long to enjoy their peace. Surely no further insurrection could be festering to ruin the prosperity Henry was striving to bring to his kingdom!

Her eyelids were almost drooping into sleep when she caught a glimpse of a faint light on the dark waters of the river. Instantly aroused she pressed against the casement and watched as the glimmer became stronger and eventually lit up the shape of the barge coming swiftly towards the house on the ebbtide. When she heard the watch challenge the boatman she drew the hangings and returned to the fireside.

In impatience she waited while she heard the opening and closing of doors and the sound of voices getting nearer.

'Come!' she called to the knock and glimpsed her half-brother's face, grey and tired, as he ushered Jasper himself into the chamber. Before John Welles shut the door firmly after the Duke of Bedford Margaret had time to see other members of her household crowded together outside in the passage way.

'What is it Jasper?' she pleaded as she led him to the hearth. Jasper took her hands and held them firmly within his own.

'Derby's brother has been arraigned for high treason!'

'William Stanley?' Margaret gasped. 'How can this be? Brother to my husband and Henry's own Lord Chamberlain! Surely it is not possible?'

'Unfortunately it is only too possible. Come, sit down and I will tell you briefly what I understand to be the correct story.'

'Where is Thomas? Does Henry suspect him of dour designs against him?'

'No, I think not. Derby has been at pains to make his position clear and refuses to stand beside his brother.'

'I do not know whether to admire or condemn him for that.'

'When it becomes the question of preserving one's neck even brotherly affection pales into insignificance.'

'Then you think William Stanley is in danger of losing his life?' Margaret asked incredulously.

'Unless a miracle happens I can see no other course open to Henry.'

'But Jasper, William Stanley is Henry's relative by my marriage!'

'Closer relationships than that have suffered in the cause of Justice,' Jasper told her grimly. 'And Stanley's actions do not speak of the man deserving pity.'

'What has he done?'

'Do you remember the traitors Henry had named at St. Paul's during the spring of last year?'

'Yes, but I do not recall the name of Stanley among them!'

'No, of course not, but you will perhaps remember that of Sir Robert Clifford?'

'Very well. I was distressed to think he had taken the hospitality of my roof and turned traitor to my son — ' She stopped as the full portent of her words struck her. 'How could William Stanley set his hand against Henry?'

'It seems Henry had his suspicions some time ago but was unable to find direct proof. He hit upon the scheme of naming Clifford as a traitor and sending him to the Low Countries to make contact with those who were giving their support to Perkin Warbeck. While Clifford was living in Flanders he made himself known in the court of the Dowager Duchess and was shocked to discover Stanley among the conspirators.'

'As well he might. I take it from what you are telling me that Clifford is now returned to England — '

'This very night. With him he brought sufficient evidence to destroy Stanley.'

'By Our Lady!' Margaret cried, looking wide eyed at Jasper. 'During our lifetime it has been possible to number those we could trust upon the fingers of one hand. It makes me fear for the future.'

Jasper turned towards her on the oaken, high backed settle and put his arm about her shoulders drawing her head down to nestle against him.

'I think you have less cause to fear now than at any other time since Bosworth. Henry has been gradually showing the strength he has amassed and if he makes an example of Stanley it will prove even further he is not a man to trifle with. You must not lose sight of the fact the Stanley family were an unknown quantity right up to the very battle of Bosworth. Even your marriage to Derby, sacrificial as it was, did not make certain the support of the Stanleys for Henry's side. Not until the fighting actually began were we sure they would assist us. I still believe if Richard of Gloucester had looked like being the victor both Sir William and Derby would have thrown in their lot with him.'

'Think you so?' Margaret said wonderingly. 'But Thomas had visited Henry two days earlier and promised his help — '

'Then why did he not come immediately to the forefront of the battle?'

'Perhaps he thought to fool Richard. What reason has Sir William given now for his disaffection?'

'He refuses to commit himself, but Robert Clifford believes he is dissatisfied with the rewards Henry gave him for his support at Bosworth.'

'Surely he is among the richest men in England!'

'Yes, I know but wealth was not all he craved; he expected to be named Earl of Chester and has been harbouring a grievance ever since he discovered he was not to be so called.'

'I see,' Margaret said slowly. 'Like most of us he had a stake in the limbus of the moon.'

'As you and I have done over the years?'

'Yes; but I am certain now that you and I have been given something deeper and infinitely more satisfying than the gratification of our lust. At this moment I am convinced there is no greater satisfaction than the perfect trust we have enjoyed. Where would I have been during the decades since Edmund died without your guidance and love? Where would I be now without you to help and support, comfort and spoil me? Oh, Jasper, I can never begin to tell you of my

265

gratitude and the overwhelming affection for you that lies within the centre of my being.'

'There is no need to tell me, for in you lies the meaning of life, the *raison d'être*,' Jasper told her simply. 'You are the personification of earthly happiness and have enriched my days with the very knowledge of your existence.'

He broke off, biting his lip and looking into the embers of the fire. Margaret could not trust herself to speak and stayed quietly within the circle of his arm until Jasper put his hand under her chin and kissed her on the mouth.

'There is no more I can tell you tonight. I had best be returning to Westminster to see if Henry should need me. I will keep you informed of all that befalls.'

Margaret glanced at the clock and saw it was close on three o'clock. She hesitated to suggest Jasper should remain at Coldeharbour but was anxious for him going out again into the bitter chill of the February night. Jasper stood up and gave her his hand; with a smothered exclamation he gripped her arm and turned quickly to grasp the mantelshelf.

'My dearest! What ails you?' Margaret asked as her heart began to pound uncomfortably in her breast.

'It is nothing — a momentary dizziness — nothing more.'

But a glance at his face told Margaret he spoke only half the truth. 'Don't go for a moment, I will get you some wine.'

'No it has passed and I am quite recovered. You must go to your bed — '

'Will you not stay here? You will take a chill if you venture out feeling as you do. Let me call Bedell and have him escort you to a chamber.'

'Thank you, Margaret. The prospect of remaining here is sufficient to tempt me into feigning illness but I have two of my squires with me and some of Henry's yeomen and I had best be returning. If I should need them — '

'Do not go!' Margaret pleaded. 'Stay where I can minister to you.'

Jasper smiled at her. A little colour had come back into his face and he straightened his shoulders and walked steadily to the door.

'See. I am quite recovered and nothing ails me that some rest will not put right. Promise me you will go straight to your bedchamber, for I shall not rest if I think you are anxious. Goodnight, my love.' He pulled open the door and was gone. Margaret went swiftly to the window and watched as he boarded the barge and was borne away up stream.

She went to her room and climbed into the high bed, huddling her chamber-robe about her and gratefully touching the hot bricks Betsey had wrapped in flannel and put to warm the sheets.

She was wide awake and knew sleep would not come to relieve her of the unease that had deepened throughout the day. Trying to comfort herself that Jasper's sudden spasm of illness was due to the tension and the lateness of the hour she forced herself to concentrate on the backsliding of Derby's brother but although she realised the seriousness of his offence and the far reaching implications it might have for her husband she discovered it meant nothing to her against the possibility of Jasper stricken with some pestilence or disease. She determined to spend the following morning consulting her physician and her own herbal book to find some remedy for the giddiness he had tried to hide from her. In moments of self torture she relived the terrible hours when she had nursed Edmund in a hopeless effort to save him from the plague that had cut short his young life in one day. As the cocks crowed from the yards of the houses across the river she pushed from her again and again the horrifying prospect of facing a future that left her without either the young husband she had adored or his brother who had come to mean so very much to her over the years.

Betsey, coming in to call her mistress to the prayers she attended each morning, found Margaret asleep at last, her face pale and the bedclothes in disarray. The waiting woman tiptoed away and in the chapel of the house prayed, beside her usual offices, that Margaret would see fit to forgive her for disobeying the strict rule she imposed that she should always be woken to attend her devotions.

When, several hours later, the silver bell summoned Betsey to Margaret's bedchamber Betsey was greatly relieved to find no mention was made of her omission and she was encouraged to help her mistress dress with the greatest possible speed.

'Send Perrot or one of the other women to fetch my physician.'

'You are not ill, my Lady?'

Margaret looked at Betsey in something approaching bewilderment.

'Ill? No. Why should I be? Oh, I see — .'

Betsey went to the door and as she opened it a page stood outside with his hand ready to knock upon the panelling.

'Yes?' Betsey asked.

'My lord the Duke of Bedford is in the

parlour and wishes to speak with you, Madame.'

Margaret was on her feet and accompanying the youth before Betsey fully appreciated what he had been saying.

'Don't send any of the women for the physician unless I send this child to you,' Margaret called over her shoulder as she turned the corner at the head of the stairway.

Jasper was standing at the casement looking down at the numerous craft plying up and down and back and forth across the Thames. He came quickly to Margaret and crushed her to him with strong arms.

'I am perfectly well!' he said quickly. 'I am as strong as the dragon on the Tudor badge!'

'Thank God,' Margaret said fervently. 'Come to the light and let me examine you, that you do not jest with me.'

Jasper laughingly suffered her to lead him to the casement and watched her with mock solemnity as she regarded him head tilted on one side.

'Do I pass your severe standards?'

'You look very well to me,' she said at length.

'If I know you, you have hardly slept — ah! I see by that swiftly veiled look that I am right. My dearest,' he pulled her down on to the seat under the window. 'I was embarking

270

at the water steps of your house and it was all I could do to restrain myself from telling the others to return to the Palace and leave me here with you. When I did come to my room at Westminster I paced the floor until cockcrow wishing I had not been fool enough to leave your roof. But, as you can see, I am quite recovered and am come to tell you of the developments in the Stanley affair.'

'Where is William?'

'He has been taken to the Tower.'

'For what?' The question was swift and a little breathless.

'To await Henry's decision. Henry called me to him this morning and it was obvious he had not slept very much either. He is torn between the magnanimity he has always favoured and the obvious necessity of making an example to potential followers of Perkin Warbeck.'

'You are of the mind that Warbeck is becoming more of a menace than he was?'

'If he is attracting the dormant Yorkists of our kingdom he is not a force to be underestimated.'

'And you see no evidence of the miracle you spoke of last night?'

'None whatever. The evidence against Sir William is damning and the man himself has made no effort to clear his name.'

'What will Derby think of us? Not only is William his brother but William's wife is a cousin of Henry's and mine.'

'I should not dwell upon the matter more than you can help. You are powerless to avert whatever may befall and your hopes are in the future of your son's succession, are they not?'

'Yes.'

'Well then. I fell in with John Fisher as I left the Palace and he told me he was sending his servant with some letters for you to study about the Chair of Divinity you are considering founding in Cambridge. Why do you not devote your energies to them?'

'By that I take it you are returning to Henry?'

'Yes,' he told her gently. 'Pray, dearest, that we shall be spared to spend at least a few more days in one another's company before — too long!' he added hastily as she looked at him apprehensively.

Obedient as a child she closeted herself with William Elmer and her other advisers while they scanned the long missive John Fisher had written. She was surprised when pages came to light the sconces and draw the curtains against the winter night.

She took her supper quietly and went early to bed. She was asleep almost as soon as she pulled the heavy coverlets over her and awoke

272

feeling refreshed and able to face the new day.

When the morning's offices were done she sat in her parlour and before noon Jasper came to her and told her William Stanley had been beheaded in the Tower in the early hours of the morning.

Margaret regarded him silently while waves of nausea welled into her throat.

'Although I knew this was most probably the only outcome of the affair now that I have heard you speak of its verity I am deeply shocked. To think the man was dining in this house not two days ago! Oh, Jasper to what lengths does a monarch have to go to keep order in his realm? How will this affect Henry?'

'Stanley was a potentially dangerous man. Keep that fact in your mind and try to put out of your head any sense of shared guilt in the matter.'

'How can I do that?' she cried. 'Henry is my son and I cannot help feeling responsible in some way for his actions. How will he meet his Maker with the blood of a kinsman on his hands?'

Margaret walked to the casement where she looked down on the Thames, flowing by unconcerned for the agitation stirring her breast.

'Have you spoken with Derby?'

'Yes, and he has retained his usual calm and speaks of coming here to you later in the day to speak with you on the matter. His sons also have left Henry in no doubt they uphold the judgement given against their uncle and have sworn to bear him no grudge.'

'That is well, but I could wish with all my heart some other method might have been discovered to clip the wings of the foolish Stanley. Do you think Henry will still make Lathom the culminating point of his progress this year?'

'I do not see why he should alter his mind. It was to be a state visit to Derby's house, more honouring him as your husband than as a Stanley, and he will probably be anxious to placate Derby in so much as he is able.'

Margaret thought of Jasper's philosophy many times during the days following the execution of William Stanley. Henry seemed to be doing everything within his power to propitiate the family of the dead man and began by paying for a most elaborate and costly funeral. To his mother it was obvious Henry was suffering a tremendous self-abasement for he avoided her as much as possible, only meeting her with others present and striving by every known method to speak of any matter but the one touching everyone's mind at the moment. Margaret bore with him, forbearing to mention anything political or moral, and spoke only of family concerns and interests.

It was with a sense of relief she saw him set out with his household on the first stages of the royal progress. He had made it known he intended to carry through his visit to Lathom and Margaret gave her word to Derby she would come to his house before the proposed date of Henry's arrival and act as hostess.

Margaret made a tour through her own manors before going to Collyweston. At Woking she left Perrot behind with the task of producing new hangings and covers for the bedchambers. The Frenchwoman had met her request with an enigmatic smile but had discussed fabrics and colours as if she were interested. Margaret left her feeling she was sufficiently occupied to be less cause for anxiety than if she had accompanied the rest of the establishment.

Jasper departed from Westminster with Henry but was to leave him at Stamford to make for the Marches of Wales where he would hold the customary courts of Oyer and Terminer. He promised Margaret he was completely recovered from the exhaustion which had given her such anxiety earlier in the year and said he would come to

Collyweston to be with her when Henry visited her home in the autumn.

'Will you go to Lathom?' she had asked him when he came to bid her farewell.

He regarded her for a moment without speaking. 'No, I have many cases to hear and estates to inspect that should keep me busy until Christmas and I should rather not be with you under Derby's roof.'

Margaret went to Lathom towards the end of July. She found the house much altered since her last visit. Derby had almost rebuilt the original fortified house and it was now a beautifully appointed mansion filled with treasures gleaned from all over Europe. There was much evidence of the new art filtering through from Florence to England. The Steward of the Household took her on a tour of inspection and proudly paraded his master's display of gold plate and hangings. As tactfully as she could Margaret gave her advice on the entertaining of the large host Henry was expected to bring with him. Although she encountered a certain amount of ingrained opposition she discovered most of her suggestions were put into practice and realised with amusement her reputation for orderliness in domestic matters had travelled to her husband's domains.

The royal party arrived in the evening of

the last day of the month. Almost at the last the waiting household at Lathom had been informed by Richmond Herald it might be necessary for the visit to be cancelled as tidings had been brought to Henry, while on his way to the house, of ships believed to be those of Perkin Warbeck off the Kent coast. Further messengers had come to say the King had received news that had set his mind at rest and he was resuming his journey to Lathom. Those who had laid in vast stores of extra food greeted this with relief and set to to bake and prepare with extra energy.

Henry did not speak much of the scare that had almost caused him to abandon his visit to his step-father's house in the presence of Derby but brought Elizabeth to Margaret's chamber and told her what had befallen.

'A force appeared off Sandwich made up of about fourteen ships. Perkin had not the countenance to put foot upon my kingdom but sent ashore nigh on a hundred of his followers. From what I understand they were ill equipped and not very warlike. The loyal men of Kent made short shrift of them and brought those who survived before the Sheriff of the County who ordered them to be brought to London in ignominy.'

'I believe you intended returning to Westminster,' Margaret said.

'Yes, but when I heard Perkin had sailed away towards the west I decided there was no need.'

'What will become of Perkin's followers in London?'

Elizabeth who had so far not spoken very much said tonelessly, 'They have been executed.'

Margaret drew in her breath sharply.

'They sought to disrupt the peace of our realm and there was no other course open to us,' Henry told her quickly. 'Let us speak of other things; we are come to Lathom to enjoy the hospitality of my step-father and we do not wish to disturb the peace by recriminations. Do you not think Lathom is now a very fine house, ma mère?'

'Very fine indeed. Tomorrow doubtless you will be taken on a tour to inspect the full scope of what has been accomplished but for tonight there is a feast and mummers with a new play. But before we go to join the others, tell me of the children — they are well?'

The smile Elizabeth gave her transformed the almost mask-like face of her daughter-in-law.

'They are very well, Madame. They enjoined me to give you many messages of love and esteem and asked me to say they are already making preparations to receive you at Christmastide!'

'They look far ahead,' Margaret replied, 'but the feast of St. Nicholas and the excitement of the twelve days of the nativity never lose their appeal to the young.'

'Have I told you I am considering offering Meg's hand to the young King of the Scots?'

'To James Stewart! But this is a change of policy for you Henry!'

'I have tried by many means to establish peace on the border with Scotland and as you know James has been slippery enough to deal with. I am now minded that only by marriage with our own family can we hope to have any lasting peace. There is too, the very real risk of Warbeck trying to enlist the Scots to his cause.'

'Do you really think James would be bamboozled into giving any considerable aid to the Pretender?'

'One can never be certain what the Scots would do to discomfort us. We must be prepared for any contingency.'

'But did you not offer the hand of the Lady Katherine Wiltshire only to have it refused?' Elizabeth asked her husband.

'That is true. Obviously it was not accepted because James thought the marriage of insignificance; our daughter would be a very different matter.'

'You are not thinking of making the match yet?' Margaret asked in some concern.

'Oh, no,' Henry assured her. 'There is time enough to consider when Meg would have to leave us.'

'What of the Spanish marriage?' Margaret asked.

'The treaty is not formally ratified; but it will be,' Henry told her with confidence. He seemed to brood on something and then rounded on Margaret.

'Jasper is not to be of our number?'

'No.'

'I cannot say I blame him,' Henry said with a chuckle. 'Come, let us go down and enjoy the hospitality of our esteemed step-father.'

As Margaret had prophesied Derby had organised a party to inspect his new dwelling house. The ladies said they would sit in the walled garden and enjoy the warmth of the sun and gossip about the happenings since they had parted in the spring.

They were interrupted about half an hour later by Lord Welles and Henry coming across the lawn and speaking of finding grooms to go riding.

'Henry looked rather white,' Margaret said to Elizabeth as they watched their retreating figures pass through the gate.

'I thought the house was very large and has many chambers?' Elizabeth said inquiringly.

'It is,' Margaret answered. 'The tour they made must have been very rapid to have completed it so quickly — .' She stopped as she saw Oxford coming across the grass towards them.

'There has been a change of plans, your Grace,' he said to Elizabeth. 'The King has decided we leave for Knowsley tomorrow morning — .'

'Derby's other house? Why, he was planning to stay here for a week, I thought!' Margaret tried with difficulty to repress the irritation she felt.

Ormond regarded her uncomfortably.

'My Lady — ,' he hesitated.

'Out with it Thomas! It is best you tell me what has befallen that makes my son change his mind.'

'Well, as you know we were to inspect the house and we went through the Hall and armoury and climbed on to the roof and were looking over the countryside from this vantage point when — ,' he took a breath and stopped.

'When?' Margaret queried.

'The King was hanging over the leads where there is no protecting parapet and unseen to anyone the Earl of Derby's jester came up to his master and said in a voice which carried to all present — 'Tom! Remember Will!'.'

Margaret and Elizabeth stared at the Chamberlain in bewilderment. The King's mother was the first to recover her voice.

'What happened then?'

'There was a most embarrassed silence while Derby made ineffective efforts to despatch his fool below broken by the King making all speed for the stairway muttering he and his household had best continue their stay at Knowsley.'

'I can well understand his disposition,' Elizabeth said quickly.

'I also,' Margaret agreed a little sadly. 'Forgive me but I had better return to the house and do what I can to ease what must be a very difficult situation.'

14

She was to find much to occupy her during the following days until the end of the state visit. Not only were relations between her son and her husband somewhat strained but news came in all the time of the activities of Warbeck. Defeated and sent from the English coast he had sailed for Ireland and after a battle with the townsfolk of Dublin, who, heartened by Henry's Deputy, repulsed the would-be invader he was reported sailing in a southerly direction. By the time Margaret left to go to Collyweston it was not ascertained if Warbeck was making for the Welsh coast or the harbour of Cork in southern Ireland.

The Welsh would make short shrift of him! Margaret thought as she rode through the dales and wooded countryside to her home. She longed with an almost physical ache to be at Collyweston and reunited with Jasper. She had missed him more than she had believed possible and during the unpleasant weeks now behind her had needed his comforting assurance and heartening common sense. What stature Jasper enjoyed that not once in all the years since his half-brother, Henry VI had rescued him and Edmund from the obscurity of the Barking Abbey where the boys had spent their childhood, had his loyalty been in doubt. He had given unstintingly of his service and the wealth bestowed upon him by his half-brother to further his hopeless cause against the Yorkists and even when at odds with Margaret of Anjou, Henry VI's hot-headed Queen, had rallied to her support with the men he had charmed from the hearths. What love and devotion he had poured out on herself and the orphaned Henry; thinking only of them and forgoing the pleasure of marriage and the begetting of a family. What other man would have cut himself off from his homeland at the height of his powers and taken his nephew to safety across the Channel. In the misty September mornings that held the first bite of autumn Margaret permitted herself the luxury of living as a separate entity, divorced from the position of wife, mother to the King and grandparent. She read no books but the religious ones she had constantly beside her and spoke little with those who formed her escort to Rutland. She was content to dwell on the beauties of the white stubbled fields and the wreaths of old man's beard in the hedgerows. She indulged in a pleasant relaxation of mind that allowed her to think of the past and conjure up memories of halcyon days where her senses had been attuned to the joy of living. When they rested in the evenings she insisted upon little or no recognition of her dignity and ate with the nuns in their refectories and prayed with them in the cold chapels they favoured.

In some subtle way she found herself happier than she had been for years and was not very surprised when she discovered on her arrival at Collyweston Jasper was already within the house.

He met her at the door and helped her alight from the mare she had ridden from Stamford.

'You are alone as I hoped you would be,' he said smiling down at her. 'When I learnt Henry was going to Knowsley I adjourned the courts until the beginning of October and made my way towards Collyweston. I prayed I might find you arriving before Henry and Elizabeth and that we might be permitted to spend perhaps a day as people instead of Henry's mother and uncle.'

'Strangely, you echo the thoughts I have had on my way home. I have shed my worries and Court duties like raiment that has suddenly become irksome and have indulged myself in a manner I am certain my confessor would find sinful in the extreme.'

'If he did that it is time you found a new confessor! Of recent times you have not been allowed to forget your position and it can only be good for you to remember that under the panoply of royalty there lives womanhood at its best.'

'You are balm to my heart,' she replied softly. 'Heaven alone knows how I have craved your wisdom and understanding during the past weeks.'

'You have been taxed by the Lathom and Knowsley visits?'

'Yes, but there is more to it than the ordeal of entertaining a vast number of extra people.' Jasper looked at her quickly. 'I will tell you about it when we sup. Will it please you to eat with me in my parlour?'

'Do you need to ask?'

She dressed in a simple homespun robe but Betsey was not deceived into thinking this meant any letting up in the fastidious attention given to the dressing of her hair or the application of salves and touches of rouge.

'You'll not be wanting to wear a coif, will you?' she asked. 'There is that pearled caul that would look very well with the dress you are wearing.'

Margaret allowed her to fix the head-dress and admitted when she saw the result in her hand mirror it was as appropriate as Betsey had said it would be.

'It is a pity you can't spend more of your time quietly in Collyweston and not have to go gadding about the countryside acting as peacemaker between half the men in the kingdom.'

'It is largely due to your care I feel so rested now. You did very well to aid me in my attempt to secure a quiet journey home; without you to fend off all the supplicants I should have had no chance to unbend as I did. Oh, Betsey, what would life be without those who have enriched it over the years?'

'Only God knows that and if I were you I should enjoy the present and allow the future to take care of itself.'

Although it was only September the evenings were chilly and Margaret noted with pleasure the fire had been lit in her parlour. She stood at the window, looking down into the valley where already spirals of mist were gathering on the banks of the river and hanging suspended in the motionless air. She did not move when she heard Jasper come to the door and join her at the casement but leant back against his shoulder when his arms encircled her and drew her towards him. They stayed there until servants came bringing food and wine.

They ate in companionable quiet, not speaking very much and then only of the merits of the dish or matters of the immediate household. They had dispensed with the ritual handwashing required by protocol and had told their respective squires and waiting women their services would not be required for the rest of the day.

'I can imagine they were not sorry to hear that,' Jasper said as the last of the pages and menials carried away the silver dishes and linen. 'What news is there of your Perrot?'

'She was left behind in Woking to oversee the making of new furnishings for beds and windows. I was not very popular with her but she is artistic enough to be interested in creating a harmony of colour and fabrics and will probably be occupied until we meet again at Christmastide. William is with me as you saw and I understand your stepsons are profiting from the tutelage of Maurice Westbury.'

'They seem very happy and contented with being here and Westbury says they give as much attention to book learning as can be expected from healthy lads who are growing fast. While we are on the subject of families have you heard I am become a grandfather?'

'Jasper! I had quite forgot in the tension of the recent weeks Helen was near her time. Is all well with her? Is it a son or a daughter?'

'All is very well, I am happy to tell you, and her son is lusty and should thrive well also. As you understand I was not made easy when she told me she was expecting a child and it was with much relief news came to from Bury St. Edmunds of her safe delivery.'

'Has she said what she will call the child?'

'Stephen; a name I must confess I cannot connect with either our family or Myvanwy's.'

The name of Jasper's long dead mistress dropped in the stillness of the room like water on the embers of a log, glistening momentarily with taut heat and dying quickly.

'We must visit her when Henry makes a progress through East Anglia as he is sure to do in the coming year. We have not seen as much of Helen as we should have done.'

'She is happy enough in her marriage and will always be grateful and beholden to you for bringing her up as your own.'

'It has been our fortune to care for the other's orphaned child and it must have been Heaven meant we were on hand to fill the gap caused by Edmund and Myvanwy's deaths. I never cease to praise God for his goodness in giving Henry your devotion through all these years.'

'Henry has been to me like my own son. The son you and I would have had had the fates decreed in our favour.'

'It has always seemed like that to me; but he is not like you — or Edmund — for that matter. I am only bound to believe he inherits his dominating desire for power from my side of the family!'

'Beaufort blood was never content to sit idly by while the glittering promise of success was but a few yards distant as we both know very well, yet in your case you cannot reproach yourself for you had the perfect opportunity given you to snatch the reins of government for yourself and you handed them to your son.'

'That was merely my feminine instincts coming to my rescue. Had I been born a man it is quite possible I should have fought tooth and nail for my inheritance. As it is I watch Henry's progress on the throne with over anxious eyes. I am afraid he grows hard and too calculating.'

'His strong religious beliefs will keep him from becoming too wilful and scheming — .'

'But what of those he has had put to death?'

'You are still worrying about that? I might have guessed. William Stanley is best out of the way. From what I hear from all quarters with his going the possibility of rebellion in the country has diminished considerably.'

'Yes,' she agreed doubtfully, 'but there are the added numbers of those who landed in Kent for Perkin and have lost their lives because of it.'

'My dearest,' Jasper cried in mock desperation. 'Stop tormenting yourself! Henry is best fitted to deal with these situations and I am sure it would be well for you to shut your mind to the actions he takes and use your outstanding talents for creating the happiness you bring to all those about you.'

'I realised with a sense of shock, while coming here from Knowsley, I am denied the pleasure of doing that which I crave most.'

She sat back in her chair and closed her eyes unable to continue speaking of something touching her very being as closely as the words she had uttered.

Jasper leant over her and pulled her to her feet.

'So you believe all other joys pale beside the delight of living for one other person?' he asked softly.

'Yes,' she whispered. 'What has the pomp of royalty to do with the business of our real lives? What does Margaret, Countess of Richmond and Derby and the Duke of Bedford mean when the burning sun strikes into my very heart and fills me with the longing to hold you in my arms? It is as

Jasper and Margaret we matter; as people under God's heaven.'

'Over the years we have fought against the alleged sin of our marriage, do you begin to think now our right to happiness was greater than the law of the Church which forbade it?'

'I do not know what I think. We have been honourable and straightforward but I wish, with all the fire and spirit left me, it could have been otherwise. If I had not fallen in with Buckingham on the illfated pilgrimage I was making and had not taken Stanley for my husband who knows perhaps you and I and Henry could have been reunited and lived out our lives in blissful obscurity.'

'My love, it had to be as it was; you know that as well as I do. We both made sacrifices for our country because we believed in Henry the kingdom could find peace. Do not upset yourself now when you see our hopes coming to fruition.'

'Forgive me. I grow old and am weary of my vanity and busyness with matters of little importance. Of course, I know we did that which was right and I am greedy to cry for my own happiness to be added to all I have been given. But do you not ever,' she cried in a burst of near anger, 'long to be allowed the privilege of closing our door against the world?'

'Every day of my life,' Jasper said simply. 'There is nothing I wanted from life more than you as my wife. That desire has coloured every action and every thought and every thing else I have done fades into insignificance. I have loved you more as the years have come and gone and craving for the impossible have thanked God for the hours, few as they have been, we have been permitted to enjoy together.'

'I am sorry,' she said miserably. 'I am humbled by your good common sense and my own stupidity.'

'You do not know the meaning of stupidity,' he told her lightly as he caressed the nape of her neck with tender fingers. 'Do you expect Henry tomorrow?'

'I do not think he will be here until the following day.'

'What do you say to us taking horse and riding out together as we used to do?'

'Oh, yes! I should like that more than anything, although I cannot now ride with the abandon I knew in Pembroke.'

'Neither can I. But what does that matter? If the day is fine you can show me some of the corners of your domain we have not visited together. Come, sit here beside me and tell me of what befell at Lathom.'

She awoke early and found the mists still

clinging to the valley below the house.

'That will soon be gone,' Betsey told her as she and the other waiting women came to bring her food and help her prepare for the day.

'Good; for I am riding out this morning and am hoping for fine weather.'

'Riding out?' Betsey echoed. 'When you have been in the saddle for almost the whole of last week? I thought you were hoping for a rest.'

'This will be a rest for I am visiting the farms and mills on the estate with Lord Jasper.'

'Ah, well, I hope it will be a fine day so you can enjoy it the more.'

'Do you really hope that?'

'Yes,' Betsey said simply. 'You have little enough time for the simple pleasures of this life. Shall I ask the Steward to make ready some food for you to take with you?'

Before noon the sun had cleared the veils of white vapour from the surrounding countryside and the air was warm and still. Margaret and Jasper rode out through the manor gateway with two grooms following behind. Passing the slate quarry which gave an income to the estate and had provided the slates to roof the manor house they climbed down to the wooded valley beyond and followed the path of the river to the furthest outskirts of the domain.

When they felt hungry the menservants unstrapped the food baskets and spreading covers upon the ground laid the cold fare ready for them. In the small hollow they had selected the light wind touched only the tree tops and the sun shone palely on the golden fronds of bracken. It was very quiet, the only sounds coming from the subdued voices of the grooms as they sat at a little distance and the breaking of an occasional twig beneath the hooves of the horses.

After they had eaten they sat back against the bank looking up into the thin translucence of the sky filled with a delicious languor that made speech unnecessary. Margaret experienced a feeling of belonging to the very earth itself; wrapped in a wholesome cocoon of contentment she was happy to share the joy of the moment with Jasper. At times they looked at one another without smiling, their thoughts in harmony.

At last, reluctantly, he helped her to her feet.

They came homeward through the westernmost fields of Collyweston both of them renewed in body and spirit. Once more they supped together, savouring the rare pleasure of intimacy.

Jasper kissed her good night, lovingly and tenderly.

'I can face tomorrow and all the tomorrows with good heart. Just to know you are alive and encircle me with your love is sufficient to help me in whatever task I am called to do.'

'Do you go to Westminster for the meeting of Parliament?'

'I think not. The cases I have still to hear should occupy me until Christmastide and if God is willing I shall be with you then.'

Her hands tightened on his arms.

'May God go with you and keep you safe, Jasper.'

'And you, dearest Margaret.'

As he reached for the latch to open the door she put out her arms and called him back to her side.

'Jasper!'

Putting her hands behind his neck she pulled his face close to hers and kissed him on the mouth.

'Goodnight,' she whispered.

Henry came the following afternoon and she played the perfect hostess and mother to her son and his wife, providing good food, music and an ear ready to listen.

When Jasper came to bid them all farewell as he left for Hereford they stood in a semicircle on the main steps to the house door and watched as he put his foot in the cupped hands of his squire and sat in the saddle.

'Jasper bears his years with ease,' Henry said.

'But I find him stooped and a little distrait,' Elizabeth said kindly. Margaret glanced at her quickly and then at Jasper. Sitting his horse with his accustomed grace and smiling fondly on his family as they came to wish him Godspeed he certainly gave no appearance of either slouching or preoccupation.

She stayed on the steps until the banner of the Earl of Bedford, embroidered with the fleur-de-lis of his Valois mother, was borne round the corner at the top of the steeply sloping roadway and was lost to her view. Hugging the warm memory of the two perfect days she had spent in Jasper's company she went in to her house.

In October she returned to Sheen and visited her grandchildren in Eltham and Windsor. Henry was kept busy with ambassadors from Spain, the Netherlands and Scotland. In November, Bothwell, James Stewart's councillor, came hastening to the Court in London to tell of Perkin Warbeck's arrival in the Scottish Kingdom and his marriage with Lady Catherine Gordon a kinswoman of the Scottish monarch. Henry took the news calmly enough and apart from fortifying the border towns sat back to await events. He told his mother he did not fear any invasion the Pretender might try upon English soil for he felt assured Perkin would not meet with the support from the northern English barons he desperately needed to fight Henry's armies.

At St. Nicholas's feast Margaret received from Jasper two covered gold cups to put with the one he had given her some years earlier. They were decorated with a band chased with portcullis' and marguerites and with deep pleasure she displayed them with the first. She waited as patiently as she was able to go to Westminster where the family would be united.

She came to the Palace on the evening of the twentieth of December and climbed the water steps glad to be out of the raw cold. A blustering wind blew from the north east and low clouds scuttered across the sky. She supped quietly with Henry and Elizabeth and went early to bed. Overtired with the travelling in the searching cold she found she could not sleep and huddling herself in her bedrobe lit a branch of candles and read until she heard the watch call the hour of two in the morning. Her eyes aching with the bad light she still lay for a long time restlessly turning from side to side. Once or twice she was minded to wake Betsey and ask her to send someone for some scalded milk but thought twice about asking anybody to traverse the icy passages to the kitchens in search of it. At last, exhausted, she slept.

She awoke with aching limbs and a pain in her head but refused to allow Betsey to mix her a potion of poppy juice. She had asked John Fisher to come and see her about the progress he had made in setting up her chair of Divinity in the University of Cambridge and she did not want to feel sleepy when he came.

Henry had told her Jasper was expected on the following day and she made her excuses not to join the others to dine and went to bed after a light supper on her own. William had told her during the day that several members of her estates in Ware and Cheshunt were coming to seek an audience with her the next afternoon and she had instructed him to set out the papers and rolls dealing with their affairs for her to scan before she slept.

The deputation arrived at noon and they had just departed after an hour of discussion and revision of methods employed for the livery of her horses at Ware and the stocking of the fish pens at Cheshunt when without knocking Henry came into the parlour.

'Henry!' she cried as she saw the perplexed look on his face, 'Henry, are you ill? What is it?'

The King signed to the pages and William to leave them. With mounting anxiety Margaret watched as he came and knelt beside her chair. More gentle than she had seen him for many months he took her hands between his own.

'Ma Mère, I bring you sad tidings — '

'Not one of the children?' she cried in an agony of apprehension.

'No; my Uncle Jasper died two days ago.'

Somewhere, a very long way off, a small hammering beat against Margaret's brain.

'Jasper?' she whispered. 'Not Jasper?' she clutched Henry's hands to her mouth, fighting against the pounding of noise she dimly realised was her heart threatening to burst in her breast. Choking tears welled in her throat and in an abandonment of grief she had not thought possible she sobbed against her son's shoulders. Henry held her murmuring the forgotten words of childhood she had used to comfort him in times of need. At last she grew quieter and he put her head back against the chair and rubbed the limp hands. Her face was livid with purple blotches beneath her eyes and he wished he had not sent her servants away from her.

Seeing her silver hand bell on the table beside her he rang it and was grateful when Betsey Massey came almost immediately to answer it. The devoted woman took one look at Margaret.

'The Lord Jasper?'

Henry nodded.

'May I summon her other ladies and send for the physician, your Grace?' Betsey asked.

'Do what ever you think fit.'

Henry gave no heed when pages, summoned by Betsey, came in and piled extra wood on the fire. With carefully averted eyes the boys stole from the chamber. Margaret still lay lifelessly against the chair her breast rising and falling in agitation while the hands in her lap were cold and clammy. After what seemed a very long time Betsey returned with four of Margaret's ladies who curtsied to the King and then bent to their mistress when he waved away their courtesies. As Henry went out of the room he saw his mother being lifted from the chair and carried to her bedchamber.

In the morning she sent word through her half-brother, Lord Welles, requesting Henry to come to her. To his surprise he found her dressed and sitting in the chair she had occupied the previous evening. Although she was still deathly pale her voice was steady as she asked him to come and sit with her.

'Tell me now what happened.'

'It seems he was on his way to Thornbury to fetch Catherine to bring her here for — for Christmas when he first complained of feeling unwell. When he came to his manor he protested he was recovered and began to make preparation to set out on the journey to Westminster. The next day he was stricken with severe pains in his chest and could not keep his feet. For several days he fought to recover but he was in great pain and the messengers who came from Thornbury said it became plain to those who watched over him he was mortally ill. He died on the twenty-first of this month.'

'Thank you,' Margaret said tonelessly.

'I have cancelled all the festivities for I can find no heart to enjoy them. I hope you will remain here with us for the present.'

'If it pleases you.'

'Mother,' Henry said gently, 'shall I send Meg to you? She has been asking for you since she arrived at Westminster.'

'Yes, have the child brought to me.'

Meg came into the room followed by a nurse and page. With great care she brought from under her cloak a much handled piece of needlework. Margaret felt the tears pricking at her eyelids but she forced them back and accepted the child's gift in a voice thick with emotion. Meg glanced at her curiously but prattled on about her life since she had last seen her grandmother. Margaret murmured words of encouragement and sent Betsey to her chest to find the St. Nicholas gift she had chosen for Meg from a Chepe jeweller she had commissioned. The little girl held her breath for pleasure as she saw the jewelled shoe buckles and bending down held them against her velvet shoes.

'Shall I fetch thread and sew them on for you?' Betsey hovering near at hand asked.

'I will do it,' Margaret said. Hardly able to see in the gloom of the winter's day she went to the casement and with some difficulty sewed the pearl adorned ornaments on to the slippers. Meg put them on and executed a few dancing steps before kissing Margaret and, at Betsey's signal, curtseying and taking her leave. At the door Betsey gave her in to the charge of the waiting nurse and page.

Margaret sank down on to the window seat and leant her throbbing head against the ice cold pane.

I hope I die, she thought fiercely. Life holds no joy if I have to live it without him. Why could I not have been with him? How much did he suffer?

The tears she had not been able to push far

below the surface flooded her eyes and she abandoned herself to the sobs racking her body. Betsey, not liking to speak but frightened to leave her mistress, went out as far as the passage and sent a page for some hot broth.

When it came Margaret made an attempt to swallow a little but it choked her and she handed the bowl back to Betsey.

'Try to eat, my Lady.'

'I am not hungry.'

'It is Christmas Eve and you need your strength for all the masses you will be hearing.'

'I have strength enough and to spare. I am sorry Betsey.'

Margaret turned again to the casement. Outside the short daylight was already fading and the opposite bank of the Thames was lost to view. She felt a nameless and hopeless dejection that robbed her of the will to move.

She was still sitting in the same position when Ormond came from the Queen to request the King's mother should take supper with her family.

'Thank you,' she said quietly. 'Give my love to my son and say I thank him for his courtesy and will come when I am ready.'

She suffered her waiting women to fetch the mourning robes kept in readiness and by great effort of will stood erect while hooks were fastened and the head-dress covering her hair completely was fixed in place. No one handed her the silver mirror and she made no comment, dismissing all the ladies except Betsey.

She knelt for a long time in the small chamber she used as a private chapel and head held high walked to the door of her apartments. Suddenly her courage failed her and with hand to her mouth she sat heavily in her chair at the fire.

'I cannot go; it is too early to parade my grief before the curious gaze of the household. Send word to say I have taken a chill; it is no lie, for I am cold to the heart.'

Betsey searched desperately for words of comfort but there seemed nothing appropriate to say. She was poignantly reminded of the time, over thirty years before, when her mistress had returned from Carmarthen after the death of Edmund. Then Margaret had been young, broken hearted to be bereft of love in its first flowering but there had been the child to consider and there had been Jasper. Jasper riding the two hundred miles from Westminster in record time to come to the aid of his desolate sister-in-law and taking upon himself, as the years past, the mantle of his dead brother. Where now could they search for comfort and succour? The King, loving his mother with unaccustomed tenderness, would doubtless give her his sympathy and complete understanding, but more than this would be required to fill the gap of the steadfast support of his uncle. Would to God He would send in His wisdom a sign of His compassion for this woman who followed His ordinances with such devotion. For now it was no child who mourned the death of a lover but a mature woman, poised, elegant but single-minded in her devotion.

'Would you have me send for your physician?' she asked Margaret.

Margaret shook her head.

'I will go to bed and perhaps sleep will give me the blessing of oblivion.'

She did not protest when Betsey brought her a cup of wine and if she suspected it was drugged said nothing but drained it.

'Whatever befalls I must be woken as is customary at five o'clock to go to St. Stephen's.'

'Very well, my Lady.'

Making an effort which robbed her of her reserves of strength she attended services on Christmas day and the feast of St. Stephen, dressing with utmost care and keeping within the circle of her family.

Derby came to her and offered his formal

sympathies for her bereavement and she was grateful to him for his kindness and spoke of every subject but that which clouded her vision and cloaked her thoughts in misery.

She was beset with the futility of living. On the first day of January William came to tell her John Fisher wished permission to speak with her.

'Tell him I have not given sufficient thought to the documents he sent me, and express the hope I shall be able to give him an answer before he returns to Cambridge.'

'Very well.'

The door was closing behind him when she called out, 'William!'

'My Lady?' The ugly attractive face regarded her keenly, searching for signs of returning interest.

'I will see Master Fisher.'

William returned in a few minutes with the young priest and the letters concerning the Chairs of Divinity. William hesitated while Fisher knelt to Margaret and then went from the room.

Margaret breathlessly rushed into a discussion on how she intended to find the necessary money to finance her new office in the University and listened with as much concentration as she could muster while John Fisher told her of the candidates he had in mind. In the middle of a sentence she rose abruptly from her chair and walked over to the window. For no reason she could understand her eyes were filling with tears and the empty, sick sensation in the pit of her stomach was causing her physical discomfort. She stood with her back to Fisher until she realised he was no longer speaking.

'Forgive me,' she said quietly and sat down on the window seat.

'My Lady, with the greatest possible respect and humility may I offer my sympathy in your brother-in-law's death?'

'Thank you.'

'If I speak what I feel in my heart will you pardon me for overstepping the barrier between your exalted position and my lowly estate?'

'You are a man of God, Master Fisher, and that ranks you with the angels.'

Fisher smiled and Margaret saw a strange softening of the thin, heavy jawed face.

'My Lady, in the saddest times of our lives there is One who is ever ready to offer comfort.'

'God?' Margaret queried.

Fisher nodded.

'I have lost God,' Margaret said turning away from him.

'A woman of your piety could never lose

Him. For the moment you are bound up in the appalling prospect of living without someone who, for many years, has been your closest and dearest relation. All your thoughts are clouded with this loss. May I be allowed to express the belief you are doing both yourself and the Lord Jasper a disservice in continuing to nurse your grief?'

As if she had been struck Margaret rounded on Fisher.

'Disservice? How so Master Fisher?'

'Now, surely, is the time to comport yourself in the sure knowledge of the Duke of Bedford's affection for you and act as he would have wanted,' he hesitated, suddenly losing the courage enabling him to have said so much, but Margaret was giving him her complete attention.

'How do you know so much?' she asked in a whisper.

'It was obvious to me when I had been but a short hour in your company that night at Coldeharbour how your thoughts and those of the Lord Jasper were closely attuned. It is not difficult to conjecture your reliance upon him who had guarded you since childhood and it is for this reason my sympathy is aroused for you now.'

Margaret relaxed against the back of her chair; for the first time for over a week she felt the warmth of the fire creep into her limbs.

'What would you have me do?'

'What does your Confessor tell you?'

'To think of God.'

'There is no better advice than that but you have an especial gift to offer God.'

'And that is?'

'You are wise, beyond the usual in women, well read and learned and coupled with this you have been blessed with compassion for those less fortunate than yourself. I venture to tell you of the plans, half-formed only, I have in my mind for encouraging the search for the truth of God's word in my university. There is so much to be done to help those who have gifts but are unable to use them through lack of proper places of study — .'

'And you think I might be able to help you?'

'I do,' Fisher told her simply. 'Other royal ladies have attempted to give their patronage to Cambridge but none of them have the benefit of your understanding. You and I could accomplish much together!'

'You bring me a ray of hope, Master Fisher. Come soon again, when I have had a little time to put into practice your kindly counsel.'

15

On the twenty-first of January Henry held the service marking the month's mind for Jasper. The Court attended, clad in the strict mourning garments laid down by Margaret herself for just such an occasion.

Afterwards in the privacy of the King's parlour the Chancellor read the Will Jasper had signed on the tenth of December. After bequeathing the majority of his estate to Henry he left the manor at Thornbury to his step-son, the young Duke of Buckingham, with provision for his widow to live there while she so desired, and beside the setting aside of monies for the chantry priests who would sing each day for the souls of his departed mother, father and Edmund, asked that his cloak of cloth of gold worn at the little Duke of York's knighting should be made into a cope for the use of the priests in the house of the Grayfriars at Haverfordwest where Owen had been interred. With characteristic generosity he provided a substantial sum to be given to the poor.

Margaret sat detached from the rest of the family, her back straight and her head held high. In the weeks since she had listened to the kindly and stringent advice of the young Oxford priest she had worked hard to accept it. With great difficulty she brought herself to realise she stood alone; the long years she had passed when Henry and Jasper were prisoners in Brittany helped her but then she had been young and lived in hope of their restoration to her. Now she was advancing in age and Jasper was dead. The bald fact struck her almost as a physical blow each time she awoke to the grey, winter mornings. She had always spent time in prayer and meditation but she now began the habit of spending several hours kneeling in the solitude of her chapel which was to last for the rest of her life. With conscious effort she pushed away from her the self-pity threatening to engulf her and concentrated on asking strength to accomplish whatever designs God especially wished her to encompass. At first her grief precluded any awareness of divine purpose but gradually she came to accept she was endowed with gifts that might be turned to the advantage of others. The well-ordered mind she had developed over the difficult years of her life helped her now to channel her energies into the paths Fisher had suggested.

She returned to Collyweston after Easter spent with her family and although she dreaded coming to the place where she had spent her last happy days with Jasper she found a curious sense of peace descend upon her once the great doors had closed behind her. In some intangible way she was surrounded with an aura of happiness experienced and shared.

With this balm she discovered a reawakening of interests that had lain dormant since Christmastide. Calling William Elmer to her she composed letters to the King and to Cambridge asking her son for a licence to endow the two readerships she had previously mooted to him and telling the Master of Michaelhouse she was prepared to listen to his plans for the advancement of learning in the University of Cambridge.

John Fisher wasted no time and came at once to Collyweston, bringing with him a scheme to suppress a nunnery in Cambridge called St. Rhadegund where he had learnt from his Bishop in Ely of conduct not in accordance with the teaching or training expected of persons who had taken the vows of Christ. He spoke long and eloquently to Margaret of his belief that here was a place which could be altered to become an academical foundation where young men could be trained properly in the Christian faith. Fisher told Margaret of the need to instruct priests in the almost forgotten art of preaching.

'There must be those who are competent to expound the Scriptures for if men are to be able to read the Bible they must have its meaning made clear to them. With the new learning coming to us from Italy it is vital to help men to understand how the ancient ways of Greece and Rome were perfected in Jesus Christ.'

'You do not think this growing education of the mind in the philosophies of Plato and Socrates is a dangerous new element?' she asked him.

'It could very well prove to be so unless the old faiths were shown to be better and more progressive still. My main desire is to promote the study of Divinity.'

He returned to Cambridge with Margaret's promise to provide funds for the commencement of the new college when they were required. When Fisher asked her she said she would be honoured to visit him in the University to inspect the buildings he proposed to use.

After Fisher left Collyweston she discovered she was once more able to read other books than her book of the Hours and Caxton's translations of the Gospels. The almost sensual pleasure of poetry no longer filled her with a desperate sense of loss but delighted the eye and the ear with the metrical pattern of its composition. For the first time in her life she set down words in an attempt to create for herself some of the magic poetry commanded.

In this new frame of mind she found the months slipped by. Returning to Sheen or Richmond, as the old manor was now called, she took up the ties of her family life, searching in the faces of her grandchildren for a resemblance to their grandfather or Jasper. Only in her goddaughter did she find any likeness either to them or to herself. Arthur with his fair colouring and delicate looks favoured Henry but bore the unmistakable stamp of his mother's family while the little Harry, growing fast was considered by all those who had known Edward IV to be a perfect replica of his maternal grandfather.

Henry and his wife greeted her with her unfeigned pleasure while those of the Court made no secret of their delight in having her in their midst. When the King set out on the yearly progress she accompanied him intending to stay part of the time in Cambridge and hoping to encourage her son to give audience to those who wished to expand the university.

Henry made first for Windsor and visited the school at Eton founded by the monkish

Henry VI where he had received tuition during the brief months of that monarch's restoration. Margaret was reminded of the first time she had been brought to view the progress of the building of the chapel when she had been a small girl. Now the newly cut stone was mellowing and shone golden in the September sunshine and more building was under way. Margaret noted the interest Henry took and determined to broach the matter of Fisher's proposals.

But the Progress was cut short by news from Scotland of an invasion by Perkin Warbeck backed up by the young King James.

Henry received the tidings with equanimity.

'Are you not anxious?' Margaret asked him.

'No. My informants tell me Perkin has not been able to amass much equipment and I have a strong force ready in the north for just such an eventuality.'

'Do you think you will have to make preparations to go north?'

'I hope not. I cannot believe James Stewart is in earnest when he breaks truce to further the cause of Warbeck.'

'Have you thought more of sending little Meg to those wild, mist-covered desolations?'

Henry regarded his mother for a time without speaking, then smiled and bending forward kissed her lightly.

'Even if I have it will not be for a long time to come. It is all important to keep good relationships with Scotland.'

'It is difficult to say that when James is giving aid to an impostor and besides, I hear the Stewart has a most unsavoury reputation.'

'Do not underestimate Meg. Her nurses tell me she has plenty of spirit!'

'She will need that to marry James of Scotland.'

Returning to Westminster Henry summonsed both his Council and the aldermen and wealthy men of the great towns. He told them, at once, that his object in calling them together was to find the best means of raising money to finance any further menace to the realm. Rather to his surprise, although he pledged considerable sums of his own the country was not quick in granting him aid.

Grumbling was heard from all quarters, and although Henry tried to keep this fact from his mother, she nevertheless came to know of it through Sir Reginald Bray and Derby. More than once she almost brought herself to the point of warning Henry of the dangers of asking too much from his people; her senses at this particular stage in her life seemed particularly sharp and she disliked thinking there were those who had genuine reason to be against her son.

To her distress she found her fears proved when the Cornish rose in rebellion when Henry's demands were made known to them. These independent people beyond the Tamar could see no reason for tax levied against them to provide money for an army to fight the Scots, who had always shown a dislike for knuckling under. The Cornish banded together and with a discontented noble who had hoped to enrich himself in the abortive French War and had been bitterly disappointed when the early truce had been made, marched towards London. With his lieutenants Henry set up forces at Hounslow and Henley, causing the rebels to change course and head for Kent; here, in the home of past malcontents they hoped to gain more support.

Hearing this Henry issued orders for his wife, Margaret and the young Harry to be taken to the Tower for safety and hurried to meet the Cornishmen. He set up his headquarters at Lambeth and waited to see the rebels' next move. Spies came in to tell they were encamped at Blackheath and he launched a sudden attack, which, taking the Cornishmen by surprise, proved entirely successful. The fighting was sharp and both sides suffered killed and wounded; the windswept heath that had seen many similar engagements was littered with the sprawling bodies of men who had come sleepily from their resting places at the unexpected bugle alarms. The leaders of the rebels realised their hopeless position as soon as they grasped they were heavily outnumbered and lacked any proper training against the superior forces of the Kings' army. When they hoisted the white flag Henry, with swift justice, hanged the leaders and sent the rest packing to Cornwall.

He returned to Richmond, bringing Elizabeth and Margaret with him.

Morton hurried to greet him with despatches from Scotland telling of Perkin Warbeck's dismissal from court with his wife and only a small entourage.

'I must send an emissary to James Stewart with all speed for it would seem he is as anxious as I am to promote good relationships between our countries,' Henry told Margaret and Elizabeth as they supped in the privacy of her parlour.

'Will you offer him again the hand of my granddaughter?' Margaret asked.

'Yes,' Henry told them. 'But you need have no fear I shall even consider sending the child for some years to come.'

'What do you think has brought about this

volte-face?' Elizabeth said with a puzzled frown, 'and where do you think Perkin will try to land this time?'

'To answer your first question I think Ferdinand and Isabella have sent their ambassador, Ayala, as often to Scotland as they have to me and as he is such an able negotiator he has probably caused James to see the wisdom of being on good terms with us rather than with the more distant French.' Henry smiled on his wife as he continued. 'If I am any judge where Perkin is concerned I believe he will make for Cornwall, where he will be fully aware of the uprising that has taken place and will hope to arouse much sympathy. There is always the possibility he might attempt a landing in Wales and seek out Arthur, but I do not think you need be afraid of that for you may rest assured no Welshman will allow him to set foot on the soil of my birthplace let alone penetrate the country-side as far as Ludlow.'

It was not to be long before Henry was proved correct in his beliefs and he received news of Warbeck's arrival near Land's End where he quickly set up an establishment on St. Michael's Mount. Henry immediately called up the levies of South Wales and the western counties of England and placed them under the command of Lord Daubeny; in a comparatively short space of time they were ready to march out to meet Warbeck.

'Go you to meet the Pretender?' Margaret asked her son; wondering how many times in the years since he had come to the throne he had been called to defend his country. This time there was no Jasper to counsel and bolster his nephew with his flare for rapid decisions on the battlefield. Neither was he able to comfort her with his unruffled advice and patient understanding.

She did not miss him less as the months since his death passed. Life, or the part in which she had lived with her senses, was bereft of the essence of joy; now there was no one with whom a shared glance or a swift touch of hands sent a glow of pleasure through her veins. As a token of her abandonment of physical awareness she elected to wear, at least once a week, a chemise of hair. Betsey and her other ladies protested with horror when they saw her delicate skin covered with a tracery of angry red scratches.

'My Lady!' Betsey cried, 'this is in no way necessary. Never, in this age, has there been a woman equal to you in piety and good living. What need is there to subject yourself to this torture?'

'Be it sufficient I felt the need to suffer bodily pinpricks.'

'Have you not suffered enough without adding to your burden?'

'In all I have borne, my own discomfort has not been apparent; let me know what is best for my soul.'

She had discovered in those who served her a sympathy she had not thought possible. No words were spoken but each member of her large household made gestures of goodwill. William Elmer was particularly helpful in an unobtrusive way. Since Perrot had remained at Woking she saw no signs of his attention to other women and was constantly at Margaret's elbow anticipating her wants and smoothing out difficulties with her tenants and overseers. Margaret thought he had aged considerably in the last two years; the fine auburn hair receding from the intelligent forehead and the high cheekbones protruding more noticeably through the thin, pinkish skin. He had become good friends with John Fisher who came with more and more frequency to Richmond or wherever Margaret was living with the Court.

The plans he had submitted to Margaret were now in operation at Cambridge and the preachers selected for the first year of office had given the requisite number of sermons they had decided upon together. With John Fisher to help her she had asked that daily masses should be said for those she loved and could no longer see in the Abbey Church at Westminster and also in the magnificent chapel of St. George at Windsor, begun by Edward IV and now nearing completion.

She had also given thought to the founding of a grammar school at Wimborne where both her parents were entombed in the Minster. It seemed as if she must exercise her ability to further the interests of the living as a thanksgiving for the dead.

She was glad of these preoccupations, when, with Elizabeth, she watched as the King set out for the West Country. He took with him an army, well accoutred, glittering in polished armour, their brave banners flashing in brilliant silks and damasks.

'They make a goodly sight,' Margaret said with a sigh as the men clattered out of sight on the dusty road.

'Suppose this Perkin Warbeck is really my lost brother?' Elizabeth asked her.

Shocked, Margaret turned quickly to face her.

'Surely you, above all people, cannot harbour thoughts of that kind?'

'But Madame,' Elizabeth answered her quietly. 'It is I, more than anyone else, who would like to believe it was my brother Richard.'

'To the detriment of your husband's throne?'

'I would not wish him to take anything from Henry which is the King's but I should be made happy if I thought one at least of my brothers had escaped the cruel fate of death in the Tower at the hands of some unknown accomplice.'

'Of course,' Margaret said gently, 'there is no one living who would deny you that happiness; but I feel you must put away from you any hopes that this might be the case; you would only be sadly disappointed if you should ever come face to face with the Pretender.'

'You are right of course, Madame, and it is stupid of me to harbour such thoughts, but there are those who swear Perkin bears the likeness of my family and with my mother still shut away in a convent, I have not anyone to call my own.'

'You have your children! And what of Henry?'

'Henry is a good husband, my Lady, but as you know well is much taken up with affairs of state. My children are my life, but they have their nurses and their tutors and they are not very much with me. I am selfish to wish it were otherwise — ,' her voice trailed off.

It was a wonder, Margaret thought, the Queen was not tempted to take a lover; the frustrating restlessness from which she was suffering naturally found outlet in submitting to the temptation of intrigue and the added danger of being the King's wife might add to the situation rather than dissuade Elizabeth.

Aloud she said: 'Can you not interest yourself in books and perhaps some studies?'

'I am not like you, Madame, and had not the benefit of a mother whose wisdom trained you in scholarly pursuits.'

'Your mother had more difficulties than mine,' Margaret told her quietly, 'but it is not too late for you to be taught whatever you would know. Henry's court is filled with those who are acquainted with men of the new learning sweeping across Europe who would be only too willing to make the Queen their pupil.'

Elizabeth moved restlessly. 'I could not concentrate upon books. Music is another matter but one cannot sing and play the lute all day!'

No! Margaret thought. Music seeks out and finds the very substance of our being; twisting with knife-edged sureness into the places which hurt the most. How often have I wished I were deaf to the evocative sweetness of a too remembered melody when I hear the court band play it!

She changed the theme of the conversation.

'There is the marriage of Arthur and the little Catherine to think about. There will be plenty of opportunity for you to help devise the masques and tableaux and you will need many new gowns to enhance your good looks — '

'The wedding is still a long way off and of what use is it to plan so far ahead? In this intransient life so much is uncertain.'

Margaret was to remember her daughter-in-law's wistful conversation many times in the days following. Days when she and the Queen waited with all the patience they could muster for tidings of what happened between the King's armies and that of Warbeck.

At first they received reports of large numbers of Cornishmen flocking to the banner of the Pretender and Elizabeth began to wonder if she should take the little Harry to the safety of the Tower once more; but a few days later special messengers came to tell them Perkin was diverted from his main objective of capturing Exeter and was believed heading for Taunton. His army had received heavy casualties and those who resisted his attacks did so with a willing loyalty.

A week passed and Richmond Herald came to the manor with despatches for the Queen from Henry. Elizabeth brought them to Margaret.

'Madame! Henry is sending the wife of Perkin here to be one of my ladies!'

'Warbeck is in Henry's hands?'

'He must be if his wife is to come to us here! Now, I shall hear the truth of the matter from someone who really knows this Perkin.'

The Lady Catherine Gordon came to Richmond bringing with her a handful of women, who went about with downcast eyes and spoke as little as possible. Perkin's wife was a girl of great beauty, possessing a perfect complexion and auburn hair. She curtsied with respect to the Queen and did not speak until Elizabeth addressed her.

'You are welcome here, my lady.'

A hush fell on the cluster of waiting women and courtiers.

'Thank you, your Grace; I am fortunate to have met with the clemency of the King of England and to be allowed to come to you and begin a new life.'

Elizabeth signalled for her to rise and took her first to Margaret, who had watched the proceedings from behind the Queen, and then presented her to each member of the household who was present.

As she made the tour of the room, smiling with touching humility to those who bowed before her, Margaret could not help wondering what had been Lady Catherine's motive in marrying the Pretender. Did the selfefacement conceal a strong urge to climb the dizzy heights of power or had the comely body sought satisfaction in the charms of Perkin's manhood? Time only would tell.

The round of the room completed Elizabeth touched Catherine's arm and drew her towards her own private parlour. The Queen turned to see if Margaret were following and discovering her still where she had left her, motioned for her to come also. Margaret hesitated, but realising her daughter-in-law must need her support, went after her into the chamber. Once in the small, pleasant room Elizabeth bade the girl be seated and handed her a goblet of wine.

'There is much I would ask,' she began, 'and I hope you will not think me prying.'

'No, your Grace, I am well aware there is much you would know of — .'

'Of Perkin — have you any cause to think he might be my brother?'

The air in the silk hung chamber seemed very heavy of a sudden as Catherine took a few moments to reply.

'Perkin Warbeck is not your brother, my Lady.' Catherine looked up as she heard the Queen take in her breath sharply. 'Do not think ill of me that I have believed in an impostor all this time and have not communicated this fact to you — but you will understand this was impossible.'

'How do you know, now, that the young man has been acting a part?'

'After the siege of Exeter, Richard — Perkin that is — went to Taunton with but a remnant of the large force he had at first commanded and from what I learnt later he was disheartened by the thought of a further fiasco and decided to make a bid for Southampton and find a ship for France.'

'He did not discover one?' Margaret asked from the seat she had taken by the window.

'No, Madame,' Catherine replied, 'he heard, while at the port of a large force coming to apprehend him and ran to Beaulieu Abbey for Sanctuary. While safe within the walls of the abbey he sent out an emissary to ask what would happen if he threw himself on your son's mercy.'

'This is what they did?' Elizabeth cried.

'Yes. On receiving his assurances of safe conduct they came out of Sanctuary and were conveyed to the King's grace at Taunton.'

'What happened then?' Elizabeth's voice was controlled.

'He made a full confession of the deception he had practised over the last five years.' The soft Scot's voice dropped a little but Catherine braced herself and continued; 'He told how he had been born at Tournai, the son of a man called John Osbeck. He spent his early youth in the Low Countries and later sailed to Portugal and entered the service of a merchant named Meno. This man used the boy — as he then was — as a tailor's mannikin to show off the clothes he made and sold. The simple Irish in Cork, where their travels took them first, insisted that only a prince could dress in the fine raiment Perkin sported and began to murmur that here was the son of Clarence — '

'Son of Clarence?' Margaret echoed, 'surely that rumour was put down for ever when my son paraded the true Edward of Warwick outside St. Paul's that Easter day?'

'Yes; no one could prove Edward of Warwick had escaped from England so it was decided this must be the younger of the sons of King Edward. Forgive me, your Grace,' Catherine said with a quick upward look into Elizabeth's face, 'I know what I have to tell must cause you pain, but it is best you should know how Perkin explained himself to your husband.'

'How came he to accept this masquerade?' Margaret asked as Elizabeth remained silent.

'If what he says is the truth he would not agree at first to perpetrate the deceit — but, who knows, his head was probably turned with all the attention he received and he found it most agreeable to be hailed as of royal English blood.'

'Did he speak English?' Elizabeth asked suddenly.

'With the faintest trace of accent. He claimed he had been taught the Flemish tongue by the family who befriended him when he escaped from England and over the years forgot his native language and had to relearn it.'

'Was he personable to look upon?' Elizabeth asked with difficulty.

'Very, my Lady,' Catherine agreed shyly. 'Not only is he handsome but he has a most appealing charm of manner.' So we know the lovely young thing was attracted to him, Margaret thought wryly. 'From those who had known your father and mother I learned they would have thought of him quite naturally as a sprig of the Yorkist house.'

Elizabeth moved uneasily in her chair.

'And you say this fraud started in Ireland?'

Margaret asked musingly.

'Yes, my Lady the King's Mother; it was in Cork the deception was started.'

'What puzzles me is why Perkin should have gone to Portugal in the first place. With whom did you say he travelled?'

'With an English knight's lady — one Sir Edward Brampton's wife.'

'Ah!' Margaret said quickly. 'A Yorkist man who defected to the court of your aunt in Burgundy. I think we can say safely that it was by no mere chance your husband was placed in the employ of the Portuguese merchant who brought him to Cork. To me it smacks altogether too much of the Lambert Simnel plot to be a simple matter of a handsome youth being persuaded to think he was a Yorkist prince solely because he paraded the streets of Cork clad in sumptuous clothing. My dear,' she said rising from her chair and placing her hand lightly on Elizabeth's shoulder, 'I believe you may rest assured that this Perkin is an impostor — and was very probably trained from the beginning to ape your brother.'

'Think you so?' Elizabeth asked huskily, laying her hand over that of her mother-in-law. 'How then do you explain the acceptance of my aunt of Burgundy of this boy?'

Margaret took a deep breath. Blood was

undoubtedly thicker than the bond tied by marriage but in this moment of seeking for truth it was better to be frank.

'I think you cannot rule out completely the possibility that Margaret of Burgundy instigated the whole business.' She saw Elizabeth bite her lip and went on more gently. 'But putting that interpretation aside you must bear in mind your aunt had not set eyes on her brother's children and she — like you — would be eager to accept the contingency of his survival. It would not do, either, to rule out absolutely the faint chance of Perkin being a bastard son of your father's or even one of your uncles who was secreted abroad to await an opportunity of making claims upon the English throne. This I find difficult to accept for it is unlikely someone would not have known of the existence of such a child and spoken of it long before this; such information would be hard to suppress.'

'Bearing in mind my father was notorious for his amours?'

'Yes,' Margaret said simply, 'but your uncles had their mistresses also. I shall leave you now to speak with the Lady Catherine. There is, no doubt, much else she will have to tell you.'

Henry did not return to London until almost the end of November and when he came he brought Perkin Warbeck with him. All the way, on the long journey from Taunton, the young man had proved a draw to the people of the towns they passed through and men, women and children crowded the narrow streets to catch a glimpse of the self-styled Duke of York.

At Westminster a stage was erected and the Pretender made to mount it and speak, once again, the confession he had signed and given earlier to Henry. The royal ladies, watching from a screened window, saw an elegantly groomed, good looking youth with a gentle mouth and flashing eyes hold himself proudly while he did, with good grace, what was asked of him. When the reading was finished he made no effort to make contact with the gaping crowds about the dais but suffered himself to be led to the waiting escort and marched off in the direction of the Tower.

Margaret saw tears in the eyes of her daughter-in-law. She found herself touched also by the futile waste of the Pretender's cause and at loss for appropriate words to comfort Elizabeth.

They rejoined Henry as he stood in the anteroom of the Hall with Archbishop Morton, Oxford and other members of the King's household. Henry came quickly to his wife and with most unusual outward affection took her hand and held it to his lips. He looked at her questioningly and Margaret saw her shake her head and suffer Henry to lead her to join the other men.

Derby and Reginald Bray moved to Margaret's side and spoke quietly of the event they had just witnessed. Margaret enquired if they knew what Henry intended to do with the offender.

'I believe it is the King's intention to release him fairly soon to live quietly with some obscure knight's family where he may make himself useful and forget his grandiose schemes of winning the Crown,' Bray told her.

'I am so glad,' Margaret said. 'What will become of those who aided him?' She experienced a great sense of relief that Henry was showing such leniency in sparing the life of the handsome Pretender, but wondered what Derby must think of his brother's execution for allegiance to Perkin while the boy himself went free.

Bray obviously shared her misgivings for he answered deliberately, weighing his words. 'He has already levied huge fines on those who took part in the rebellion — and indeed, this is why our return to Court has been so long delayed. His Grace drew up the list of Cornish and Devonian offenders himself and personally assessed the amount each should pay him for a pardon. I am of the mind that most will think very deeply before involving themselves against the King at any future date.'

'Meaning their pockets hurt them most?' Margaret said ingenuosuly. She made her excuses and left the company pleading fatigue. Coming into her own apartments she shook her head at the waiting women who would have accompanied her and closing the door against them leant against the solid oak.

The room looked very empty and her eyes filled with the tears threatening her since she had first seen Warbeck. She thought, with an aching longing, of the many times Jasper had come swiftly to her when he had known she was troubled and had taken her aching head on his shoulder and soothed her with the familiar words of their mutual affection. Trying not to abandon herself in a wallowing of self-pity she looked back on the forty years of devotion he had bestowed upon her and counted herself blessed to have been endowed with his unfaltering love. How many women there were she could name who had not once, even in a plethora of marriages, known such happiness as she had enjoyed; and she had been fortunate enough to marry the hero of her childhood and have his brother as her champion until his death almost four years ago. Four years! Her heart thudded and missed several beats as once again the misery the day had engendered welled within her breast. I grow old, she told herself, I should be thinking only now of sitting beside the fire with embroidery and the idle chatter of women's gossip to fill out the hours.

But she knew this could never be for her. Apart from Betsey and her waiting women she had no especial friends among the women of the Court and thought it dangerous to speak too freely with the wives of Henry's ministers and councillors. She understood perfectly that they regarded her with curiosity and were sometimes stiff and unnatural in her presence when they first met although they later confided to one another she was sympathetic and understanding once the initial barrier was down.

Thank God, she told herself somewhat wearily as she went to kneel before her private altar, my faith has returned with abundance to be my comforter!

16

Margaret was delighted when Elizabeth told her she was expecting another child; her happiness in her daughter-in-law finding solace in the fulfilment of her natural function turning to gratitude on Elizabeth's and her own behalf when the birth of a son at Greenwich in February, 1499, distracted them both from the course of events following the capture of Warbeck.

The foolish young man, unable to accept the extraordinary light captivity imposed upon him, escaped from his captors who behaved more as hosts than jailors and threw himself into sanctuary in the Charterhouse in Richmond. From here he attempted to reach the coast but was recaptured almost at once. This time he made his confession twice; once again outside the Abbey at Westminster and then in the Chepe. Crowds watched, shaking their heads at his folly, and watched silently as he was taken away to an uncomfortable cell in the Tower.

What followed was predictable; almost too predictable Margaret was to think in the uncompromising darkness of the sleepless nights that seemed to become more and more part of her life. Perkin soon discovered that within the confines of the Tower the Duke of Clarence, Edward of Warwick, still lingered in endless captivity. It did not take the silver tongued Pretender long to bribe his warders and arrange a meeting between the pale-faced Warwick and himself. Warwick was almost too easily persuaded escape was possible; his despair at a life spent virtually all in imprisonment making him grasp eagerly at the first opportunity of freedom he had been offered. When Perkin led the way he followed with almost pitiful trust and together they were miserably apprehended and returned with ignominy to wait Henry's pleasure.

Margaret knew her son suffered agonies of conscience about the fate he decided for his two prisoners but nevertheless he did not hesitate when he gave the final command for their execution. Margaret found it impossible to dismiss from her mind the suspicion that the recently confirmed marriage treaty between Prince Arthur and Catherine of Aragon had any bearing upon Henry's decree and knew it was not only feminine intuition which told her the Spanish monarchs hesitated to sign the agreement while two Pretenders to the throne lived to command supporters to their cause.

Whatever dark truths lay behind the King of England's action divine judgement was to make him pay the price. The infant prince, named Edmund after Henry's father and another of Margaret's godchildren, died soon after his birth. The blow was slightly mitigated and Margaret hoped showed heavenly forgiveness when the Queen found while she was still mourning her latest born that she was once more pregnant.

With the birth of the Lady Mary, Elizabeth regained some of her vitality and seemed more contented than Margaret could remember. The Queen insisted upon tending the child herself and although she tired easily spent much of her day with her new little daughter. The royal nurses came to Margaret and spoke of their anxiety for their mistress but Margaret told them to help Elizabeth as unobtrusively as possible without taking the baby away from her; in the care of her child she was able to forget some of the harrowing events of the past year.

When Elizabeth's hollow cheeks filled slightly and her happier frame of mind continued, Margaret asked her son to release her to go to Collyweston. She had spent only fleeting visits of late and longed to remain there for some months to rest and devote her time to her own affairs. With reluctance

Henry granted her permission to leave.

She made the journey in leisurely stages, calling at Cheshunt, Ware and Hatfield on the way. She lingered longest at the Bishop of Ely's Palace at Hatfield, making the better accommodation of her almsfolk the pretext for staying in the house almost a week. But she knew it was not the old men and women, grateful as they were for her concern, that held her but the knowledge that here, in this pleasant hillside house Jasper had been born. It was here he and Edmund had passed the first tranquil years of their lives: lives tragically interrupted when Henry V's evil brother had broken up the idyllic happiness of Owen Tudor's family and scattered them, never to be united again. While she lingered she chided herself for sentimentality but, nevertheless, hugged to herself the thought of the two men she had loved throughout her life. As she stood and gazed into the distant, grey hills, she could almost hear the childish voices of the Tudor family as they played among the oak trees and imagined the magnificent Owen as he crashed through the dried leaves of the Hertfordshire woodlands and bent from the saddle to scoop one of his sons to sit before him and enjoy the chase. She remembered her father-in-law as he had ridden beside her down the Pembroke coast and conjured up for her, in the musical English that was peculiarly his own, past splendours of Agincourt. With the thought of Owen came the grim majesty of the Welsh coast and the waves of the Atlantic ocean breaking in splendour against the towering cliffs of Jasper's domain. Softly across the years she heard again the music of the magician's pipe as it had threaded her dreams with those of Jasper and she closed her eyes and allowed herself the indulgence of reliving the brief time they had spent together in the haven bound castle.

At last she tore herself away from her memories and set out for Collyweston. She spent two days at Bletsoe, her own birthplace, where she stayed talking deep into the night with her St. John half-brothers. Earlier in the year they had lost their mutual uterine brother, Lord Welles, and this was the first time they had had opportunity of speaking freely of purely family matters. Margaret found a simple pleasure in reviving her own childhood with these white-haired men who were her mother's children by her first marriage.

Margaret realised with something akin to amazement Oliver and John must be over sixty, while she was not so far from that age herself. She had to admit she found travelling very much more exhausting than before and her limbs were beset with aches and pains that at times she found difficult to bear. She discovered also of late that Betsey, who had never left her service since she had become her waiting woman in this very house, was often quiet and although she gave her the same devoted attention she had lavished on her since her childhood her actions were slower and she could not be hurried. Margaret tried to share out the daily duties between her other ladies but Betsey was jealous of her position and resented any suggestion she was incapable of fulfilling her daily offices.

Perrot was accompanying her on this journey; a pale ghost of the vivacious girl she had been, her dark eyes glowing in the brittle beauty of her face. She spoke neither to William as they went north or Maurice when they arrived at Collyweston.

Margaret found her manor in the same orderly routine she craved and settled down as if she had only been absent for a few weeks. Westbury had only the younger Buckingham child and the young Northumberland to tutor for Edward had gone to Thornbury to claim his estate and be near his widowed mother, returning to Henry's Court when Catherine had married Sir Robert

Wingfield. Margaret was not very surprised when Jasper's widow was wedded again; was it Wingfield who had awoken the dormant passion Jasper had confided in her on that long ago day? Subtly, with Catherine's remarriage Jasper became completely Margaret's again, the legal formality of his union with Buckingham's widow sloughing off as she went to Wingfield's bed. Margaret allowed the tranquillity of Collyweston to wrap her in its special magic and when the day's work was concluded sat in her parlour with books as her most constant companions. She was coming more and more to enjoy the beauty of the written word and when her eyes were very tired would send for the Buckingham boy to read to her. He sat at her feet, shyly at first, but with growing confidence and read to her from her growing collection of volumes. Now and again he would stumble over an unusual word but she prompted him with patience and the boy confided to Westbury he enjoyed the sessions and found pleasure in what he had anticipated would be dull and uninteresting.

She corresponded regularly with Fisher, enjoying the simplicity and pungency of his writing and looked forward to a visit he was to make to Collyweston later in the year. Their plans for the new college had prospered and they began to look around for other buildings that might serve their turn as houses of learning.

Margaret wrote also to Henry; long letters concerned with the many and varied interests they shared and homely enquiries for the health of his family. Quite content in the well-ordered daily round of Collyweston she knew she looked forward to the reunion when they all met to celebrate the wedding of Arthur and Catherine which was becoming the dominant theme of correspondence passing between her son and herself.

The arrival of the infanta was expected in the autumn. After many years of uncertainty Isabella and Ferdinand had consented to the formal betrothal of their daughter and their ambassador reported to Henry all preparations, including the amassing of her enormous dowry, were nearing completion.

Margaret pushed away from her the conviction the monarchs of Spain had held back the despatch of their child until they were absolutely certain she would one day become Queen of England in undisputed right. Before she had left Westminster she and Elizabeth had composed a letter to Catherine, welcoming her and giving her motherly counsel on the subject of dress in the northern dampness and advising her to learn some English as her new subjects were not easily disposed to speak foreign tongues. Margaret wondered how Arthur, now fifteen years of age, anticipated his forthcoming marriage to a completely unknown girl. He had written to her in the gracious, stilted phraseology of Court etiquette and had received a reply couched in the same eulogistic prose but he really could know nothing of the young woman who would one day, share his throne and his bed. From all accounts Catherine was comely and desirable but ambassadors with marriageable heirs to their master's thrones were notoriously easy to please.

When the summer came Margaret sat in her walled garden with her ladies working together on a large tapestry she intended as part of her wedding gift to her grandson. She found the rhythmical plunging of the needle and the matching of silks and wool a happy pastime and she sewed with the stitches her profound hope for the happiness of the young couple.

When the time came to leave Collyweston she experienced a more than usual pang of regret at leaving her home. How soon would she be able to take herself quietly away from Court and return to its mind-healing tranquillity? She determined to tell Henry she would like to make her forthcoming visit to Court her swansong and devote the rest of her years to her Rutland manor and the pursuits of her academic concerns.

London, she discovered on her arrival, was already in the grip of a fever of preparation for the royal wedding. Outside St. Paul's church where the ceremony was to take place stands were being erected while other joiners and carpenters prepared the elaborate set pieces for the tableaux. Sempstresses were working until their eyes ached to finish the costumes for the set pieces and the masques that would take place over a week of festivities.

Unfortunately Margaret was not able to enjoy the arrangements with the pleasure she had anticipated for she had other matters to occupy her mind. Betsey had disquieting news to tell her and she broached the matter during the nightly ritual of the hairbrushing.

'Have you seen anything unusual in Perrot's behaviour?' Betsey asked as the brush went through the mass of silver sparked auburn.

'No!'

'She is with child.'

'Betsey! What makes you say this?'

'It is common talk in the household and although she has tried to hide it with tight lacing it is not difficult to see.'

'Why did you not tell me before?'

'I would not disturb your peace in Collyweston.'

'Do you — ?'

'Know who is the father?' Betsey prompted. 'No, my Lady. I would not think it is any member of the household but where bedsport is concerned there is no accounting for taste.'

'This distresses me beyond measure!' Margaret said in a troubled voice, 'I thought to have the well-being and discipline of those in my house easily within my compass and yet here I find one of my own waiting women overtaken by a mortal sin and I am not aware of it.'

On the following day she sat in the window seat of her parlour. She had been going through the details of the banquet she was to hold in honour of the Spanish Ambassadors to mark the occasion of the wedding with her new controller of the household and William Elmer. She waited until the major domo had left the chamber and William was tying documents at the table. Without lifting her head she said quietly:

'William, I understand Mistress Perrot is with child!'

'Yes, my Lady,' William spoke evenly.

'You know then?'

'All know of it.'

'Except I,' Margaret told him heavily.

'You are anxious that it is possibly I who am the father?' William said coming to stand directly in front of her.

'Yes,' Margaret replied looking up at him.

'Then you may rest content, Madame; Perrot has not disturbed my peace of mind for many a long day.' His voice rose a little. 'As you are well aware, there was time when I saw her face on every page as I wrote, or sensed her presence in the lilac blossom or the soft summer air, but I have grown since then and am no longer to be ensnared only by the heady promises of the flesh.'

'I am glad,' Margaret said simply, 'I have much trust in you, William Elmer, and I would not have my opinion shattered.'

'You are very kind.'

'No, it is not only kindness; I, too, was young once, and have known the temptation of succumbing to the overriding calls of the flesh — made more difficult in this instance by the involvement of the heart also — ' she stopped amazed at her frank confession.

'Madame,' William said with great humility, 'only those who have suffered understand the true meaning of self-sacrifice. May I — ' he hesitated, 'may I tell you how deeply

349

honoured I am to serve one with such compassion for human nature?'

'Thank you,' Margaret said, her eyes threatening to fill with tears. Biting them back she continued, 'I had thought my household considered me a dry-as-a-bone only taken up with duties and academic matters.'

'There are the very young who might think in that way, but we, who have served you over the years, know otherwise.'

'Even when I make journeys to Calais chasing debts owed to my long dead mother by the King of France?' she said with a little laugh.

She had doubted the wisdom of the journey across the rough Channel in the previous winter many times. What those about her thought of her facing perilous seas to try and settle the matter of monies owed her family for the ransom of the Duke of Orleans after Agincourt she had hardly dare imagine. She had only known, at the time, she was experiencing a restlessness that threatened to engulf her in the confining walls of Court life and she had seized the opportunity to visit Calais when Sir Reginald Bray had drawn her attention to the outstanding debt.

She had met with no success in obtaining gold she had hoped to give to Meg as part of her dowry but she had known a release of spirit engendered by the swiftly flying spray and the proud battling of the ship against the unleashed strength of the sea. She had stood, during the daylight hours, in front of the mast and allowed the wind to blow over her in a cleansing exultation. Betsey had pleaded with her to come below but she had shaken her head and stayed on deck until the winter daylight was lost in the dark clouds of night.

She brought herself back with some difficulty to the young man who still stood looking down at her.

'Forgive me, William, I wander.'

William smiled, the ugly attractive face tender with affection. 'Is there anything more I can do for you before I take these accounts to Sir Reginald?'

'No thank you. I have the sempstresses coming to try on the robes I shall wear for Lord Arthur's wedding and I shall rest here until they come.'

She was happy to have heard William deny any interest in Perrot's coming child for although she had not thought their liaison continued no one could be sure of what passed between a man and a woman in the privacy of locked doors or in the concealment of a hollow in unfrequented country woodlands. Although there was still the possibility the child might be Westbury's Margaret could not bring herself to see the dark, handsome tutor engaged in underhand coupling with any of her waiting women. She put the matter from her mind as Betsey came in with several girls, their arms piled high with velvets and furs.

A week later she was about to retire when one of her ladies, Elizabeth Zouche, hurried into her parlour and whispered something to Betsey. Although Betsey registered no particular emotion Margaret recognised in the heightening of colour on her cheekbones her faithful tiring maid was put out about something.

'What is the matter?' Margaret asked quietly. Elizabeth and Betsey exchanged rapid glances.

'Perrot is ill, my lady!'

'Sufficiently so to send for the physician?'

'We did not know what to do — '

'Send for Dr. Morgan to attend her at once and I shall go to her room also.'

'But — Madame!'

Margaret took a cloak from a chair and led the way to the quarters occupied by the ladies of her household. Betsey made several inadequate attempts to speak and detain her mistress but Margaret hurried on as if she did not hear until she stopped before a low door and asked if this were Perrot's room.

Betsey nodded and Margaret went in. The room was lit by a single rush light and was cold with a curious smell of sickness. Perrot, white and shaken with pain, lay on the narrow bed. She made an effort to sit as she saw Margaret but Margaret motioned her to lie back and going to her side took her hand in hers. Perrot rolled helplessly against the pillows.

'Send for the midwife,' Margaret said over her shoulder, then to Perrot, 'How near to your time are you?'

'Two months, Madame,' Perrot said, very low. Margaret felt a surge of fearful anxiety grip the walls of her stomach but she said nothing and grasped the other's damp hand more strongly within her own.

She stayed with Perrot until she gave birth to a stillborn daughter in the hushed hours after midnight. The waiting woman lay with eyes closed, spent and exhausted. Throughout the difficult labour she had buried her head in the pillow rather than cry out and had not spoken to those who tended her. Margaret bent over her before she returned to her chambers.

'Try to rest.'

'I can never forget your kindness, my Lady — '

'Do not speak of it,' Margaret said. 'Reserve your strength and you and I shall speak another time.'

Betsey moved from the fireside where she had remained throughout the night, replenishing the blaze and providing water from a cauldron suspended in the hearth. Without speaking she wrapped Margaret's cloak around her shoulders and walked with her down the wide staircase to Margaret's rooms.

'I never cease to marvel at what you will do next,' she said at last as she helped Margaret to undress. 'I should have thought you would have censored Perrot for her behaviour rather than nurse her through a night of sickness.'

'Would you have me desert one of my own household in her hour of greatest need? Betsey! Jesus Christ had compassion on women who strayed from the path of virtue — would you have had me turn on her in the pangs of labour?'

'No, of course not,' Betsey said reluctantly, with the candour of forty years' service, 'but I should think there are others who might have ministered to her without you taxing your strength.'

'Perhaps in some way I feel responsible for what has happened to Perrot. My household are as my children to me and I should have taken stronger measures to see Perrot did not fall from grace. The moral responsibility must rest with me.'

'Moral responsibility or not, you look tired out to me. I shall bring you some warm milk and you must sleep late tomorrow morning.'

'I must hear Mass — '

'You can attend a later one for once,' Betsey retorted with the touch of asperity Margaret recognised as true concern and she made murmurs of agreement and sank gratefully into her goosedown mattress.

Perrot recovered slowly but before the day when the high ranking officials of the Court set out for Plymouth to welcome Arthur's bride she was on her feet and making an attempt to carry out her duties. Margaret sent for her and the woman came into the parlour, her face stiff with a mixture of pride and shame.

'I am glad to see you recovered; sit down.'

Perrot looked at her, startled. Margaret waved her, a trifle impatiently, to a stool by the fire.

'Do not be afraid, I am not going to preach. Neither shall I pry into the matter of the father of the child. That will remain a secret between your conscience and your God. All I ask is that you put your trust in me and for the future give your undivided loyalty to God and the service of my household.'

'Oh, Madame,' Perrot cried in an outburst of weeping, throwing herself on her knees in front of Margaret, 'I can never thank you enough — I do not deserve your forgiveness or your pity — ' Margaret's mind flew back to the distant day when she and Jasper had watched the lovely young creature Perrot had been diving naked from the river bank at Torrington. Much of what had happened to her waiting woman might have been avoided if Margaret had put a stop, there and then, to what she had known went on between William Elmer and the girl. She realised now, what she had not fully understood then, that she had turned an unseeing eye to the liaison for it had been symbolic of the union existing between herself and Jasper. When she had spoken to Betsey of her moral obligations to Perrot she had spoken the stark truth.

'You have been punished enough,' Margaret went on in a voice threatening to break slightly, as Perrot begged her to deal with her as she deserved, 'later perhaps, when you are stronger, your confessor may devise some penance if you so desire.'

'My Lady, my Lady, how can I ever thank you?'

'There, child, dry your eyes and have done.' Margaret put out her hand and helped the woman to stand.

From then until the festivities began Margaret wore the hair shirt close to her body. Betsey and the others protested in vain but nothing would shake her from her self punishment. She longed for the wisdom of someone to pour out the suffering she was experiencing and spent hours on her knees in her private chapel, rising stiff and aching with pain.

About the time Henry and the Prince of Wales set out to greet the Princess of Spain as she made slow progress from Plymouth to Exeter and across the windswept Plain of Salisbury towards London Margaret commanded a litter to be brought to convey her through the city streets to see the preparations being made to welcome Catherine of Aragon. Wrapped in a sable cloak she was carried through the town and was rewarded with an unhampered view of the set pieces nearing construction. She stopped and spoke with the workmen who were putting the finishing touches to the castles, bowers of red and white roses and a truly magnificent representation of the signs of the Zodiac. This was sited at the end of Cornhill and she was in time to see a rehearsal of the pageant that would take place on the day of Catherine's entry into the City. Margaret listened with pleasure as citizens, dressed in sober garb and not the costumes depicting their various roles, acted the parts of notable astronomers of the past, declaiming verses especially written for the occasion. One man, obviously the producer of the pageant, stood on one side with a handful of papers and testily prompted those who forgot their lines. The performance finished, Margaret called the players to her and invited them to return with her to Coldeharbour for hot soup and cold viands. When they left her, later in the day, she had extracted a promise from them to attend her dinner party for the Spanish Ambassadors and re-enact their pageant.

Margaret noticed Perrot's interest in the actors and while they were still at Coldeharbour asked her if she would care to assist them in their last minute rush to complete the costumes they required. After an almost imperceptible hesitation Perrot agreed and went off with another waiting woman, quite happily, to the producer's house. Later, sitting in the window seat and watching the cold, autumnal dusk fall on the river Margaret thought again of the slight reluctance she had sensed in Perrot. In a sudden flash of intuition she recalled the players who had come to Collyweston and had intrigued the King's household with their display of necromancy and leger de main. Was it perhaps here she should look for the father of Perrot's child? Margaret recalled now the talk there had been at the time of Harry's knighting of profane orgies taking place in the ruined chapel on the south bank. Could it be the magicians had pursued Perrot until last year and she had fallen victim to their rites? It were better if I did not discover the truth, Margaret told herself and gazed bleakly at the darkening sky; as she watched a flight of ducks echeloned over the river and dipped towards the water. Diverted she returned to the fireside and rang the bell to summon pages to shut out the night.

A week later William Elmer brought Sir Reginald Bray to her parlour. She greeted him warmly and bade him sit while he told her of the meeting between Henry and his future daughter-in-law.

'What is the Lady Catherine like to look upon?' she asked eagerly.

'She is beautiful,' Bray said simply. 'All who have seen her agree with me she is both elegant and high spirited.'

'Healthy and strong also?'

'The Lady Catherine has the clear complexion that speaks of a good constitution and she has delighted us with exhibitions of her country's dances.'

'It is good to know she is not frail or

delicate for my heart misgives me where the Lord Arthur is concerned. His wife will need the strength of two to fend for him and protect him.'

'Come my Lady!' Bray told her smiling, 'this is not the time for the mopes. If you could have seen Lord Arthur leading her in the dance and leaping as high as she you would have had no cause for alarm. The Prince of Wales and his little bride made as pretty a picture as ever I hope to see.'

'Could they converse very much together?'

'More by sign language than by speaking — '

'Then she did not give great heed to the advice the Queen and I gave her to learn a little English,' Margaret said wistfully.

'She will soon learn. The young are quick to put their tongue to a language when they are living amongst it.'

'Has she brought many courtiers with her?'

'A goodly number; dark and with formal manners. They did not take too kindly to the King's wish to see the Lady Catherine before the wedding service!'

'Indeed? What did my son say to that? I cannot think he would tolerate travelling such a distance only to be met with a complete denial of his hopes to meet his future daughter-in-law?'

'You are right, my Lady. His Grace let it be known he intended to see the Princess and waited at her lodging until her duenna and other advisers brought her to pay her courtesies.'

'Was my son pleased with what he saw?'

'He told me afterwards he was delighted and I wrote a letter for him to King Ferdinand and Queen Isabella telling them of his great pleasure and utter satisfaction in his son's bride.'

'That is well, then.'

On the 12th November Catherine rode into the city of London from Lambeth Palace where she had been lodged and showed herself to the people. She was allowed to enjoy the sole honours of the day as she rode on a beautifully caparisoned mare through the gaily decorated streets. The royal family awaited her in a house on the Chepe and only Arthur, as the centre of one of the most ambitious tableaux, greeted her and escorted her the remainder of the journey. Everywhere the brown haired princess was greeted with affection and given a tumultuous reception by the city folk. Catherine smiled on them, her grey eyes alight with pleasure and in halting English thanked the Mayor when he presented her with a wedding gift of fine plate. Tired but very happy she alighted at the house in the Chepe and met those members of her bridegroom's family she had not yet seen. The sixteen-year-old curtsied gravely to Margaret and was warmly kissed on both cheeks by Elizabeth and Meg and the baby Mary. Young Harry, stocky and glowing with vibrant health, doffed his feathered hat with a flourish and bowed low to his future sister-in-law.

'She is lovely!' he whispered to Margaret as Catherine was escorted below to rejoin her procession back to Lambeth. 'My Lady grandmother, do you not think Catherine is a fitting bride for any man?' His golden-brown eyes were sparked with enthusiasm. Margaret smiled at his exuberance.

'I agree with you,' she said fondly. Although she would not admit it she had a very tender spot for the handsome ten-year-old beside her and next to Meg he was her favourite grandchild.

In the days of the wedding festivities that followed Henry was very much in evidence. His was the right to bring Catherine from the Bishop of Lambeth's Palace to the door of St. Paul's and he afterwards said he had never enjoyed anything as much as the brief sail down the Thames in the King's barge while he and Catherine had acknowledged the excited cheers of those who crammed the craft pushed together on the broad river. All too soon it seemed he was helping her alight at the Paul's wharf and walking with her to the Cathedral where he handed her to his brother.

Margaret with Henry and Elizabeth waited inside the Gothic arched church on a dais especially constructed for them and craned forward when trumpets pealed to announce the entrance of the bride and bridegroom. Margaret found herself in tears and fumbled in the velvet purse at her waist for a handkerchief to stem the tears flooding her eyes. The young people looked so vulnerable and other-worldy as they came down the wide aisle and waited for the service to begin, and she found herself praying desperately for their happiness in each other.

While fountains gushed wine and the populace prepared to feast into the night the King and his Court repaired to the Palace where a magnificent banquet was given in the newly married Prince and Princess of Wales's honour. At last, those who could still stand, accompanied them to Baynard's Castle and assisted in the Bedding. The King and Elizabeth were the last to leave the nuptial chamber, beaming happily on the beautiful young couple as they sat, demurely enough, against the heaped pillows of their marriage bed. Margaret had not been of the company and she had left the feast early for Coldeharbour. She found she became exhausted with too much excitement and nearly always slipped quietly away to rest.

Before the tournaments and masques began to mark a fortnight of celebrations Henry paid his mother an unexpected visit. He brought in with him some of the raw November cold and Margaret, looking sharply at her son, thought he looked thinner than ever now the marriage he had worked so hard to bring about had actually taken place.

But the King was by no means despondent nor showed any signs of tiredness.

After giving his mother a jewelled perfume phial to mark the occasion of the wedding he sat down in the chair opposite her before the hearth and drank deeply of the mulled wine she had offered him.

'So you are well pleased,' she prompted.

The light grey eyes twinkled. 'Very,' Henry said. 'Especially since Arthur's gentlemen came with haste to tell me this morning the marriage was truly consummated.'

'Whose word have you for that?'

'Arthur's own.'

'Then it should be true enough. But are you not a little concerned he is over young for too much indulgence in wedded bliss?'

'No, no!' Henry said more jovially than she had heard him for a long time. 'If you cast your mind back, my Lady Mother, you were not so very much older than Arthur when you conceived me!'

'That is as may be!' Margaret said tartly, 'but your father was almost ten years older than Arthur is now, which is quite different.'

'God's Blood, Mother!' Henry cried, then crossed himself hastily as the unusual oath slipped from him. 'You worry too much. Now is the time to rejoice in our good fortune in bringing about this highly desirable marriage; this is not the moment to indulge in morbid fancies.'

'Perhaps you are right,' Margaret agreed with a smile. 'Tell me of the plans for the day's events.'

The dinner party she gave for the Ambassadors was one of the brightest spots of the ensuing festivities only rivalled by the coming of the Scottish Ambassadors to mark the betrothal of their King James to Meg. Henry and his family went from jousting field to banqueting table in an aura of complete happiness. Margaret was delighted her son should at last see the fulfilment of the hopes he had carefully tended for so long. Only at night, in the solitary splendour of her great bed, was she beset with the remembrance of the handsome young Warbeck and the unlucky Edward of Warwick who had lost their lives as Henry followed the relentless star of the Tudor destiny.

17

On the twentieth day of April in the year 1509, Margaret stood at the windows of the new Palace Henry had created at Richmond and waited for the physicians to summon her to the death bed of her son. She felt numb with sorrow, drained of the spark of life sustaining her during all the long years.

She was alone in the room. More than an hour before she had sent John Fisher, now her Confessor and confidant, and Betsey with her other waiting women to a belated dinner. They had all pleaded with her to eat something but she had shaken her head saying she was not hungry and would recall them when she needed them.

In the hour she had traced their lives since Arthur and Catherine's marriage with the finger of grief. The union, solemnised with such splendour and ringed about with an aura of great hope had shattered into the splintered fragments of expectation abandoned as Arthur had died of a mysterious illness in Ludlow Castle. They had spent but four short months in the place where Arthur had passed much of his childhood and had taken up residence with the joyous acclamation of the populace of London ringing in their ears.

Taut-faced messengers had brought the disastrous news to Richmond and Henry and Elizabeth had been stricken with sorrow, comforting one another as best they could in the loss of their firstborn. Margaret knew Henry suffered most as a father and looked upon the blow to his statecraft as a minor consideration. To her son, who had known nothing of family life apart from that which Jasper had lavished upon him, the breaking up of his own young family circle was an almost unbearable cross to bear. With the Queen it was the same; over the years she had become fond of Henry, wearing down the inborn resistance he felt towards her Yorkist blood, and centring upon their children the meaning of existence. She was visibly more withdrawn after Arthur's untimely death and seemed to find no joy in the expected birth of yet another baby. It had not surprised Margaret very much when, giving birth to a still-born child, the Queen had sickened with fever and without making an apparent effort to survive died less than a year after her firstborn.

Henry was distraught. For a man who had not been passionately in love with his wife his grief was almost quixotic. Margaret saw a great change in him, and for almost the first time in their relationship, was unable to communicate with him. She recalled the years following with a shudder; her undeviating mind shrinking from the duplicity of the dealings between Henry and the sovereigns of Spain.

Ferdinand and Isabella, while making surface pleas for the return of both their daughter and her dowry, nevertheless exhorted their ambassador to sue for the immediate betrothal of Catherine with the new Prince of Wales, the eleven-year-old Prince Henry.

Margaret remembered vividly the shock she had experienced when Henry had brought her, on one of his rare visits, news of Spain's desires. She had stared at him, unbelieving.

'How can this be?' she had cried, 'when you told me the marriage had been consummated?'

Avoiding her eyes the gaunt King had muttered something about Catherine swearing she was as virgin as the day she had landed on English soil.

'And you believe this when Ferdinand presses for the wedding portion as well as the dowry? Was this not only to be delivered to him when the marriage was completed?' Margaret had asked very quietly.

She was never to be quite sure what Henry did believe from this time on. Her beloved son became almost a stranger to her; straining after the call of his destiny like a soldier scaling the walls of a beleaguered town. More and more Henry became absorbed in the affairs of his kingdom, daily extorting more and more money from his people through the agency of Dudley and Empson, two of his ministers who quickly became the most hated men in the country. Margaret's fears for Henry's avarice became only too real.

Although she understood his thirst to bolster his economy she could not comprehend his attitude to his daughter-in-law. The girl had had to plead with Henry to remove her from the damp walls of Ludlow Castle where she was terrified she would fall sick of the dreaded disease that had robbed her of her young husband. Almost reluctantly, it seemed to Margaret, Henry agreed Catherine should reside in the palaces close to the capital although not with the Court. Bewildered the girl sent frantic letters to her parents asking them to intercede on her behalf and either restore her to them in Spain or insist upon her acknowledgement as bride-in-waiting of the Prince of Wales.

Margaret knew Henry was well aware of what the Princess wrote to Spain for the resident Spanish ambassador kept him acquainted of the correspondence passing between his master and mistress and their daughter. With this evidence he possessed a strong case for the diplomacy he practised and had no compunction in keeping Catherine in England while he protracted the negotiations for her future betrothal.

Margaret remembered with a rush of shame how Henry had even contemplated his own marriage with Catherine when Elizabeth died. All she could say in his favour was that he recognised the urgency of providing another heir to the throne for as Arthur had been snatched away from them what was there to prevent Prince Henry being taken by any of the other mortal illnesses so prevalent? It was not sufficiently comforting to know Prince Henry was strong and enjoyed an abundance of good health for some diseases struck the hale and hearty as well as those who were sickly. Where would lie the succession should this calamity befall the throne?

The little Meg, sent with many misgivings from her own manor at Collyweston to be the bride of the gallant but libertine King James of Scotland, had as yet no heir while Mary

371

was too young to contemplate marriage although Henry had succeeded in making for her the ambitious match of wedding Charles, the heir of the Emperor.

Fortunately Henry had reverted to his former wisdom and had rejected the idea of marrying his daughter-in-law and turned his attention to other appropriate ladies. He made exhaustive enquiries about the women suggested to him and sent his ambassadors with lists to check the type of face of the would be bride along with other very much more intimate details of her personal features. Margaret, who was unhappily made aware of these facts, had been unable to unburden herself even to Fisher who had become a growing solace to her since he had accepted her office of Confessor. She wrestled with the problem of her son's daemon alone.

To her concern he had finally agreed to the betrothal of Prince Henry and Catherine. Margaret absented herself from the proceedings while Ferdinand publicly stated his daughter was still a virgin and the treaty of marriage asked for a Papal dispensation as the Princess's first wedding had not been consummated.

There had now come a ray of hope for the Pope would not give the dispensation without hearing more evidence and for many months clerics journeyed between Spain, London and Rome. The new young Prince of Wales declared he thought the marriage could not be anything but invalid and his grandmother breathed more freely as Henry turned his attentions to alliances with French Princesses.

These, she strongly believed, would have taken place had not Isabella chosen this most inconvenient moment to die and leave Ferdinand free to enter again the lists of matrimony. Hardly waiting for a decent period of mourning he married Germaine de Foix, a niece of the King of France, and turned the diplomatic tables on Henry.

Margaret could not help being aware of the strain this was on the Princess Catherine. Not sure of what lay in store for her in England or elsewhere she became desperate when her mother died and wrote even more urgently to her father beseeching him to bring her home to Spain or else to send her more money to help her live in England. She pleaded dire poverty which was not strictly the case for Henry had set her up in a small establishment of her own where she had plenty of servants and food. Her health had suffered severely over the years since Arthur's death and she had lost the vivacity all had spoken of at her wedding. Margaret, while feeling very sympathetically towards the young woman, could not repress a certain impatience with her sufferings for Catherine could not, even after five years in England, either read or write the language.

Catherine's fortunes had improved slightly when Henry, to Margaret's dismay, resumed the marriage arrangements with Ferdinand of Prince Henry and Catherine and agreed to accept most of the jewels and plate the bride had brought with her for her first marriage as part of the settlement for the second. But still Henry hesitated to set the date of his son's marriage. Could it be, Margaret asked herself again and again, Henry was not too certain of the advisability of such a marriage? Was he troubled by the moral issues more than he cared to admit? She, who through her long life, had withstood the temptation to marry Jasper although she had loved him deeply and with passion, saw in the permitting of this marriage her sacrifice made a mockery. She prayed long and earnestly for Henry to be guided away from taking the fatal step. Now it seemed as if death would settle the matter for in his bedchamber Henry fought to keep breath within the frail bones of his chest and had made no decision.

As she thought she would gladly have given

the remaining days of her own life to have had Jasper here to share her anxiety, she heard a knock on the door.

Fisher came in to her answering call and told her the King's physicians were requesting her to come to her son's bedside. Leaning heavily on the arm of Fisher she went to the King's apartments.

In the bedchamber the curtains were drawn and tapers guttered in the silver sconces. Henry lay propped against a mound of pillows, yellow and ravished with fever. His hair, prematurely white, straggled from a woollen cap and lay damp on his forehead. Her heart aching with the piteous sight of her only child in extremis, Margaret let go of Fisher's supporting arm and fell on her knees beside the bed. Henry seemed dimly aware of her presence and the hands, plucking at the silken sheets, strove to find hers. With tears filling her eyes and flowing unheeded down her cheeks Margaret took his hands between her own, trying to warm the brittle fingers with some of her own life.

While physicians and ministers hovered in the background she strained to hear any word he might say to her and was rewarded with a whispered; 'Ma mère — do not think — too badly of me — I have tried to do — that which is right for England.' The inarticulate

375

words fluttered in the close air of the sickroom and with the slightest pressure on her enfolding hands Henry said, 'I have loved you and Uncle Jasper — ' Sobbing she brought one of the blue veined hands to her lips and kissed it, aware as she did so of another person kneeling beside her. Looking up through the blinding tears she recognised the handsome and comforting young man as Prince Henry. Prince Henry — ? Only for the very briefest moment for as she watched her son made an effort to sit up and clutch her before he sank back against the pillows. The physicians hurried to him and turned to her shaking their heads sadly.

'The King is dead!' cried the Archbishop of Canterbury, William Warham, 'Long live the King!'

How can the man be so stupid? Margaret thought as she had her face in the bedclothes, still on her knees until she realised all those in the bedchamber had rustled to kneel also. From a distance she heard the rather high voice of her grandson thank those about him before he bent, with a charming gesture, to help her to her feet.

Of course! Margaret knew now the men about her were not stupid but acknowledging her grandson as the new King of England. Hastily collecting her wits she stood and then, as gracefully as her rheumatism would allow, sank in a curtsey.

*   *   *

Some unsuspected source of nervous energy sustained her throughout the ordeal of the long state funeral and she followed in a litter both the procession to St. Paul's where black horses drew the maroon velvet covered hearse and the later one to the Abbey Church where Henry had directed he should be interred, beside Elizabeth, in the new as yet uncompleted chapel. Feeling very alone, without even Derby who had died five years before to support her, she followed the draped coffin with its ring of guttering torches through the city streets and beside the Thames to the Cathedral. Here, ghost white, she leaned on the arm of her chamberlain and watched as the ministers of the crown broke their wands of office and threw them down into the tomb and listened while the pure voices of the choirboys sang some of the anthems Henry had enjoyed.

Her grandson escorted her to Coldeharbour where she had protested she would rather be than anywhere else while he went, with his Chancellor and other great officials to the Tower to hammer out the smooth succession from one reign to the next.

As the new King bent to kiss her good night she thought how very little she really new of the fair headed young giant who was now King. Henry had kept his son in the background to give him ample opportunity of studying and fitting himself for his new role. In the rare visits he had made to the Court he had shown remarkable skill at all sports, dancing and winning the hearts of the women who obviously admired his personable charm. He was the only one, when they were allowed to meet, who could coax a smile to the face of Catherine.

She longed now to ask him what his plans were concerning his marriage but could not bring herself to speak of the matter. She said, instead, that she was glad to see Catherine was among the royal ladies who mourned in the Abbey and that she hoped Mary had not been exhausted by the day's demanding ceremonies. Her grandson murmured some conversational replies and made his farewells.

Margaret retired early. Betsey, now seventy, was helped by two of the younger waiting women but lingered to talk over with her mistress the happenings of the day. Margaret was grateful to her and had some difficulty in persuading her to go to her own rest.

She awoke aching in every limb and when

she arose found her knees stiff and her feet locked. She forced herself to put on her clothes and sent for Fisher.

With him she talked over the necessity for altering her will now her son had died before her and asked Fisher, frankly, if he thought the new King would hamper any of the plans they had already put into motion for the founding of two colleges in Cambridge.

'The King is young, my Lady,' Fisher told her in the direct way she had found so easy to understand, 'he is also at an impressionable age where pleasure seems to be the mainspring of life. Shall we say he will probably view the last few years of your son's reign as a time of gloom and might easily wish to spend a great deal of money in the pursuit of merriment.'

'You think it would be advisable to ensure my fortune is properly disposed of?'

'I do. If you bear in mind there is a Coronation and a royal wedding to celebrate you will realise much money will be needed.'

'I had not yet thought of a crowning! It seems so very soon to speak of rejoicing when — my son has so very recently died.'

'Of course, but it is a good thing to give the people a happier prospect to look forward to.'

'You are right. I heard you speak of a

wedding — has anything been said about the marriage?'

Fisher regarded her with his penetrating eyes.

'Yes, my Lady. I have heard it from the Chancellor and Bishop Fox that the late King gave orders it was to take place as soon as possible and that Princess Catherine's father has sent, by Italian bankers, the second part of her dowry to show his willingness for the early solemnisation of the union.'

'So, after all, the thing which I have dreaded is to come about,' Margaret spoke heavily. 'Did you hear my son express this wish as he lay dying?'

'No. I was not present but I do not doubt the word of those who told me. Try not to disturb yourself too much.'

'Disturb myself!' Margaret rounded on him with a flash of her old fire.

'There has been Papal Dispensation,' Fisher said quietly.

'Granted after years of difficulties. No, my friend, I see this as a disastrous union that could one day cause much unhappiness to my grandson.'

Always, when she was disquieted she liked to go to the casement and look out onto the world beyond the confines of her own rooms. Now she was startled to see the May trees on the other bank white with blossom while in the cloudless blue skies swallows dived towards the water and swooped effortlessly up again.

'I have lived too long,' she said almost to herself. 'The earth has reawakened and I have been completely unaware of it. I wish I could go to Collyweston and pass the remainder of my days in the tranquillity which is especially its own.'

'When the Coronation is over you will be free to go where you wish; but now, come with me to the chapel and you and I shall pray together.'

As the days passed and the June sun failed to warm her bones she discovered she lived more often in the days of old than the present. She sat for hours with a piece of tapestry on her knees and dreamt of Pembroke, Bletsoe and Collyweston; somehow all merged in an earthly paradise.

Betsey and Perrot privately expressed their dismay when she refused to have a new robe for the Coronation. Never, in all the years they had served her, had she not gladly accepted the excuse of celebration to order a magnificent gown. She showed little or no interest in the ones they brought and sent them away saying the mourning dress she was wearing was sufficient for the present.

Secretly she resented their intrusion into her private world where she was once more young and needed. Quite often she heard again the weird, plaintive tune of the magician's pipe and could smell the sharp Pembroke mud and the wild flowers clustered on the Haven's shores. Occasionally she was tossed in the small boat in which she had escaped down that very Haven with Henry and Jasper when David ap Thomas had rescued them from the beseiging forces of the Yorkists. Her youth had died on the following day when her son and Jasper had sailed away from her to France and had left her for fourteen endless years. But what were those endless days when they held the promise of a possible reunion? Now, she was alone again and only in the Heaven the Bible promised her could she hope to meet again with those she loved.

Reaching these morbid levels she made an effort to stop herself wallowing in self-pity.

On occasions she worked incessantly, signing documents and discussing her many interests with those who advised her. Those about her, William Elmer, Maurice Westbury, Betsey and the rest of her devoted household, watched with anxiety and did what they could to cheer her.

On the 11th June the new King came to

tell her that he and Catherine had been wedded that day in the Palace at Greenwich.

'I hope I may have your blessing, my Lady Grandmother,' he said kneeling to her.

'You will always have that and I pray to God that you are blessed with strong heirs to perpetrate the line your father has begun.'

When he had gone, the room dimmed by his vitality, she abandoned herself to helpless tears.

The day before the Coronation Margaret stood on the Thames Street balcony of her house and watched the King and Queen's procession pass below. The young Henry drew loud cheers from the people who flocked the roadway as he rode by in crimson velvet beneath a canopy of gold and a long stream of gold and silver clad courtiers followed on horses trapped in silk and damask. After them came the Queen's procession with Catherine carried in a litter borne by white palfreys. The girl had regained the beauty she had frittered away during the frustrating years since she had come to England and she acknowledged the delight of her husband's subjects with radiant smiles and flowers plucked from the multitude surrounding her in her conveyance. When she came abreast of the balcony where Margaret stood she commanded the horsemen to stop and waved and called out greetings to her husband's grandmother. Margaret watched as the procession started up again in the direction of Westminster.

She was carried to the Cathedral the following morning and watched the Coronation, in all its ancient and elaborate ritual. Later, although very tired, she insisted upon attending at least part of the banquet in Westminster Hall. In vain, Dr. Morgan pleaded with her to think of her health.

'I am,' she told him enigmatically and simply.

She had agreed to spend the night at the Abbot's House at Westminster to save her the tiring journey back to Coldeharbour and she went to bed when she thought she had seen enough of the merriment and avoided meeting the eye of her physician.

She awoke to find the tapers burning and the curtains undrawn. Making an effort to sit she was smitten with an agonising pain under her left breast. She cried out sharply and Betsey and several of the other people she faintly grasped were in the room hurried to her side. As Betsey put her arms about her Dr. Morgan poured a sharp liquid between her teeth. She tried to protest but had to gulp it down before it choked her. The pain easing a little she asked what hour it was and Perrot told her it was almost midnight.

'I have slept but a very short time!'

'No, dearest Lady,' Betsey said gently, 'you have slept for a day and a night.'

'Indeed,' Margaret pondered the extraordinary happening. Suddenly the pain gripped her again and she drew her arms and legs together in an effort to ease the knife like thrust in her chest.

She was only dimly aware of the days that followed. She could not distinguish between the night and hours of daylight. At times the pain left her and at others her hands were cramped in torment. She sometimes knew those about her and called them by name but at other times she was confused and spoke to them as if they were the dead ones she had loved.

On the morning of the twenty-ninth day of June, 1509, she knew she was dying. Mercifully she was completely without pain and knew an ease of spirit long since forgotten.

'John Fisher!' she whispered from the soft pillows. 'Wilt thou administer the Blessed Sacrament to me?'

Fisher came swiftly to the bedside and without speaking went to the altar and brought the silver platten and chalice.

Assisted by Betsey and Perrot who wept

unashamedly Margaret sat upright and took the wafer on her tongue and sipped the wine.

'Now truly I know,' she whispered, 'that Jesus died to save us and in Him I put my trust. May He bless all of you who have given me the benefit and comfort of your devotion.'

A little later they crossed her hands on her breast and looked with wonder on the calm sweetness of her face, now free from the pain that had racked her for almost a week.

As they looked, Fisher said softly, 'All England hath cause for weeping at her death for she was the epitome of merciful goodness and it is not often mankind has the opportunity of seeing her like. Our lives will be the poorer by her going. May she rest in the peace she so richly deserves.'

THE END

We do hope that you have enjoyed reading this large print book.

Did you know that all of our titles are available for purchase?

We publish a wide range of high quality large print books including:
Romances, Mysteries, Classics
General Fiction
Non Fiction and Westerns

Special interest titles available in large print are:
The Little Oxford Dictionary
Music Book
Song Book
Hymn Book
Service Book

Also available from us courtesy of Oxford University Press:
Young Readers' Dictionary
(large print edition)
Young Readers' Thesaurus
(large print edition)

For further information or a free brochure, please contact us at:
Ulverscroft Large Print Books Ltd.,
The Green, Bradgate Road, Anstey,
Leicester, LE7 7FU, England.
Tel: (00 44) **0116 236 4325**
Fax: (00 44) **0116 234 0205**

Other titles in the
Ulverscroft Large Print Series:

STRANGER IN THE PLACE

Anne Doughty

Elizabeth Stewart, a Belfast student and only daughter of hardline Protestant parents, sets out on a study visit to the remote west coast of Ireland. Delighted as she is by the beauty of her new surroundings and the small community which welcomes her, she soon discovers she has more to learn than the details of the old country way of life. She comes to reappraise so much that is slighted and dismissed by her family — not least in regard to herself. But it is her relationship with a much older, Catholic man, Patrick Delargy, which compels her to decide what kind of life she really wants.

PAINTED LADY

Delia Ellis

Miss Eleanor Needwood was about to be married to a most unsuitable suitor when Philip Markham came to her rescue. He arranged for Eleanor to be in London for the Season, a guest of his sister, who decided that everyone would benefit if Markham married Eleanor. And thus the rumour started. The surprised couple decided to play along with the mistaken impression until a scandal-free way to end the betrothal could be found. But when Eleanor agreed to pose for a daring artist, the result was far more scandalous than any broken engagement.

RUN WILD MY HEART

Maureen Child

For beautiful Margaret Allen, travelling alone across the western plains was her only escape from a loveless marriage — a marriage secretly arranged by her father as part of a heartless business scheme. In a fury, she left her quiet, unassuming life behind and ventured out on her own . . . Cheyenne Boder set out to claim a cash reward for finding Margaret and bringing her home. But the handsome frontiersman found a promise of love in her sweet smile and vowed to unearth the hidden passions that made her a bold, proud woman of the west!

SECRET OF WERE

Susan Clitheroe

Blessed with wealth and beauty, Miss Sylvestra Harvey makes her debut in the spring of 1812, and she seems destined to take London society by storm. Sylvestra, however, has other ideas; she is set upon marrying her childhood friend, Perry Maynard. What better way, then, to cool the ardour of her admirers than to nurture rumours of a scandalous liaison between herself and the dangerous Marquis of Derwent? This daring plan is to lead Sylvestra into mortal danger before she finally discovers the secrets of her own heart.

ONE BRIGHT CHILD

Patricia Cumper

1936: Leaving behind her favourite perch in the family mango tree in Kingston, Jamaica, little Gloria Carter is sent to a girls' school in England, to receive the finest education money can buy. Gloria discovers two things — one, that in mainly white England she will always need to be twice as good as everyone else in order to be considered half as good; and two, that her ambition is to become a barrister and right the wrongs of her own people. Ahead lies struggle — and joy. The road stretches to Cambridge University, to academic triumph and a controversial mixed marriage. Based on a real-life story.